D1329816

# Land of Their Own
## from Russia to South Dakota

**A Historical Novel**

**by**

**Ruth Richert Jones**

*Ruth Richert Jones*

**Thorne Tree Publishers**
**P.O. Box 6536**
**Omaha NE 68106-0536**

Library of Congress Control Number: 2001129083

ISBN 0-9712325-0-4

Additional copies of this book are available by mail. Send $10.95 each plus $2.00 postage and handling for first book, $.75 for each additional book. Make checks payable to Ruth Richert Jones.

Send to:

THORNE TREE PUBLISHERS
P.O. Box 6536
Omaha NE 68106-0536
(402) 556-2365


Printed in the U.S.A. by
Morris Publishing
3212 East Highway 30
Kearney, NE 68847
1-800-650-7888

This book is dedicated to my husband, Dr. Russell G. Jones, himself an author (*Our God*) and a retired professor of Bible at Grace University, where he taught for thirty-six years. Without his continuing encouragement, his editorial expertise and other active involvement this book would not be in print.

This book is also dedicated to our children, their spouses, our grandchildren and our nieces and nephews to remind them that their great heritage did not come without price. First it was God who gave His Son and then it was our ancestors who kept the faith alive and immigrated to the United States at great cost.

\* \* \*

"Great is the Lord and most worthy of praise; his greatness no one can fathom. *One generation will commend your works to another; they will tell of your mighty acts*," Psalm 145:4 (NIV).

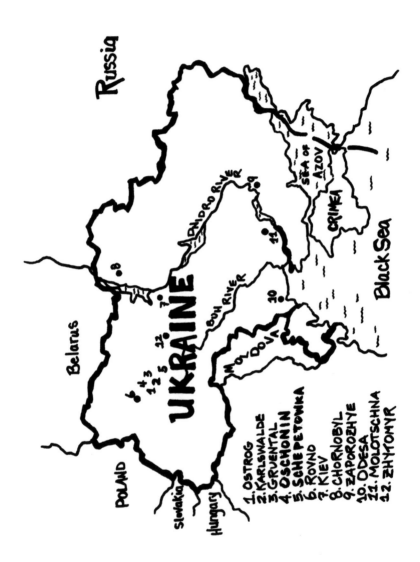

1. OSTROG
2. KARLSWALDE
3. GRUENTAL
4. OSCHONIN
5. SCHEPETOWKA
6. ROVND
7. KIEV
8. CHORNOBYL
9. ZAPOROZHYE
10. ODESA
11. MOLOTSCHNA
12. ZHYTOMYR

# List of Illustrations

Front Cover and illustrations by
Emily R. Brown
Great-great-Granddaughter
of
Ben and Nettie Richert

# Prologue

It is thought that Nettie Richert's people originated in the Netherlands, where they helped drain the lowlands and turned the land into productive farmland. During this time, Peter the Great from Russia came to the Netherlands and was favorably impressed with their accomplishments.

In 1762, Catherine the Great presented her famous *ukaz* to the Senate, which opened the door for these people to settle in Russia and develop the swamp lands there. She gave each of the immigrants sixty-five *hectors* or one hundred and sixty-two acres. The land was free from taxation for ten years. She also loaned them each five hundred *rubles*.

According to Boese, when Prussian leaders heard how successfully these people drained the land in the Netherlands, they asked them to come to Prussia and drain their lowlands. Since the Hollanders were suffering severe persecution for their faith in the Netherlands, a large group, including Nettie's people, accepted the offer and moved to Prussia. According to historians, they were successful in their endeavors in Prussia and consequently prospered.

Early in the eighteenth century, when land became scarce in Prussia, Nettie's people moved to the Volhynia Oblast in western Russia, now Ukraine.

It is not clear whether or not these later immigrants received land. They may have rented the land from the nobility. This is the stance the author has taken for this novel. We know each family lived in a combination house and barn with a narrow side yard. Each family farmed about four acres behind their buildings. All the cattle grazed in the pasture across the main road.

Nettie and Ben were born in Karlswalde. After their marriage they lived in Gruental. It was from this village that they made their first attempt to immigrate to America.

Little is known of Ben's origin. Some historians say that all Mennonites, sometimes called Hollanders, in the United States with the surname Richert are related. According to them, the boat of two brothers with the surname Richert capsized on the Rhine River. Mennonites (or Hollanders) rescued and befriended them. The Richert brothers changed their religious affiliation from Lutheran to that of their rescuers. They married women from that group and from then on identified with them.

After twenty-two pregnancies, Ben and Nettie had six living children. The author's father, Jacob, born November 2, 1881, was the first to be born in the new country.

The Hollanders separated themselves from people outside their villages. They controlled their schools and churches. They spoke *Plautdietsch* but used German in their church services and in the schools. They also practiced nonresistance. In the middle eighteen hundreds, when these freedoms were threatened, many Hollanders left Russia.

Conditions worsened and shortly after the Hollanders left, the Tsar was assassinated. Then when the Bolsheviks came into power, those who remained not only lost their religious freedom but many were relocated, some to Siberia, others to Germany and to other areas. Millions, including Russians, died during a Stalin-engineered famine. For seventy years the people living in the Union of Soviet Social Republic had limited opportunity to worship God. Many were persecuted.

The major events in this book actually took place, as well as historical events referred to in the text. The book portrays the political, economical and religious climate of this period in Russian history. The people in Karlswalde call Nettie and Ben's people Hollanders and this is what the author calls them in this novel.

The author's grandparents, Ben and Nettie Richert, and their children, Andrew and Eva, arrived in the United States in 1875. Elder Tobias Unruh, Heinrich and Helena Buller, and their five children also arrived at this time. It was Elder Unruh, Nettie's uncle, who led the Karlswalders to London. When numerous passengers broke out with small pox, he transferred to the hospital ship to accompany the sick. Except for these and historical persons mentioned in the text all other characters are fictional.

The author is indebted to John A. Boese, her father's cousin, for his book, *The Prussian Polish Mennonites Settling in South Dakota in 1874 and Soon After* (Freeman, S.D.: Pine Hill Press, 1967) and his unpublished work, *The Life Story of Henry H. Buller --1821-1913*. She is also indebted to her uncle Benjamin B. Richert, for the account he wrote of his parents' immigration and which was included in the previously mentioned unpublished work. Had these men not recorded the information, it likely would have been lost.

The author is also deeply grateful that her grandparents and great grandparents immigrated to the United States. She is thankful to God for the Christian heritage these godfearing people left behind.

# Part I

# The Dream

# Russia, April 1874

# Chapter One

Ben Richert raised himself to one elbow, then, with half-open eyes, he glanced around the shabby room. His eyes came to rest on the rays of light seeping through the dirty windows. What time was it? Had he overslept? Ben ran his hand over the mattress. Where was Nettie? Had she risen without calling him?

Then Ben remembered. He was not at home in the little *dorf* of Gruental. This was Oschonin and he was in a hotel room. Today he and Nettie with six-year-old Andrew and eighteen-month-old Eva would board the train for Antwerp, Belgium. From there they would take a ship to America.

Still fully clothed except for his boots, Ben sat up with a start. Where were Bill Schultz and Victor Gorbansky, the strangers with whom he had slept?

Ben shuddered in disgust. He hadn't wanted to sleep with them, not with perfect strangers. But there hadn't been an empty bed in town.

Oschonin wasn't that far from home but to make the train, Pappa, Nettie's father, had brought them here the day before. By the time they arrived, the hotels were filled. Now Ben knew they should have come earlier in the day.

Oschonin was bulging with people, most of them, like Ben and Nettie, on their way to America. In America they'd have freedom, freedom from tyranny, freedom to run their own *dorfs* and schools and, most important of all, freedom of religion. Not only that, they'd have land of their own, a hundred and sixty acres of it.

Ben ran his hand through his tousled brown hair. At least they had found a better place for Nettie and the children even though they shared a long ward-like room with other women and children. With Nettie in the family way, she wouldn't sleep very well anyway, especially while sharing the bed with two tossing children. Still, she hadn't shared a bed with strangers. And she had shared the room with women from their own people.

Nettie hadn't wanted Ben to sleep with these men. "With strangers?" she had exclaimed. "Is it safe?"

Ben had hesitated himself. But what could he have done? He had to sleep somewhere. Ben's powerful body had always been his source of pride. He hadn't heaved hundred-pound bags of grain for nothing. He might be under six feet tall but his strength made up for it. If anyone tried anything, he reasoned, he could handle it. Still, when he met Schultz and Gorbansky, he hadn't really worried. Seemed like decent men. Schultz was a Hollander.

Schultz and Gorbansky must have risen early. Thoughtful of them to let him sleep. But how could they have left without waking him? He must have been more tired than he had realized. He always awoke before sunup.

Ben pulled his watch from his pocket and sprang open the lid. Eight o'clock, long past time to get up. He reached for the things he had stowed under the overcoat he had used for a pillow. But there was nothing there. He unfolded his overcoat and shook it. Nothing! His money purse was missing. Two hundred and fifty *rubles* gone. The tickets weren't there either. Worst of all, the family passport and visa were gone too.

A sickening feeling came over him as the naked truth began to dawn on him. Schultz and Gorbansky had slipped them out from under his head. Thieves, common thieves. That's what they were! He should have heard them. And he should have felt them reach under his overcoat. He must have been more tired than he had realized. Little wonder. Strong as he was, his thirty-year-old body had been worn out. Even so, it had taken Ben a long time to fall asleep. But once he fell asleep, he slept like a baby. Now this. He shrugged his shoulders in disgust. On top of everything, he'd probably picked up fleas.

3

Ben sat for a moment stroking his bushy brown beard. What was he to do now? What could he do? True, there was money sewn in the lining of their coats. But that was to help them settle in America. And there wasn't very much. But there was enough to buy more tickets.

His heart sank as he remembered that they couldn't leave without a passport and visa and he couldn't get them here in Oschonin. They'd have to go back to Gruental. He shouldn't have been so pig-headed. He shouldn't have insisted on leaving this spring. He should have waited until the big group left, if they left.

Ben fought back the tears that were threatening. Grown men didn't cry. Still, going to America where he would have land of his own had been a long-time dream. And with the new law requiring young men to sign up for the draft lottery, immigrating to America seemed even more urgent. Now these swindling thugs had taken away all his hopes and dreams. Ben reached for his boot and hurled it across the room. It hit the wall with a thud.

"Thieves!" he roared. Ben's clear blue eyes turned to cold steel. "Common thieves, that's what you are!"

He sat for a moment before reaching for the other boot. Slowly he put it on then limped across the room to retrieve its mate. He looked at the boot a moment before putting it on.

"Good thing they didn't take these," he mumbled then thrust his foot into the boot. He tucked his coarse blue shirt into his trousers, straightened his suspenders, slipped into his coat then put on his heavy overcoat and hat.

He stalked out of the room. He'd report the theft, that's what he'd do. The police would catch up with them and he'd get his money and papers back. They'd put them in jail and he and Nettie would catch the morning train after all.

When he found the men, then and not before, would he tell Nettie. He couldn't face her now. How could he admit to her that he was such a fool? How could he admit that he let the men steal everything out from under his head while he slept?

On his way to the front desk, he ran into Jacob Friesen and Henry Ratzlaff. Friesen stuck out his hand, his bearded face grinning broadly.

"Good morning, Ben," he said. "How'd you sleep? Didn't sleep too well myself."

"Well, I didn't have that problem. I slept too soundly."

"Can't see that that's a problem."

"It is if you get robbed."

Friesen's mouth fell open. "Robbed?"

Ben nodded. "Woke up but the thugs were gone. So was my money, tickets, passport and visa. Everything."

"What're you going to do now?" Ratzlaff asked.

Ben shrugged. "What can I do? I'll report it to the police."

"We could take up a collection to buy more tickets," Friesen offered.

Ben shook his head. "Good of you to offer but we couldn't go without a visa and passport. And it takes time to get them. No, if they don't catch them, you'll have to leave without us."

"Maybe they'll catch them," Ratzlaff said. Friesen nodded his agreement but Ben could see they didn't believe it for one moment.

Ben grabbed Ratzlaff's arm. "Don't tell Nettie if you see her. I'd like to tell her myself."

"Of course," the men muttered then slowly walked away.

Ben stepped up to the counter. "I'd like to report a robbery," he told the clerk.

"Well, you're at the wrong place. Police station's down the street. Tell *them* your troubles."

Ben opened his mouth to give the clerk a piece of his mind, then thought better of it. He stalked through the door and out into the street. Outside the sun was shining brightly. How could things be so bright out here when he felt so gloomy inside?

But the policeman to whom he reported the theft only added to his gloom.

"Actually, it serves you right!" the officer told him. "You Germans don't know a good thing when you see it."

"Hollanders, not Germans," Ben muttered under his breath.

"What's that?" the officer wanted to know.

5

"Nothing," Ben told him, "Never mind." Better not irritate him.

The officer gave Ben a curious look then went on.

"The Tsar's been favoring you for more than a hundred years," he said, "and what thanks does he get? You're leaving! Well, don't set your hopes too high. It's happened before. These men know where to hide. There's not much chance we'll find them in this crowd but tell me what they looked like and we'll try to find them."

Ben described the men to him but he could see the officer wasn't going to try very hard.

He turned and slowly walked away. He was sure he would recognize Schultz and Gorbansky if he saw them again but like the policeman had said, they were likely gone. Probably left town long before dawn.

Several families were making their way to the hotel dining room and that reminded Ben he was hungry. Nettie had the food they brought for the journey and now that he'd reported the theft, they could eat. Just thinking of *vorscht* and *roesha zwieback* made his mouth water but he wondered how well he would have liked eating the same thing day after day. Without an occasional bowl of *komst borscht* to break the monotony, they'd probably have been sick of it.

On the way, he met Toby Beyer. Toby was taller than Ben with a slighter build. Thick dark hair and a neatly trimmed beard framed his face. Their families were good friends and his parents had only agreed to let the twenty-one-year-old go to America because Ben and Nettie were also going.

When Toby was still a child, Ben showed Toby how to carve. Last winter, when it was too cold to work outside, they spent hours together carving small objects. Ben carved a team and wagon for Andrew. Toby carved a small angel for Sophia, his fiancee.

"On your way to breakfast?" Ben asked.

Toby nodded. "Wanted to get a hot breakfast while I have a chance. Mamma packed some *roesha zwieback* for the journey but I'm afraid I'll get pretty tired of the same thing."

Ben nodded his agreement.

Toby laid his hairy hand on Ben's arm. His blue eyes searched Ben's.

"Ben, do you think Sophia's parents will ever change their mind about her? Will they ever let her come?"

Ben stroked his beard. "I don't know, Toby," he said at last. "You can't blame them, can you?"

Toby thought about that a minute. "Not really -- I guess. Still, I don't know how I'll ever live without her. Maybe if they had insisted before we made all our plans, and before we got our passports and visas, it might have made a difference. I might have stayed."

"But your parents still wouldn't approve. You know how our people feel about marrying outside of our own *dorfs*, let alone marrying Russians."

"But what'll I do if they never let her come?"

Ben's face grew sober. "Maybe you'll have to find a girl from our own people."

"Oh, but I couldn't do that. Would you have considered marrying anyone but Nettie?"

Ben paused before answering. "No, Toby," he said slowly, "to tell you the truth I wouldn't. There'll always be only one for me and that's Nettie."

"I knew you'd say so. That's how I feel about Sophia. Maybe Sophia's parents will change their minds and let her come later on."

Toby pushed back his hat. "Well, at least I'm not going alone with strangers. You'll be there."

Ben scowled. "No," he said. "We're not going."

Toby's mouth dropped open. "You're not going?"

"We're going back. Nothing else we can do."

Ben recounted the events of the previous night.

"And so we'll have to go back and start all over again," he finished.

The young man took on the look of a child. "But you'll come

7

as soon as you can, won't you?" he begged. "You won't settle back in Gruental, will you?"

Ben shrugged. "Right now I don't know. Actually, we gave up our place in Gruental and all our furnishings. We don't really have anywhere to go."

Ben shifted his foot. "It will be a while before we can leave. Takes time to get the papers. Besides, we barely have money to buy more tickets. And we'll need money when we get to America."

Toby's eyes clouded over. "And I had so counted on you being there, to give me advice. I've worked on the nobleman's farm and helped my father but there's a lot I don't know."

"But you'll be in America. You won't have to sign up for the military lottery. You'll have freedom and land of your own."

Ben laid his hand on Toby's shoulder. "Besides, you've still got the Lord."

"You're right," Toby said, "but the only reason I decided to go was because you were going."

He turned to leave then turned back again. "When are you going back? I'll see you before that, won't I?"

"It all depends on when we can get someone to take us back."

"I'll check with you later. I can help load your things."

The two parted and Ben made his way to Nettie's room.

Immigrating hadn't been easy for it meant leaving Nettie's family, knowing full well they'd probably never see them again. Ben's parents were no longer living so they hadn't had to be concerned about them.

Ben wished Nettie's parents had consented to leave but they hadn't had the money to make the trip even if they had wanted to. And they really hadn't wanted Ben and Nettie to leave.

Had their great-grandparents felt the same way when they came to Russia at the turn of the century? Was it as hard for them? The immigration of Ben's people had always followed persecution. It began hundreds of years before in Holland. Now this monster was once again raising its ugly head.

# Chapter Two

William Schultz breathed a sigh of relief as he closed the door behind him and Gorbansky. They slipped down the back stairs of the hotel without meeting anyone. Once outside, they waited a moment to make sure no one had seen them. Then they started down the dusty street.

Schultz elbowed Gorbansky. "Pretty good haul, eh?" he whispered.

Gorbansky gave him a toothy grin. "How much?"

"Don't know yet. Better wait to check 'til we get out of here."

"Yeah, someone might have seen us."

They moved cautiously away from the hotel and proceeded along the dusty, deserted street leading out of town.

"Better lay low 'til people start movin' around. When the dray-house opens, we'll get our horses and get out'a here."

On the edge of town the street dwindled into a narrow path.

"This is it," Schultz said. "We'll follow it into the woods. They'll never find us here in this thick underbrush. If anyone comes, we'll see them before they see us."

When they were deep in the forest, they sat down on a fallen log to rest. Only then did Schultz take the money purse out of his pocket. He held the *rubles* out for Gorbansky to see.

"Can you believe it?" Gorbansky exclaimed. "Look at all those *rubles*, must be two hundred and fifty of 'em!"

"Didn't I tell you these Hollanders had money? They act like they're poor but they pinch their *kopecks*. Talked to plenty of 'em when I was workin' for the railroad. Some of 'em claimed they got help from America but I'm not so sure. They live frugally and stash away their money. That's why they have

9

money to emigrate. I'm a Hollander myself. I know."

Schultz riffled through the papers. "Here's their passport and visa and their train and steamship tickets. And all that money besides. Quite a haul, eh?"

Gorbansky nodded. "Maybe we ought to use that stuff ourselves."

"What would we do with a family visa and tickets for four people? They'd be suspicious for sure. Besides, people are leaving all the time. If we can make this kind of haul each time, we'll be rich." Schultz nudged Gorbansky again.

"Yeah. I guess you're right. But what if he doesn't come?"

"Why wouldn't he?"

"Might've gotten suspicious and called the police."

Schultz shook his head. "He doesn't dare go to the police. Not with his reputation. Besides, he can't get tickets any cheaper, not as cheap. He'll come."

Schultz was right. It wasn't long before they heard snapping twigs.

Gorbansky poked Schultz with his elbow. "There he is," he whispered. Schultz nodded. They waited, listening to the approaching footsteps.

"Over here," Schultz called in a hushed whisper.

Both men watched as the man broke through the underbrush. The man was tall and wiry and wore a rumpled overcoat. His hair was dark and he wore a scruffy dark beard. A felt hat with a ring of sweat perched on his head at a crooked angle.

"Anybody follow you?" Schultz asked.

The man glanced over his shoulder. "Not that I know of."

"Well, we better make sure. We'll wait a few minutes to see. We'd all be in trouble."

They waited in silence.

"Did you bring the money?" Schultz asked after a while.

"Sure. But you're askin' too much."

"You won't get them cheaper anyplace else. It's a bargain. Cost you a lot more at the dock. And you can't buy a passport and visa. With your record, you know you can't get one on your own."

Schultz paused and eyed the man. "Er, do you have any other clothes? Hollanders are neat people. They firmly believe cleanliness is next to godliness. You wanna get the officials suspicious? Get something clean on and ironed. And get rid of that hat."

The man touched his hat affectionately. "I suppose I could find something else," he said slowly.

"You better."

"I still think you're askin' too much."

Schultz shook his head. "Take it or leave it. Plenty of people who want tickets not to mention the passport and visa."

Reluctantly, the man took a handful of *rubles* from his pocket and handed them to Schultz. "Still think it's too much."

Schultz shrugged. "Like I said, it's up to you."

But he took the man's money and examined each coin. Apparently satisfied, he dug in his pocket and held out the documents.

"Have a good trip," he told the man. "And, by the way, we never met you. Remember that!"

The man nodded then left for home.

# Chapter Three

Nettie sat in a straight-backed chair gently rocking Eva. Eva, her head covered with blonde ringlets, was wearing the dress Nettie had sewed for this journey. Ankle-length, it was dark blue, sprinkled with tiny blue flowers the color of Eva's eyes.

Nearby, six-year-old Andrew, also blonde, lay sprawled across the bed playing with the team and wagon Ben had carved for him. Impatiently, he shoved back the trouser strap that had slipped off his shoulder then turned to his playing again.

Suddenly Eva gurgled and squirmed out of Nettie's arms. She slid to the floor and toddled to Andrew's side. Andrew saw her coming and, with one quick motion, he spread his arms and upper body over his treasures. Eva screamed and Nettie snatched her away then set her on the floor. The doll Eva had been carrying fell to the floor and Nettie quickly picked it up and brushed off the dust.

This was the doll that Nettie stuffed with Turkey Red Wheat and she couldn't let anything happen to it. Ben had high hopes of sowing that wheat in America. The Russians forbade the Hollanders to take the wheat out of the country and Nettie asked Ben if it was right to take it.

"We Hollanders developed it," Ben said, "and I figure it's ours. And stuffed in Eva's doll, they'll never know."

Nettie guessed Ben felt a twinge of guilt himself, though he hadn't said so.

"The wheat *is* ours," he had reasoned aloud, "grown on the land we rented from the Tsar. If it hadn't been for us Hollanders, southern Russia would never have been called the Bread Basket of Europe. Besides, they'd never miss that little bit of wheat."

That small amount of wheat would cover merely a small patch of land but it would produce more each year Ben planted it. Eventually there would be enough to cover most of his hundred and sixty acres.

As Nettie raised up and leaned back in her chair, her dark blue eyes caught sight of Ben's broad shoulders filling the doorway of the ward-like room. Their eyes met and the edges of Ben's eyes crinkled with a smile. Nettie's eyes flashed with delight.

"Ben!" she said, "Good morning."

Ben crossed the floor to Nettie's side and slipped his big hand under the dark fringed scarf covering her shoulders. As he touched the *chignon* at the back of her neck, his fingers playfully pulled at one of the hairpins.

"Ben! No!" Nettie exclaimed as she grabbed his hand. "You know it's not proper for a married woman to be seen in public with her hair down."

Ben loved to see her long, honey-colored hair fall loose over her shoulders and she suspected he might actually loosen it this morning. She couldn't let him.

Ben grinned then closed his big hand over Nettie's slender shoulder.

"At least you haven't tied that thing over your head," he said. "I know proper married Hollander women wear *babushkas* but they make women look like *babushkas*. No wonder they call the scarves that. I like your hair uncovered."

He gave Nettie's shoulder a squeeze. "Did you sleep well?"

Nettie smiled her gentle smile. But they had been married long enough that Ben knew that her gentle smile could be deceptive. Nettie might be gentle at times but she was strong-willed and certainly not a pushover. Ben guessed that's what made living with her interesting.

"I'm fine," Nettie said, "just fine, though I do get stiff if I lay too long in one position. How about you, Ben?"

Before Ben could answer, Eva slipped from Nettie's arms and

held up her arms.

She gurgled as Ben tossed her into the air then caught her and set her in Nettie's lap again. He took off his heavy overcoat and lowered himself to the bed. Andrew sidled next to him and Ben absently put an arm around him.

But Nettie remembered Ben had not answered her question.

"Did you sleep well, Ben?" she asked again.

Ben hesitated.

"Very well," he answered at last.

Nettie frowned and her dark blue eyes studied his.

"Something's wrong, Ben. What is it?"

"What is it, Ben?" she repeated when he didn't immediately answer.

Ben moved closer to Nettie and took her hand. "I've got something to tell you. I, that is, they ... I've been robbed."

Nettie gasped. "Robbed? When?"

"During the night."

"While you were sleeping?"

Ben nodded.

"Then you don't know who did it?" Nettie asked.

"Oh, I know who did it," he thundered. "It was Schultz and Gorbansky, the men I slept with."

Nettie's eyes flashed. "I knew it!" she exclaimed. "They looked shifty."

"Looked like ordinary men to me," Ben answered. "And when I woke and they weren't there, I couldn't help but think how decent they were to leave without waking me.

"Then when I reached under my overcoat, (I used it for a pillow.) my money purse was gone. I shook out my coat and checked the pockets. Nothing! Two hundred and fifty *rubles* gone."

"They might have killed you!" Nettie snapped.

Andrew's eyes opened wide. "Did they have a knife, Pa, did they?"

"No, Andrew, that is, I don't know."

"They might have killed you," Nettie repeated.

14

"Killed you," Eva mimicked.

Nettie pinched her lips and gave Ben a look that said they'd better be careful what they said.

Ben nodded his agreement. "All they wanted was the money."

"I should have insisted that you leave the money with me. I was with women from our village. It's my fault."

"I take the blame, Nettie. I should have listened to you. I shouldn't have slept with them. Should have sat up in the train depot. Would have had plenty of time to sleep on the train."

"We all could have stayed in the depot."

Ben shook his head. "Too crowded. Besides, you're in the family way. You needed rest."

"You needed rest too. We've worked hard to get ready. Pappa should have brought us earlier. Oschonin isn't that far from home."

"Pappa couldn't have. He has the milking to do. But he could have brought us yesterday, right after dinner. Oschonin's bulging with people. Most of them, like us, on their way to America."

"But why'd they pick on you? How'd they know you had money?"

"If it hadn't been me, it would've been someone else." Ben's eyes turned to steel again. "At least you had a decent bed even though you had to share a room with others."

"True, thanks to you. And I didn't have to share a bed with strangers."

Nettie picked at the pleats in her skirt. "I don't know how you could sleep in the same bed with those strange men."

"We all had our clothes on, except for our boots. Didn't really want to do it but I had to sleep some place. I was sure I could handle them if they tried anything. I haven't heaved hundred-pound bags of wheat for nothing."

"You're strong. But two men?"

Ben guffawed. "My strength didn't mean a thing! They did it all on the sly. And to think, I trusted them. But they did seem like decent men. They must have gotten up before the sun came

15

up. I don't know why I didn't wake up when they reached under my coat."

"You always have slept like a log."

"But I usually wake up by sunup," Ben laughed again. "And to think when I awoke, I applauded them for being so thoughtful to let me sleep."

"We do have money sewn in the lining of our coats," Nettie said.

Eva opened her coat and looked at the lining. "Money in our coats," she mimicked.

Ben smiled absently at Eva then turned to Nettie again. "Not enough to buy tickets. Besides, I didn't tell you all of it, Nettie. They took our tickets too and our visa and passport."

Ben stroked his brown beard. "We can't go without the papers, even if we bought more tickets. And we can't get them here in Oschonin"

Nettie's eyes clouded over. "Oh, Ben, I'm so sorry. You've been dreaming so long about America."

Ben nodded. "Yes and I'd still like to go. If we stay, we won't be able to control what they teach Andrew and Eva. They'll control our *dorfs*. And we'll have to pay taxes to support the state church. Worst of all, they'll try to force us all to take up arms."

Ben's eyes brightened. "And, Nettie, if we emigrate, we'll have land of our own, a hundred and sixty acres of it."

"Maybe the police will catch up with them. Do they know?"

"I reported it but there's not much chance they'll catch up with them."

"Did you really talk to the police, Pa?" Andrew asked.

"Yes, Andrew. But don't interrupt."

"Yes, Pa." But Andrew's eyes glistened with excitement. He couldn't resist another question. "Can I go with you if you go to the police again?"

"No, Andrew."

"What do you mean it won't do any good?" Nettie interjected.

"They'll just slip out of sight. Probably they're gone already."

Ben's shoulders fell. "No, I don't expect to ever see that money again. Or the papers."

He put his arm around Nettie's slender shoulder. "I was a fool to trust them. What must you think of me?"

"Think of you? Why I love you as much as I ever did. You just ran into the wrong people."

"It was stupid of me to think I'd be safe."

Nettie laid her hand on Ben's knee. "Ben, don't blame yourself. You couldn't have known."

"I should have expected it. I don't know what we'll do."

"Do?" Nettie got a determined look on her face. "We'll just go back to Gruental."

"Aren't we going on the ship?" Andrew wanted to know.

"I told you not to interrupt." Ben shoved Andrew onto the bed. "Now sit there and shut up so we can talk."

Andrew burst into tears. Ben's face softened. He took a handkerchief out of his back pocket and wiped Andrew's face. He put his arm around him and held him tight.

"I'm sorry, Son. Got carried away. I always did have a quick temper. Your ma knows that. I shouldn't take it out on you. But do let Ma and me talk."

When Andrew had stopped crying, Ben turned to Nettie again.

"Don't forget we gave up our place and sold all the livestock and furniture."

"Then we'll go to Karlswalde and stay with Mamma and Pappa until we find a place to live."

"And where'll they put us? They have eight people living there the way it is. Besides, they didn't want us to leave in the first place. Remember how Mamma cried, Nettie? They trusted me to take care of you. And now this."

"They'll be glad to see us again. Besides, whatever anybody says, I know better."

"What'll the people at church think? They'll say we should have waited to go with the group Uncle Tobias is organizing.

17

And maybe they're right."

"But remember, Pappa doesn't think we have anything to worry about."

"That's true. He thinks things will just go on the way they always have."

"Do you suppose Pappa is right?"

Ben was silent a long moment. "Nettie, I hate to contradict Pappa but I think he's wrong. Things are bad and they're getting worse all the time. I know. I've talked to men on the road."

Nettie's face fell. "Why can't we live in peace? Just raise our families and keep to ourselves?"

Ben laid his hand on Nettie's shoulder again.

"That would be the ideal but I'm afraid it's not possible. At least not until Christ comes and sets up His kingdom."

He patted Nettie's hand. "But this is man-talk. Women shouldn't have to bother about such things."

Ben rose to his feet. "One thing I'm going to do is watch for those thieves. There's a chance, a slim chance, we'll run into them."

"But would you know them if you saw them? It was late when you went to bed."

"I'd know them anywhere!" Ben roared.

Despite himself, Andrew tugged on Ben's sleeve. "Then what'll you do, Pa? Huh? What'll you do? Will you fight 'em?"

"Fight 'em?" Eva repeated.

Ben put his arm around Andrew and Eva. "Everything's going to be all right. Don't you worry."

He pulled his watch from his pocket and sprang open the lid.

"It's late, maybe we can eat and then I'll check with the police again. I'm starved. How about you, Andrew? I could eat a horse. Let's have some *vorscht* and *zwieback*."

Nettie handed Ben the bag of food. He pulled out a chunk of each and took a huge bite of *vorscht*.

Nettie's eyes sparkled mischievously. "Well the theft didn't spoil your appetite. Have you forgotten to pray?"

Ben grinned sheepishly and swallowed the bite. He held out

18

his hand to Andrew. "Come, Andrew and Eva, we're going to pray." They all clasped hands then Ben prayed.

"We thank you for these provisions. Now bless them to our bodies' use. Take care of us as we return and help us to recover the money and papers."

Ben paused.

"And give us a forgiving heart," he added.

"The *vorscht* was supposed to last 'til we reached Antwerp and the *zwieback* all the way to America, but it doesn't matter now."

She reached over and touched Ben's hand. "I was thinking while you were praying that God will take care of us, Ben. He always has."

"You're right, Nettie. I had planned to stay a day or two to look for Schultz and Gorbansky but I'm probably a fool to even try. This isn't Gruental or even Karlswalde with its five hundred people. Oschonin's a lot bigger and it's crowded. I'm sure those thieves left a long time ago. I could spend the whole day looking for them and still not find them."

"And we'd have to pay for another night's lodging," Nettie added.

"There's that to think about but I would like to try to find them ..."

His voice trailed off as he considered what he would do to the two if he did find them.

Ben sighed. "You're right. We can't afford it. I'll check with the police and let them handle it. We'd better get back as soon as we can. We'll only stay with Mamma and Pappa a little while -- until we find a place of our own."

"Toby'll be disappointed. Does he know?"

Ben nodded. "Met him in the hotel but Toby's a grown man. He can take care of himself."

"But his parents had counted on us to look after him."

"Nothing we can do about it."

"Too bad he couldn't have taken Sophia with him. He'll be awfully lonesome." Nettie looked up into Ben's clear blue eyes.

"Ben, do you think they'll ever let her go? Will Toby ever see Sophia again?"

Ben's eyes saddened. "I don't know, Nettie. I just don't know."

Ben tucked his coarse blue shirt into his trousers, straightened his suspenders, slipped on his heavy overcoat and hat then he left.

# Chapter Four

With a sad heart, Ben watched Nettie's nimble fingers rip open the seam of her coat. Nettie paused, still holding the lining in her hand.

"In a way I'm glad this happened," she said.

Ben raised his eyebrow. "You really didn't want to leave, did you?"

Nettie shook her head. "I didn't want to leave Pappa and Mamma. I'd probably never see them again." She paused. "And then this baby ..."

"I know. You were good to come anyway. If only your pappa and mamma had come with us. Do you suppose our great-grandparents felt the same way when they came to Russia seventy years ago? Was it as hard for them to leave their families?"

"That was different. They left because of persecution. And everyone came."

"It's no different now. I may be less than thirty but I'm sure persecution's coming. And very soon. They've passed this new law and I'm sure we're the real reason. Those of us who refuse to take up arms will be in trouble."

"I know. That's the only reason I consented to go. But Pappa says they'll give you alternative work."

"I don't trust 'em."

Nettie gave Ben a worried look then reached through the open seam and pulled out several *rubles*. She laid them in his hand.

Ben studied them a moment.

"This probably would have been enough to buy a horse in

America," he said at last.

He held them for a moment longer. "Now we'll have to use them to get back to Karlswalde."

Ben reached for his money purse then grimaced, remembering that the thieves had taken that too.

His clear blue eyes again turned to cold steel but he said nothing.

He dropped the coins into his pocket, gave Nettie a quick glance then left the room. There were tears in his eyes. Nettie could understand his frustration.

Ben was a complex man — soft and gentle at times but tough with a quick and fiery temper. Sometimes he was patient. At other times a minor incident could set him off.

He'd feel better outside. Something about the great out-of-doors had always appealed to him. Nettie guessed that's why he enjoyed farming. Their ancestors were men of the soil and they had become experts at draining swampland and tilling it. That expertise must have been passed on to Ben. He had carefully tilled the four acres they had rented from the nobleman and had kept it looking like a garden.

What fun she had setting up housekeeping after their wedding. The three-roomed house was plenty big enough for the two of them.

The first thing Nettie did when they moved in was spread the cloth she herself had embroidered on the table. No oilcloth for them, she told Mamma. But that quickly changed when Andrew arrived. It was much easier to wipe the oilcloth than to wash and iron a tablecloth. She had folded the embroidered cloth and put it away for company. Now it was in the immigrant box with the other things they planned to take to America.

All those years Ben worked for the nobleman, Ben dreamed of farming his own land. In Russia that would never happen.

Then they heard of the vast areas of land available in America. Ben couldn't believe it at first.

But the committee the Hollanders sent on a fact-finding tour returned with glowing reports. Mamma's brother, Elder Tobias

Unruh, was one of them.

After that Ben became restless and soon shared his dreams with Nettie. But the decision to leave was difficult. To please Ben, Nettie reluctantly made preparations to leave. How disappointed Ben must be with this turn of events.

* * *

At the drayhouse, Ben met Joseph Hoffman, a drayman, who had stopped to pass the time of day with the proprietor. Hoffman had dark brown eyes and a dark beard that reached his chest. Ben asked him if he would take them to Karlswalde.

"You're going home?" Hoffman exclaimed. "Most people are going to America or at least talking about it."

"Not really going home. To Karlswalde, where my wife's parents live."

Hoffman took off his hat and ran his fingers through his dark hair, which, like his beard, was streaked with gray.

"Guess you know what you're doing but if I were you, I'd leave Russia while I had the chance. If I weren't so old and didn't have a business to run, I'd leave too."

"That's what I intended to do until two thugs came along."

"And?"

"Took our papers and our tickets, our money too."

"So that's why you're going back. Too bad. But what'll you do when everybody else from Karlswalde leaves? Heard the whole *dorf's* leaving."

"That's just talk. Some of them aren't going. My wife's parents aren't."

"Why not?"

"Don't have the money. Besides, her father thinks things aren't as bad as they seem."

Hoffman slowly shook his head. "Hope they don't find out the hard way. Besides, I wouldn't let that stop me from going, if

23

I were you."

Hoffman turned to the business at hand. "You can ride along if there's room. How many of you are there?"

"My wife and two small children."

"Sure, there's room if you don't mind being a little cramped. I'm on my way to Schepetowka with some freight. Since you lost everything, I won't charge you much."

Hoffman turned to his restless horses. He stepped between them and stroked their necks, mumbling reassuring sounds to them.

Ben eyed Hoffman's wagon. The floor was about three feet wide with two-foot sloping sides. The sloping sides made it useful for hauling loose hay. Except for a small space directly behind the driver's seat, the wagon was filled with packing boxes.

"Not as big as the Hollanders' wagons," Hoffman said. "That Buller from Karlswalde drives a big wagon, all painted and shiny."

"You know him?"

"Sure. Often meet him on the road."

"Well, Buller's my father-in-law."

"You don't say!" Hoffman stuck out a hand. "Then we're friends!" He climbed into the seat. "Get in and we'll pick up your family and things and be on our way. It's late and I need to get going."

Ben climbed up into the wagon and seated himself beside Hoffman.

\* \* \*

Nettie helped Andrew pick up his toys then gathered their belongings and put them into the immigrant box. She closed the lid with a bang.

She stared at the box before helping Eva with her coat. This

24

was all they had except for the clothes they were wearing and their bedding.

Toby's sudden appearance in the doorway, brought her back to reality. "Morning, Nettie."

"Why good morning, Toby."

Toby sat down on the immigrant box. His head drooped dejectedly. Andrew and Eva ran to his side but he hardly noticed them.

"Hear you're going back," he said. "When are you leaving?"

"Soon as Ben can find someone to take us."

"I had hoped you'd change your mind."

"Nothing else we can do."

"Yeah, I guess you're right but I wish you were going."

"No more than Ben does. He's very disappointed."

Before they could say more, Ben walked into the room.

"Are you ready?" he asked. "Driver's anxious to get started."

Toby rose and picked up the immigrant box. Ben took the bed roll. Nettie and the children followed.

Toby swung the heavy box over the side of the wagon and shoved it in front of the boxes already there. There would barely be room for Nettie's feet.

"Want to sit up front with the driver?" Ben asked.

Nettie's mouth dropped open. "Oh, no!" she said. "We'll sit on our box."

Ben frowned. "Got a long ways to go and the box is hard."

Nettie smiled. "I'll be all right."

Hoffman leaped into the wagon and stacked two boxes on top of each other then set them behind the immigrant box.

"That'll give you something to lean on," he said. "Doesn't have springs like the seat but I'll try to miss the holes."

He ruffled Andrew's blonde hair. "The boy can sit in front with us."

Hoffman climbed over the back of the seat and took the reins. When Hoffman turned his back, Nettie hiked up her ankle-length dress, stepped on the hub of the front wheel then, with Ben's help, she climbed into the wagon.

25

"You sure you want to sit there?" Ben asked as he swung Eva over the side and set her on Nettie's lap.

"We'll be just fine."

"All right then, but if you get too tired, say so and we'll trade seats for a while."

Ben helped Andrew onto the seat. Before climbing up himself, he extended a hand to Toby.

Toby's big, hairy hand wrapped itself around Ben's and held it like a vise. He reached out with the other hand and clutched Ben's arm. "You'll look after Sophia, won't you?" he asked.

"Why sure, that is as much as we can. You know the Russians and our people don't have much to do with each other."

"But you'll keep an eye out for her, listen for anything about her, won't you?"

"Sure."

"And you'll come as soon as you can, won't you?" Toby asked.

Ben nodded.

"They say it's a big country. How will we ever find each other?"

"Most of our people are settling in a place called Kansas so I suppose that's as good a place to meet as any."

"All right then."

Toby was still clutching Ben's arm. "You *will* come, won't you?"

"If we can get the money."

"You have to! And when you come, bring Sophia."

The wagon pulled away and left Toby staring after them.

# Chapter Five

Toby's dark eyes stung as he watched the departing wagon. He brushed his sleeve across his eyes and whisked away a tear. This wasn't the way he and Sophia had imagined things to happen. They dreamed of making the trip together and of spending the rest of their lives with each other. They planned to marry as soon as they got to America or maybe before on board the ship.

But Sophia's father had ruined all that. He ordered Sophia to remain behind even though she'd already had her passport and visa. Toby didn't know when he'd ever see Sophia again or *if* he'd ever see her again. To make matters worse, now that Ben and Nettie weren't going, he had to go alone with people he hardly knew.

Long after the wagon disappeared from sight, Toby stood and stared after the wagon. A shrill whistle jolted him back to the present. Then another blast sounded, this time a little more impatiently. Toby picked up his immigrant box and in a few long strides he reached the hissing train. His feet had barely touched the inside of the car when the train lurched forward. Toby lunged through the door and chose the first empty seat he saw.

The train quickly picked up speed and before long they left Russia and were traveling through Poland. Toby stared out the window but he saw nothing. He was thinking of Sophia, beautiful, brown-eyed Sophia. Was she thinking of him too?

* * *

Sophia *was* thinking of Toby but she was at home patching a pair of her brother's trousers.

"Why can't they watch what they're doing?" she wondered aloud as she cut a patch to fit the hole.

Sophia was sure if they had to patch the holes they tore in their trousers, they'd be more careful. She usually hated patching but today was different. While she stitched, she could think about other things. And today she wanted to think of Toby.

Sophia looked up at the clock standing on the shelf with the icons beside it. It was almost time for Toby's train to leave. How she wished she were there with him. But at least Ben and Nettie Richert would be there. He wouldn't have to travel alone with strangers. She glanced again at the icons and prayed for Toby's safety.

She thrust her hand into her pocket and drew out the little angel Toby had carved for her then traced the fine lines with her fingers. Then she planted a kiss on the angel's head.

A tear rolled down her cheek and then another and another. She took a handkerchief from her pocket and wiped them away. She couldn't let Mother see her crying again. She would never understand. Even when Sophia's heart was breaking because Father had set his foot down, Mother didn't seem to understand. Had Mother ever loved Father as much as Sophia loved Toby? Impossible!

Sophia remembered how angry Father was when she and Toby shared their plans with them.

"I will not allow it!" he shouted. "Aren't our young men good enough for you? Must you choose a Hollander? He doesn't even belong to the Church."

"Please, Father," Sophia had begged.

But Father was firm. "At sixteen you are too young to decide for yourself. Someday you will understand and will thank me."

"Never!" she declared in a loud voice. "Never! I do know what I'm doing."

"Maybe they'll change their mind," Toby told her.

But they hadn't.

And yesterday, when Toby came to say goodbye, they would not even let her talk to him.

Now as Sophia remembered those encounters, she burst into fresh tears.

Mother chose that moment to come into the room. Sophia slipped the little angel into her pocket.

Mother put her hand on Sophia's shoulder. "You aren't still crying about that ... that Hollander, are you?" she asked.

There was a touch of empathy in Mother's voice but Sophia knew that didn't mean that Mother would side with her. She would always support Father.

Mother put her hand on Sophia's shoulder. "Just remember, Father knows best and like he said, someday you will thank him."

Sophia dropped the trousers she was mending and covering her face with her hands, she burst into more tears.

Mother put her arm around her sobbing daughter. But Sophia knew she and Father would stand by their decision.

Sophia remembered the first time she saw Toby. It was just after his youngest sister was born. Toby came for Sophia in his father's wagon so she could help his mother.

Toby, so strong and handsome, helped her into the wagon. Their eyes met and their lives changed forever. For two wonderful weeks she stayed in the Beyer home. For fourteen days they saw each other every day. They ate at the same table. Their eyes met across the room a thousand times. Their bodies often touched as they secretly brushed against each other in passing. At the time, although they never said so in words, they both knew there would never be anyone else for either of them. And they also knew neither of their parents would approve. Marriages between Russians and Hollanders just didn't take place.

Then the day came when Toby's mother no longer needed Sophia's help and Toby took her home. On the way, they stopped in a grove of trees and Toby took Sophia in his arms and declared his love for her. Sophia could still feel his powerful arms around her.

"Somehow, sometime," he promised, "I'll make you my wife."

The time ended all too soon and they moved on. After that they saw each other only occasionally. But always in secret.

Then, one day when they could bear it no longer, they decided to emigrate to America and secretly they applied for passports and visas. Since Sophia was only sixteen, they falsified her age. They talked about that a long time but in the end they decided this lie was justified. Still, Toby felt a pang of guilt and said so. When the documents arrived, Sophia told her parents of their plans. Father was furious.

"I will not let you go," he bellowed. "He isn't a Russian. Besides, it isn't proper for you to travel together when you're not married."

In the end, he sent Toby away and Sophia rushed to her room crying.

Sophia brushed away another tear. Did Toby miss her as much as she missed him?

# Chapter Six

Nettie settled back on the immigrant box and looked straight ahead. She forced back the tears that threatened. She couldn't let Ben down. He had dreamed too long of America. And they had worked too hard. It wasn't Ben's fault that the thugs robbed him. Couldn't blame Ben for catching up on much-needed sleep. Still, she couldn't help thinking it was carelessness. If only she had kept the money and papers with her. They would be on their way to America.

Nettie couldn't forget all the work that had gone into their leaving, the baking and *vorscht*-making, the sorting, the selling and all the scrubbing so the house would be clean for the next family. And all the time, she hadn't felt well. The morning sickness had lasted far longer than it should have. And then there were the false labor pains. She couldn't help wondering if something was wrong with this pregnancy.

She still wasn't feeling well and now the work was all for nothing. The first thing they needed to do was find a house. And they'd have to have furniture too, not a lot but enough to get by. Ben could make more in the wintertime. Worst of all, Ben might have to serve in the military.

Nettie had mixed feelings about going to America. She wanted to go for Ben's sake but she also wanted to stay. She thought of the new life growing inside of her. Tears welled up in her eyes as she remembered the two little ones, a girl and a boy, whom they had buried in the church yard. Maybe this time the baby would live, especially now that she would be where Mamma could attend her.

31

The wagon had barely pulled out of Oschonin, when the train whistle echoed across the valley. Ben winced. They would have been on that train leaving for America if it hadn't been for those thieves.

No one in Karlswalde would be looking for them. The home folks couldn't know they were coming back. Ben and Nettie had no way of letting them know.

Hoffman broke into Ben's reverie. "You want me to take you to Karlswalde?" he asked.

Ben nodded. "Know where that is?"

"Been there lots of times. You folks raise mighty fine cattle and hogs too. Your cows produce more milk than any cows in the country. 'Milk-boats,' they call them."

"It's the acorns."

"You're too modest. You Hollanders are excellent farmers. Your people were the first to use a one-share plow instead of a wooden hook. And you were the first to use a cradle with the sickle. It's little wonder you raised small grains better than the Russians. And we can't forget the potatoes."

"And what did the Russians use them for?"

"Making vodka!" Hoffman guffawed. "Leave it to the Russians."

Did they raise potatoes in America? Nettie wondered. Potatoes were a main-stay for the Hollanders. How many different ways had Nettie cooked them? She had fried them and mashed them and served them whole. Ben liked fried potatoes best, that is, it was a toss-up between fried potatoes and the mashed potatoes and gravy she served at special meals.

But Hoffman was still talking. Nettie strained to listen. "Anyway," Hoffman was saying, "you Hollanders have done very well for yourselves."

Ben frowned. "Don't forget down through the centuries, with every move, the Hollanders gave up their land and most of their possessions. Nettie's father is fifty-one and all he owns is some livestock, his wagon and their household goods. Even the few acres they farm and the house they live in don't belong to them. They're just renting."

"But you have to admit that the Tsar's treated you Hollanders better than they have their own people and better than the Germans who immigrated here. The National Party isn't happy about that. They want everyone to be treated alike. 'Russification' they call it."

Ben shrugged. "But the Tsar's freed the serfs."

"And it took him years to do it. But just wait. The National Party will push until you Hollanders will be treated the same as everybody else. The fact that your people didn't serve in the Crimean War in fifty-four did not sit well with them. That's why, starting in October, every man will have to register for the military lottery."

Hoffman took his eyes off the road and looked at Ben. "That includes you Hollanders, too."

"But it's not right. Catherine, the Great, said freedom from the military was forever."

"Ah, but that's where you're wrong. The forever in the *ukaz* means ninety-nine years. The ninety-nine years are up, have been for several years. This new law includes *everybody*."

"But they've only drafted the serfs in the past."

"That won't be true anymore. The Tsar's caved in to the National Party on a number of things. They'll keep putting the pressure on. If they have their way, the government will control everything. And to get the support of the state church, they'll push to make everyone pay taxes to support it."

"Surely not. We have our own church to take care of."

"Won't matter."

"Our people scrimped and saved to build our church. How can they expect us to support the state church too?"

Hoffman nodded. "That's not all. They're saying the Germans used the Kaiser's money to get the best land in the country. And don't forget, they classify us all as Germans,

33

including you Hollanders."

"Everyone knows that the Kaiser didn't pay us to settle here. Catherine the Great lured our people here then told them where to live. Besides, our people went to Prussia before they came here. "

Hoffman snapped the reins and the horses lurched forward.

"You know it and I know it but if they say it loud enough and often enough they'll have everyone else believing that you're German sympathizers, especially the Tsar's officials. Besides, they believe the Kaiser will start a war between Russia and the Germans,"

Hoffman turned to look Ben full in the face. "And you Hollanders will side with the Kaiser."

Ben shook his head. "But we're not Germans. We're Hollanders. We're not loyal to the Kaiser. Never have been. You know that! Besides, you Germans came to get land. Our people are pacifists. They came so they could practice their faith."

"Again, we all know that but will the Tsar listen to us or will he listen to the National Party? As far as they're concerned, you're Germans too. I think the Tsar's sorry his grandmother, Catherine the Great, gave you Hollanders all that good land and he's only too willing to take it away from you. Besides, the Tsar has to keep the nobility happy too. They haven't forgotten that he took away some of their land and set the serfs free."

"But it wasn't good land. When our people came, they cleared and drained it then built it up."

Hoffman snapped the reins again and the horses trotted a little faster.

"Yes, sir, I think the Tsar will buckle under to the National Party. Freedom will be restricted."

Ben frowned. "There's talk that since we practice non-resistance, they might let our men work for the forestry division."

Hoffman waved away the thought. "Talk, just talk. You'll see, my friend. Like I said, I'm German too, though not of your people. I hope you're right. The military's no picnic. You serve for twenty-five years and when you're finished, there's no pension. If you get drafted, it's doubtful if your family will ever see you again. Sometimes they hire you out to fight for some other country. Worse yet, if you get crippled up, you're on your own. Plenty of beggars in Rovno. You've seen them. They're all soldiers who've been hurt so bad they're no use to the army. They muster them out to look after themselves."

Nettie shuddered. What if Ben were forced to go into the military? Could she live without him for twenty-five years? And how would she feel if he came back a cripple, if he came back at all? How would they live? There was no way she could earn a living.

"What a pity!" Ben was saying.

Hoffman nodded. "Like I said, it's not good. Talked to a man not long ago whose brother had been drafted. Terrible what the Russians do to them. Flog them for falling asleep at their post or for not answering roll call, little things like that. And the trouble is some of the Germans don't know Russian so they don't understand the commands."

Nettie kept her eyes closed but she heard every word. Could this happen to Ben? Ben really didn't understand much Russian.

Ben stirred uncomfortably and threw a worried glance over his shoulder. Fortunately, Eva was sleeping soundly in Nettie's arms. Nettie's eyes were closed too. Andrew, seated between Ben and Hoffman, was leaning heavily against Ben and was breathing deeply. Ben heaved a sigh of relief.

"Asleep, are they?" Hoffman asked.

Ben nodded.

"Like I was telling you, this man's brother said they'd strip them, then march them past a line of soldiers who hit them with knouts. The more excited the soldiers got, the faster and harder they swung their knouts."

"What's a knout?"

"You don't know what a knout is? You'll find out if your name comes up in the military lottery. It's a whip. Made of

35

leather with a piece of metal at the end."

Tears rolled down Nettie's cheeks.

"That's not all. Often they sell their armies to other countries and you'd have to fight for them," Hoffman said. "You don't want to serve in the army. If I were you, I'd get out of Russia as soon as I could. How old are you anyway? About thirty-five?"

"Be thirty in October."

"See, then you still have ten years before you're too old for the military lottery."

Ben knew Hoffman was right.

Nettie winced. She didn't want Ben to go through that. Still, the fact was she didn't want to leave.

The two men fell silent.

"It's interesting that you feel the way you do about the Tsar," Ben said after a while. "Many of our people agree with you. They fully believe persecution is right around the corner. That's one reason they're talking of immigrating to America. They don't trust the Tsar."

"Can't blame them either. I don't trust him myself. I heard your people sent delegates to America to check it out, even, asked President Grant personally for permission to settle there."

"That they did and Nettie's uncle, Elder Tobias Unruh, was one of them. They got permission and they've asked the American churches for a loan. The *dorfs* are divided about going. Nettie's parents sided with the people who wanted to stay."

Hoffman looked grim.

"The others organized a committee to plan the immigration," Ben continued. "Everybody signed a promise to remain peaceable and satisfied. They also agreed to obey orders and not to grumble or criticize the overseeing committee."

Hoffman grinned. "And those stubborn Germans agreed to it?"

"Hollanders, not Germans."

"Whatever."

"But yes they did. They even agreed to put the group's welfare ahead of their own and promised to pay back any loans."

"Sounds like they're serious about leaving."

"You bet they are. Each family will put a *ruble* a month in the church treasury to pay for the train-ride to Antwerp."

Hoffman eyed Ben. "Sounds like they have it well organized. Then why did you leave before the rest of 'em?"

"Wanted to get out while I could."

"Then you'll leave again with the others?"

"Can't. Not without money."

"You're a fool if you stay. Can't you get some of that church loan?"

"The loan hasn't come through yet."

"Well, then, I'd buy myself a team and wagon. You could probably earn enough by November."

"Only problem is I don't have the money." Ben's face tightend. "Had a little sewn in our coats but there's not enough to buy a team and wagon. Those swindling thieves took every last *kopeck* I had on me."

"Then I'd beg or borrow enough to buy an outfit! You can make more money freighting than any other way."

Behind them, the sun was slowly sinking.

Darkness set in long before they caught sight of the forest surrounding Karlswalde. Nettie saw the trees and was glad they were almost home.

Ben sat quietly thinking over Hoffman's advice. Hoffman was right, of course, but who would lend him the money to buy a team? Who *could*?

Then they reached Karlswalde. Except for the two saloons, one at the north end and the other at the south, the *dorf* was dark.

"Turn here," Ben said when they reached the saloon at the north end of town.

Hoffman turned onto the unpaved street. Dark silhouettes of long houses with steep roofs lined one side of the street. The families lived in the front part of the house. The center part housed the cattle and the far end was used to store hay.

Each yard was nearly the same. The remains of last year's

haystack and a chicken house stood at the back. Near the street was a bricked-in well.

"Sure can tell this is a Hollander *dorf*," Hoffman said. "You open your doors to the side while Russians open theirs to the front."

"Not sure why but, as far as I know, that's the way they've always built them. And they've always combined the barn and the hay mow with the house. Makes the house warm and it's handy for the boys who sleep in the hay."

The strip of land behind the houses had been cleared of timber and staked into four-acre plots. On this land, rented from the noblemen, the Hollanders raised Turkey Red Wheat and oats for their horses.

Dairy farmers, their prize herds grazed in the oak-forested pasture across the road.

"It's the fourth house," Ben said when they reached the church.

Hoffman turned off the street and Ben vaulted out of the wagon to open the gate. As the gate opened, a barking dog burst from around the corner and lunged for the horses The team shied to the right but Hoffman clutched the reins more firmly and brought them under control. But they pranced nervously and strained at the bit.

Ben stuck out his hand to the dog. "Be still, Patches! Wanna wake the neighborhood?"

At the sound of Ben's voice, the dog pricked up his ears and bounded toward him.

"Recognized my voice, did you?" Ben said as he stroked the dog's head.

For an answer, the dog lunged at Ben's face and tried to lick it.

"Down, Patches," Ben ordered but the happy dog wagged his tail and ran circles in front of Ben, nearly tripping him.

Fending himself from the dog's display of excitement Ben

**A Hollander House**

strode purposefully to the door. No one answered his first knock. He knocked a second time, this time a little harder.

Then from inside came the sound of wood scraping against wood as the security bar slid from its place. The upper half of the door opened and Pappa's face, with his night cap still in place, appeared in the opening.

His graying goatee dropped to his chest.

"Am I seeing ghosts?" he exclaimed.

"No ghosts, Pappa," Ben replied. "It's Ben and Nettie. Can we come in?"

Pappa flung open the lower half of the door and stood unashamedly in his long night shirt.

"But, of course. Come in! Come in!"

"Mamma, it's Ben and Nettie," he flung over his shoulder.

Pappa stepped aside to let the late arrivals into the small kitchen. Then Mamma, her hair hanging in a long braid down her back and wearing a long nightgown, wrapped her ample arms around Nettie. Tears gushed down Nettie's cheeks. She was home with Mamma. How could they ever have considered leaving?

Pandemonium broke out as Nettie's four sisters rushed into the little room.

"Come into the sitting room," Mamma said as she led the way into the next room. "Helena, go tell Johan."

Mamma struck a match and lit the kerosene lamp standing on the square table in the middle of the room. Then she straightened the rumpled comforter on the bed in the corner.

A settee stood against the outside wall and above it, prominently displayed, hung the framed words, "*Gott ist die liebe*." A crudely-built dresser, a rocker and several straight chairs completed the furnishings.

Just then, a small wizened woman, dressed in a long flannel nightgown and matching nightcap, came tottering through the door on the far side of the room.

"*Was ist loos*?" she asked as she peered disapprovingly at the noisy little gathering. "It's late. You should all be in bed."

40

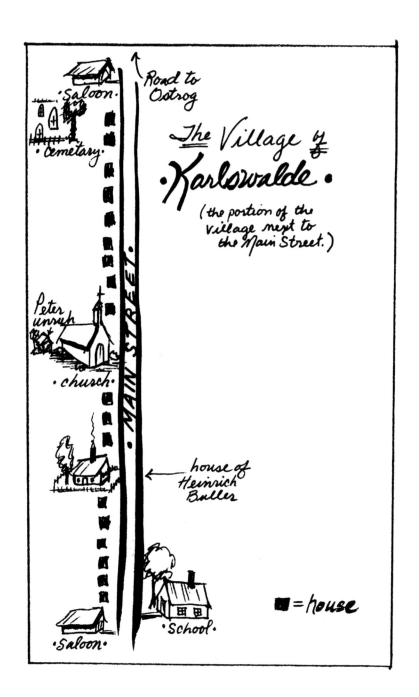

Road to Ostrog

The Village of **Karlswalde** ·

(the portion of the village next to the Main Street.)

·Saloon·

·Cemetery·

Peter unruh

·church·

MAIN STREET·

house of Heinrich Buller

·Saloon·

·School·

■ = house

Then her eyes fell on Nettie. The little woman dropped into the rocker.

"Ben and Nettie, you are back!" she exclaimed. "But why? You should be on your way to America."

Nettie put her arms around her. "Oh, Grossmom, I'm so glad to see you again."

"But why did you come back? You shouldn't have, you know. Things are not good here in Russia. We should all go. But nobody listens to me."

"It's a long story, Grossmom," Ben put in. "We'll ..."

Just then Ben remembered Joseph Hoffman still standing in the doorway. He turned and thrust some coins into his hand.

Hoffman refused the coins. "Let's say it's toward that team and wagon you'll be needing," he said.

"But ..."

"No buts about it. Consider it seed money."

"Well, if you say so," Ben said.

"I do say so."

"Well, then, why don't you spend the night here? It's late and the roads aren't safe anymore. You're welcome to sleep in the haymow."

"I'll take you up on that but first I'll have to take care of the horses."

"Johan," Pappa put in. "Take our horses out of the barn and put Hoffman's in."

"No need to do that," Hoffman protested. "I'll just tie 'em up."

"You were good enough to bring Ben and Nettie home." Pappa declared. "The least we can do is give your horses shelter."

"Well then, I'll unload Ben's box and head for bed. Have to deliver this load then go to Schepetowka for another."

With that he followed Johan out the door.

But although Hoffman retired, there was little sleep for the family that night.

"It's clear," Pappa said when he had heard the story of Ben's

42

misfortune. "You should have waited. Why else did God let you lose your papers and money?"

"But if we stay, Ben will have to serve in the army." Nettie exclaimed.

Ben looked at her in surprise. Had she been awake after all when he and Hoffman discussed the military?

Pappa waved her question away. "The Tsar's giving our young men something else to do."

Ben's eyes narrowed. "And if he doesn't?"

"You can move to Poland. It's not as far as America. Besides, by the time they settle all this you'll be too old for the military lottery."

"By that time Andrew will be almost old enough."

Pappa's face fell. "Yes, you're right," he said in a hushed tone. "Each generation has to face that question all over again."

"Well it doesn't have to be decided tonight," Mamma said. "The children have school tomorrow. They better go to bed."

"Andrew will be going to school too so he better go with Johan," Nettie put in.

"Oh, Ma, do I hafta? We just got back."

Nettie pinched her lips. "You've already missed two days."

Reluctantly, the boys made their way to the haymow. The adults talked long into the night before Pappa announced it was time to go to bed.

"Soon be time to milk the cows," Pappa said.

"Ben and Nettie, you take the girls' bed in Grossmom's room," Mamma announced. "The girls can sleep on the floor here in the living room."

Soon the house was dark and quiet again. Ben had barely touched the bed when he fell asleep. But Nettie's soft voice awakened him.

"Ben," she whispered. "Are you asleep?"

Ben sat up with a start. "What did you say?" he muttered.

"Shush. Don't wake up the others. Are you asleep?"

Ben rubbed his eyes. "I was."

"Sorry."

He put his arm around Nettie. "That's all right. The baby's not coming, is it?"

"No, thank God. It's just that I can't sleep thinking about you going into the Russian army. Do they really whip them with whatever that thing is called?"

Ben jerked to attention. "Were you awake? I was sure you were asleep."

"I had my eyes closed but I couldn't sleep. Tell me, do you really think they'd be that cruel?"

Ben shrugged. "That's what Hoffman said."

"I don't want that to happen to you."

"Don't lie awake thinking about it. They say they'll give us alternate work."

"But Hoffman said that he didn't think they'd keep their word. Anyway, you'd be away from us for seven years. Andrew would be fourteen when you got back. And then you could be called up again during the next eight years."

"That's better than now. Now it's twenty-five. Most families don't expect to see their men again once they go into the army."

"Oh, Ben," Nettie sighed. "Did you know all this when we left?"

Ben nodded. "Yes, that's the main reason we left."

"Why didn't you tell me?"

"I did."

"Not all of it. I thought they made only the serfs serve in the army. We're not serfs. And I didn't know how terrible the army was."

"The new law changes all that. They're drafting everybody, even the rich. The only difference is that the rich become officers."

Ben drew Nettie close and held her tight.

"We'll find a way to go to America. I promise."

In a moment he was sound asleep again. But Nettie saw the sun rise. She didn't want Ben to serve in the military but now that they were back, she wasn't so sure she wanted to leave Mamma and Pappa either.

# Chapter Seven

The following morning while it was still dark, Ben awoke to the clattering of the cook stove. Then the safety bar on the door slid from its place and the door opened and closed. Pappa was on his way to the pasture to bring the cows to the barn for the morning milking. He would need help.

Ben tried to slip out of bed without waking Nettie and Eva but Nettie stirred.

"What time is it?" she mumbled sleepily from under the covers.

"Don't know. Can't see my watch but Pappa's already on his way to the pasture. I'll help him so the boys won't have to get up so early. They were up late last night. So were you. Stay in bed."

Nettie did not argue. Her body ached from the many miles of rough roads. She snuggled back under the covers.

Ben slipped on his shirt and trousers then quietly left the room. Nettie had hardly closed her eyes again, when Eva raised up.

"Pa?" Eva asked.

"Helping Grandpappa."

"Me help too."

"You stay with Ma and keep her warm."

But Eva stubbornly refused to lay down. "Me wants to get up too," she insisted.

Nettie sighed. It was clear Eva wouldn't sleep anymore. Besides, Nettie could smell coffee. Mamma must be getting breakfast and with four extra people, Mamma would need Nettie's help. Besides, she would have to see that Andrew was up in time for school.

"All right then," Nettie said, "but first let me get dressed. Stay under the covers and keep warm."

Obediently, Eva sank into the featherbed. Nettie crossed the room to the immigrant box and opened the lid. There, laying on top, was the tablecloth she had embroidered for her hope chest. It was one of the few frivolous things they packed to take with them. At first Ben said they'd have to leave it but when he saw Nettie's disappointment, he reluctantly agreed to take it along.

Now Nettie carefully laid the tablecloth aside and took out fresh petticoats and underwear for herself and Eva. Then she took out an ankle-length dress made of gray calico sprinkled with tiny mauve flowers and laid it on the bed. It was one of the dresses she had made to take to America.

Beneath it lay the dress she had made for Eva using the same material. She took it out and laid it beside her own dress.

Eva sprang out of bed and grabbed the dress.

"Just like Ma's!" she exclaimed as she thrust the dress over her head.

But she missed her aim and her head became stuck in the sleeve. Frustrated, she cried out for help.

"You crawl back under the covers," Nettie said as she freed Eva. "I'll dress you after I get dressed."

But Eva shook her head. "Me get dressed now," she insisted.

"No," Nettie said in a no-nonsense voice. "You stay in bed."

She covered Eva again and tucked the covers firmly around her then continued with her own preparations.

When Nettie finished dressing, she untied the ribbon holding her hair in a pony tail and combed out her hair then fashioned it into a *chignon*.

After dressing Eva, Nettie opened the immigrant box again and took out clean clothes for Andrew. Then, with a quick glance at Grossmom's empty bed, she silently whisked Eva out the bedroom door and through the living room past the sleeping forms of her sisters.

Nettie paused in the doorway for a moment to take in the delicious aroma of fried pork and coffee.

"Mm, side-pork!" Nettie exclaimed as she stepped into the kitchen.

Mamma was turning sputtering slices of smoked pork with a two-tined fork, trying unsuccessfully to keep them from curling. Nearby a pot of coffee bubbled away.

Eva held out her arms for Mamma to take her. Mamma handed the fork to Nettie and took Eva in her arms.

"*Mein kindtlein*," Mamma said as she pressed Eva to her breast. "Grandchildren should live near their grandparents."

Mamma, forty-seven, was short and plump. Her brown hair streaked with gray was severely pulled back from her face and twisted in a coil at the back of her head.

But Eva didn't remain long in Mamma's arms. Upon hearing Nettie's sisters stirring in the living room, she wriggled out of Mamma's arms and toddled to her aunts.

Their shrieks of excitement brought back memories of Nettie's own childhood. For a moment she was no longer twenty-six and the mother of two. She was ten and still living at home.

Mamma took back the fork and Nettie turned from the warmth of the bricked-in oven and planted a kiss on Grossmom's wrinkled cheek. Grossmom, dressed in a dark blue dress and a gray apron that covered most of her dress, was seated in a rocking chair a few steps from the stove.

"Good morning," Nettie chirped.

Grossmom, her thin white hair twisted in a tiny knot near the top of her head, laid down the sock she was patching and cupped Nettie's face in her hands and kissed her.

"It's good to have you home but you should be on the train going to America."

"I know. We really didn't intend to come back."

"You must leave with Tobias's group."

"Ben wants to," Nettie said.

"And you?"

"Well, I'll go if Ben insists." Nettie paused. "But it is awfully nice to be back."

Grossmom's troubled eyes turned stern. "You must go! There's no other way."

"It takes a lot of money and there isn't much time to earn it."

"Then you'll have to borrow from the churches in America."

"But that's not certain yet. They still haven't agreed to loan the money."

"Tobias says it's only a matter of time."

"But Ben doesn't like to borrow. He's independent."

"It's a good trait. Ben is a fine boy but this borrowing is justi-fied. Helena and Heinrich should leave too."

"What?" Mamma exclaimed. "And leave everything behind?"

"Helena, you know the land is poor. Can't grow anything on it."

"Heinrich agrees with me."

"Then he's a fool." Grossmom picked up her mending again.

Mamma handed a slab of raw side-pork to Nettie.

"Put it back on the shelf, would you?"

Nettie took the meat through the door to Grossmom's left leading into the smoke room. She breathed in the heavy aroma of smoked hams and side-pork hanging from the ceiling. That meat had to last until this year's chicks were big enough to butcher.

The shelves of the closet directly behind Grossmom were filled with bread and home-canned goods. To Grossmom's right a door opened into the barn. The tantalizing aroma coming from the kitchen stove could not completely cover the odor seeping in from the barn.

A long table covered with a red and white checkered oilcloth took up most of the remaining space in the kitchen. In the middle of the table the flickering oil lamp cast a circle of light in the dim room. Starched white curtains hung at the room's only window.

Nettie slipped a flowered apron over her head then fastened it behind her back. She wiped the oil cloth with a dishcloth then, taking a stack of plates from the cupboard on the opposite wall, she set the plates around the table.

"Seems like we've been gone for weeks instead of just a couple of days" Nettie said.

"Too bad you left in the first place," Mamma said. "You'll have to start all over again with livestock and chickens. All these people leaving for America. They're foolish."

Before Nettie could answer, her sisters, Catherine and Helena, with Eva between them came clattering into the kitchen. Elizabeth and Caroline followed close behind.

"Breakfast ready?" Catherine asked.

"You lay-a-beds," Mamma exclaimed, "expecting to eat without helping. It wouldn't happen if Nettie weren't here. Elizabeth, wash your hands. Wash Eva's too. Helena, see if Andrew is up. Though he probably went with the men to milk the cows. They'll be in anytime."

Mamma turned to Nettie again. "Like I said, "all these people leaving for America. They're foolish."

Nettie frowned. "A lot of people don't agree with you, Mamma, even Ben. He says our young men might have to take up arms."

"There's nothing to worry about. Pappa says the Tsar'll be fair and let them work in the forestry."

"And if he doesn't?" Nettie asked.

"Oh, he will."

"But they've already passed the law. It starts in October."

Nettie put her arm around Mamma's shoulders.

"Why don't you emigrate with us?"

Mamma wiped her hands on the corner of her apron. She swept her arms in an arc around the small but cozy room.

"We're too old to give all this up."

Her blue eyes sparkled with pride.

"Why look at all we have. We'd have to start all over again. And in a strange land yet."

A hairpin slipped from the coil at the back of her neck and fell to the floor. She bent to pick it up then tucked it back into her hair.

"Besides, Grossmom isn't well enough to make the journey. She's seventy-eight. We couldn't leave her here all alone."

"What do you mean I can't make the journey?"

"Of course!" Nettie exclaimed. "You could come with us."

Mamma, her lips pinched tightly closed, shook her head.

"But, like I said, we can't leave all this behind. Look at this nice big house, made of wood yet, not mud like the people by the Black Sea. Why we live in the best place in Russia. Not barren like other places. We have trees. God was good to bring us here to this huge oak forest."

Mamma speared the side-pork onto a plate. "We've worked too hard to leave all this. In America, we'd have to start all over again. They say the people there dig holes in the ground and live in them like rats."

"But, Mamma, what about Johan? When he's old enough he'll be drafted into the army."

Mamma tucked a loose strand of hair back into the coil.

"Like I said, Pappa says that the Tsar will find other work for our young men."

"They might break their word and put them in the army anyway." Nettie lowered her voice. "Mamma, the Russians are cruel to the soldiers."

Mamma waved away the thought. "God will look after us. Besides, how could we afford to take all of our family? And, Nettie, you've got to think about your children and about the one that isn't born yet. What would you have done if it had been born on the ship? Can you be sure there'd be a mid-wife?"

"Ben could have helped."

Grossmom nodded. "Ben is a fine boy. He'd know what to do."

Mamma looked astounded. "Don't count on it. Men lose their heads at a time like that. I always send them off to get hot water or quilts. Gets them out of the way. Besides, you need your Mamma at a time like that."

The lock of hair had come loose again. Mamma pinned it more firmly into the coil. "We can't go. Even if we sell all we have, it wouldn't be enough to buy passage for the whole family."

Mamma opened a door in the floor and descended to the cellar for butter.

Grossmom beckoned Nettie to move closer. "You're right," she whispered. She shook her finger in the direction of the cellar door. "They could go if they wanted to. If they refuse, you and Ben must go anyway."

Nettie flung her arms around the diminutive figure. "Oh Grossmom, I love you so much."

She had hardly spoken the words when the door opened and Pappa and Ben, each carrying a bucket of milk, entered the kitchen. While the men washed up, Mamma poured milk into a pitcher and set it on the table.

She was setting the side-pork on the table when Johan and Andrew made their noisy entrance into the kitchen.

"Wash up," Mamma told them.

The boys frowned but they did as they were told.

When they were all seated at the table, Pappa prayed then they began eating.

"Too bad you gave up your house," Pappa said when he had filled his plate.

"With all the people leaving, we'll find a house."

"You can live with us until then."

Ben frowned. "I'm sorry to have to move in on you. But it will only be for a short while."

Pappa nodded. "*Ya*, until you find a house. Land too if you want it."

Ben swallowed his food. "Still there's this. We don't know what the nobleman will do with the land people leave behind. He might take it away from our people and rent it to the Russians. There are plenty who would like to lay their hands on the land we've cleared and improved."

"Don't worry. The nobleman knows we're good farmers."

Ben hesitated. "Actually, Pappa," he said at last. "I'd still like to go to America."

51

"Maybe the theft was a sign from God," Pappa's goatee trembled with every word. "Maybe you aren't supposed to go."

He shook his head hopelessly.

"Pappa, with all due respect to you, I don't think it was judgment from God that caused the theft. It was the result of my own foolishness. Next time I'll be more careful."

He hesitated then added. "Maybe you'd like to go with us this time."

Pappa shook his head. "We're too old to go to an unknown land. And we have too much to leave behind."

"Yes," Mamma chimed in. "We can't leave all this behind. It's taken years to get it."

Ben looked at them with troubled eyes. "Things are heating up here in Russia," he said. "St. Petersburg is full of crime. They've even tried to kill the Tsar."

"St. Petersburg's nearly two thousand miles away," Pappa said.

"But it's coming our way. The officials don't like us. They're rude to us. They were rude to me in Oschonin."

Pappa nodded then he added wistfully, "Actually, if we had the money we'd leave too."

Mamma jerked to attention. "What are you saying, Pappa? We can't leave all this behind."

"I don't think you have to worry, Mamma. Even if we sell our cattle and household goods, we wouldn't have enough to buy tickets. Counting Grossmom, there would be eight of us. No, we can't afford it."

"Maybe the Lord will provide another way," Ben said.

"Maybe, but then, again, we have to be practical."

The men drained their coffee cups then pushed back their chairs.

"Do you think the nobleman would loan me enough money to buy a team and wagon?" Ben asked Pappa.

"Not if he knows you're going to America."

"Maybe we wouldn't have to tell him."

Pappa nodded thoughtfully. "I see what you mean. Well, it

wouldn't hurt to try. I'd co-sign the loan if you like."

Ben's eyes mellowed. "Would you, Pappa?"

"If you like and we better go this morning. You'll be needing the wagon and horses."

He turned to Mamma. "Mamma, fix us a lunch. We're going to Ostrog to see the landlord."

Johan, who had been drinking from his bowl, set the bowl on the table with a thud.

"Can I go along, Pappa? Can I?"

"You're going to school, young man," Mamma flung over her shoulder.

"Oh, please, can't I go. Pappa, don't you think I need to go with you to help?"

"And what would you help with? We're not hauling anything. No, you better go to school."

"And it's almost time to go too," Mamma said as she cut the bread for Pappa and Ben's sandwiches. "Helena and Elizabeth, you clear the table.  Johan, you feed the chickens. And hurry or you'll be late."

"And take Andrew with you," Nettie said. "He's already missed two days."

Andrew frowned. "Oh, Ma, do I have to?"

"How else are you going to learn to cipher and speak proper German?"

"I won't be needing schooling. I'm going to be a farmer and maybe haul things like Grandpa."

Pappa rose from his chair. "You children are going to school. Only Ben and I are going to town."

Everyone knew it was settled. The boys would be going to school. Reluctantly, the boys left the table and Helena and Elizabeth  cleared it.

Soon Pappa and Ben, carrying their lunch in a bucket, climbed into Pappa's wagon then started on their way.

Reluctantly, the boys put on their coats and left for school. The girls soon followed.

"Wanna go too," Eva wailed.

Mamma picked her up and held her in her arms but Eva wriggled out of her grasp. She toddled to her coat hanging on a peg by the door and tugged at the hem.

"Wanna go to school," she whimpered.

"You can't go and that settles it," Nettie declared. She set Eva at the table with a jar of colorful buttons.

Eva, her face streaked with tears and sobbing intermittently half-heartedly sorted through the buttons. Soon she seemed completely absorbed in her play.

"Well," Mamma said when Eva had settled down, "we won't have to get dinner for the men so we'll get lots of work done. First I'll stir up a batch of bread. Then we'll hang a sheet across Grossmom's bedroom so you and Ben can have a place of your own."

So absorbed were they in their work that they forgot Eva. It wasn't until later that morning when they came to the kitchen for coffee that they noticed that Eva was missing.

"Eva. Where's Eva?" Nettie cried.

"She couldn't have gone far." Mamma said.

She turned to Grossmom. "Have you seen her?"

Grossmom shook her head. "I was with you."

Leaving her cup on the table, Nettie made a quick search of the barn and the haymow. Eva was not there. And she wasn't in the yard.

"Do you think she followed the children to school?" Mamma asked.

Nettie frowned. "How could she get out? She's not tall enough to reach the latch."

"Someone must have left the door open," Mamma decided. "Who knows how far she's gone?"

Nettie threw a coat over her shoulders and hurried to the schoolhouse. Patches, her plumed tail swishing, followed close at her heels.

But no one at the school had seen Eva. Dejectedly, Nettie walked back up the road. To her right was the pasture, where the villagers kept their cows, dozens of them. Had Eva climbed under the fence and into the pasture?

Nettie froze. The cattle seemed harmless enough but somewhere among that placid herd was a bull. More than once, he had chased the men. What would he do if he saw Eva?

"Oh, God," Nettie pled, "don't let anything happen to her. We've already buried two. Please. Not Eva, too."

Nettie wiped away a tear and hurried a little faster.

She climbed under the fence and into the wooded pasture. A few cows looked up as Nettie came toward them but they returned to their grazing.

Nettie ventured farther into the woods, calling as she went, but to no avail. By now she was hot and sweaty and her hair was hanging in untidy strands around her face. Nettie impatiently brushed back the unruly hair with her forearm. Where was Eva?

# Chapter Eight

Tired and disheveled, Nettie pondered her next move. Then a team and wagon appeared on the south horizon. It was coming her way but was still too far away to see any details. Nettie waited. Perhaps the driver had seen Eva.

As the wagon drew nearer, Nettie saw the driver silhouetted against the clear blue sky. The flaps on his cap were untied and were fluttering in the breeze.

Nettie heard Eva before she saw her. She was sitting on the seat beside the driver, gurgling happily and clapping her hands.

"Me ride in the wagon," she shouted.

Nettie flew to her side. "Thank God you're safe."

The driver, grinned then lifted Eva out of the wagon and into her mother's waiting arms.

Nettie wrapped her arms around her small daughter and wept for joy.

"Where were you going?" Nettie asked after a while.

"Me find Pappa."

"But you shouldn't have."

"Found her down the road," the farmer explained. "She was sitting on the grass crying. I figured she probably lived here in Karlswalde."

"Oh, thank you. Thank you."

"Glad to do it," the driver said. "Have to hurry now."

He snapped the reins and the horses started up the road.

Nettie knew Eva needed a talking to but she didn't have the heart to do it. Instead, she held her tightly as she carried her home.

* * *

Shortly before supper, Ben with two sleek chestnut-colored horses hitched to a wagon, swept into the yard. Pappa, driving his own rig, followed close behind.

Andrew and Johan with Patches at their heels, raced across the yard to meet them.

Ben stuck out his hand. "Slow down. Slow down. Horses get scared when you come up so fast."

Andrew came to a stop but there was excitement written all over his face.

"Pa, did you really buy them? Did you, huh?" he wanted to know. "Are they ours?"

"Did you hear what I said?"

Andrew nodded. "But are they really ours?"

"Yep," Ben said as he fastened the reins. He leaped out of the wagon. "Not the best that money can buy but a good team and they'll help earn money to emigrate."

Ben laid Andrew's hand on the horse's nose and showed him how to stroke it.

"They like to be stroked but they don't like sudden moves," he told them.

Andrew and Johan watched then stroked the other horse in the same way.

"What're their names?" Andrew wanted to know.

"Sig and Sush."

Suddenly the door to the house flew open and the women with the girls trailing behind, swept out of the house and rushed to the horses' sides. The horses whinnied and pawed nervously.

"Stand back," Ben warned. "You startled them."

Obediently, the womenfolk stepped back and admired the horses at a distance.

"Oh, Pa," Andrew exclaimed. "It's the nicest team I've ever seen."

Johan wasn't ready to accept that. "Nicer than Pappa's?" he challenged.

"A lot nicer."

"Can't be. Pappa's are better."

"Who says?" Andrew wanted to know.

Johan threw out his chest. "I do."

Andrew might be younger than Johan but Andrew wasn't ready to concede. "So?"

Johan pushed up his sleeve. Just in time, Nettie stepped between the two boys. "Supper's ready, boys, and there's fresh bread. Wash up and come in."

Johan pulled down his sleeve and started running for the house. "Beat you," he yelled over his shoulder.

"So?" Andrew said. He stayed behind to watch Ben take care of the horses.

"Well, we found Ben a good team," Pappa said when the family had gathered around the table and Pappa had prayed over the food.

"It's a good wagon too. Good prices on both. Doesn't hurt that so many people are leaving. Brings prices down."

"Pappa's right. We got a good deal." Ben turned to Nettie. His blue eyes sparkled. "And, Nettie, we have a house."

"Oh, Ben, so soon? Where is it?"

"Right here in Karlswalde."

Nettie beamed. "Really?"

Ben smiled. "I thought you'd like that. It's close enough so you can walk here to Mamma and Pappa."

Nettie smiled her gentle smile. "That'll be nice especially when you're out hauling."

"I really didn't expect to find a house so soon but I stopped in to see Albert Toaves. He's in charge of that, you know. He said there was one."

"It's the Penner house," Pappa explained. "They left when you did and probably took the same ship you were supposed to take."

"Toaves wasn't very happy about everyone leaving. Said there'll be plenty of empty houses if Uncle Tobias has his way and the whole *dorf* leaves. Said right now there aren't many

58

houses available. Just this one."

"Oh, Ben, I'm so glad. When can we move?"

"As soon as we can get packed. The house is empty. God was good to give us the house."

Nettie's eyes glistened. "I'll have time to plant a garden."

Ben took a sip of coffee. "That you will."

"What'll we do for furniture?"

"I'm taking a load to Schepetowka tomorrow. I'll bring back enough lumber to make some. We'll need a table, some benches and a bedstead. I'll bring some ticking too."

"That'll be soon enough. It'll give me time to scrub before we move in."

Ben frowned. "Seems to me the Penners were real clean. Surely, they cleaned before they moved out."

"Of course," Mamma said. "They were very clean. They wouldn't want others to think they're dirty so they'd have cleaned it properly before they left. But Nettie'll want to clean anyway. I'll help."

Ben gave a resigned sigh. "You women, you could save yourself a lot of work."

Nettie and Mamma just shrugged.

Pappa helped himself to another slice of bread then buttered it.

"We saw the overseer too. Says they're emptying their bins so there'll be room for the new crop. They can use Ben to haul wheat to Schepetowka."

"It'll mean staying overnight those days but then we can use the money," Ben said.

Schepetowka was a bustling railroad center connecting rural communities to the Black Sea. From the Black Sea, the grain was shipped by boat to other European countries. At this time of the year when the noblemen's farms were emptying their storage bins to make room for the next crop, the hauling business was booming.

"They'll also need help on the farms," Ben put in.

"I'll need help too," Pappa said, "not much, mind you. Johan is big enough to help but I might need help hauling, if the man who hauls for me can't handle it all."

"I'll take all the work I can get," Ben said. "And I'm glad we found a house. You've got a houseful without us and, besides, I don't want to be beholden to you."

"You'd never be beholden to us," Pappa declared. "You're family and you're welcome anytime."

Ben played with his fork. "Generous of you. But now we won't need to stay here. And we won't need the Penner house very long. Only 'til we have enough money to pay for the team and wagon and for more tickets. If we get the outfit paid off, we'd have that money."

Pappa leaned forward and looked Ben full in the face. "Do you really think you can earn that much money? There's lots of hauling but the nobleman doesn't pay very well"

"If not, we can probably get a loan from the American churches." Ben laid down his fork. "But I'd rather pay for the tickets myself."

"I wouldn't count on that money. They might decide not to send it," Pappa countered.

"If I get enough work and we watch what we spend, we might not have to borrow."

Pappa's eyes clouded over. "Like I've said many times, I'm not sure leaving's a good idea though, of course, if we could afford it, we might consider it."

"But we can get a hundred and sixty acres for nothing. Just think! All we need to do is live on it for five years."

"How do you know it's true? Could just be talk. Maybe the free land is all gone."

"Don't forget what Johannes Wall said when he came back a couple of years ago. He said America was the most wonderful place in the world. And it was big."

"Yes, and he almost got put in jail for it. Would have if he hadn't fled to Poland."

"But he escaped. Besides, Uncle Tobias has also been to America," Ben said.

Ben pushed his chair away from the table. "Pappa, I, that is Nettie and I, have made up our minds. We're going to try again."

Nettie looked at Ben with startled eyes but she said nothing.

Mamma stood up and started clearing the table. "Well, let's enjoy each other while we have time," she said.

Later, while preparing for bed behind the curtain, Nettie questioned Ben.

"Ben, something's wrong, isn't it?"

"Wrong? Why do you say that?"

"I can sense it."

Ben chucked Nettie under the chin. "You always can."

"What is it?"

"I guess it's the loan that bothers me. What if we can't make the payments?"

"But you sounded so certain when you talked to Pappa."

"Guess I was trying to keep up my own spirits."

"Surely you'll find freight to haul. Pappa always has."

"I don't want to take it away from him. He has eight mouths to feed. I only have four."

"Course I'll mainly haul wheat," Ben added.

"You got the team and wagon at a good price. Surely the Lord's hand was in that."

"I only hope I didn't jump ahead of His leading. That's why I don't like to borrow."

"If we decide to leave, you can always sell the team and wagon and pay off the loan."

"Who knows if there'll be anyone to buy them. There's talk that the whole *dorf* is leaving. And how much would I get for the rig if everybody's leaving? Another thing, if I don't get hauling, I won't earn any money."

Nettie laid her hand on Ben's. "Let's trust God to supply the work."

Ben's eyes shown with admiration. "I wish I had your faith, Nettie."

# Chapter Nine

The following morning, Mamma and Nettie, with Eva in her arms, set out for the new house.

"Looks pretty clean," Mamma said as she set down the bucket containing two odd-shaped chunks of homemade soap and some old rags.

Nettie also set down her bucket then lowered Eva to the floor. Eva toddled off into the other room.

"As I said, I'm sure Bertha scrubbed it thoroughly before they left," Nettie said. "Wouldn't want anyone to say she was a sloppy housekeeper."

"No, not Bertha."

They stepped into the living room. "House is just like ours. Isn't any bigger," Mamma said. "But then, they build these houses all alike. You'd think they'd add another bedroom for bigger families."

"The way things are going, we won't need a bigger house," Nettie said with faint bitterness. "God hasn't seen fit to let us keep but two babies."

She sighed wistfully.

"*Ya*, but you have another one coming."

"True but the house'll still be plenty big enough for all of us. The baby can sleep with us and when Andrew is older, he can sleep in the hay. Unless ..." She let her voice trail.

"Yes, unless you decide to leave," Mamma finished.

Nettie nodded then continued her planning.

"Ben won't come home until tomorrow and when he comes, I'll sew up the ticking he brings and we can sleep on the floor."

"No big hurry," Mamma said. "The girls don't mind sleeping

on the floor."

"But they need a room of their own."

"Yes, I've been thinking of that. I think we'll leave that sheet we put up for you. That'll give Grossmom space to herself, too."

Mamma picked up a bucket. "I'll get some water while you start the fire," she said.

Nettie brought in some wood she found stacked against the barn and started the fire in the firebox. She set the wash kettle on the stove and Mamma filled it with water from the well. Then, while the water heated, she and Mamma examined the smoke room and the barn.

The two women spent most of the day scrubbing walls and floors, breaking only long enough to eat the thick slices of bread and ham they had brought with them. Grossmom would feed the school children when they came home for lunch.

After lunch, Nettie piled their coats in one corner and laid Eva down for a nap. Eva slept until they had finished cleaning.

"Good thing I baked bread yesterday," Mamma said as they walked home. "You can take a loaf with you."

"And starter, if you don't mind," Nettie said. "If you let me borrow the extra mixing bowl, I'll bake Saturday. Ben will be expecting *zwieback*."

"You'll need an oil lamp too," Mamma said.

"Just oil. We packed a lamp in the immigrant box. We can use that. But I'll need a few pans and a few dishes. It's a lot to buy all at one time. We'll have to wait 'til Ben earns some money."

"I hope he gives up the idea of going to America."

"Mamma, we've talked about that before. I don't think he will." Nettie paused. "I'd really like to stay. You know that, don't you, Mamma?"

"I know. I hope he changes his mind." She turned to leave. "I'll get some things together for you while you do your packing."

"I don't have much to pack — just the quilts and bedding and the things that we took out of the immigrant box."

"It'll give you time to sew up the ticking when he comes. You get that done and I'll get the other things together then start supper."

Nettie had laid the last item into the immigrant box when Grossmom came to Nettie's side of the curtain. She was holding a flat object wrapped in a towel. She placed it into Nettie's hands.

"Open it," she whispered.

Nettie carefully unfolded the towel and there in the folds of the towel lay a beautiful dinner plate. Nettie's face beamed.

It was the plate that had hung on Grossmom's wall all those years before she had moved in with Mamma and Pappa. White with a translucent quality, the plate was edged with gold. Roses in various shades of pink formed a colorful border.

"Made in Germany by the Meissens," Grossmom explained. "It was my mother's. A wedding present. I want you to have it."

She stepped a little closer. "I want you to take it to America," she whispered. "When you get to America, hang it on the wall. It'll remind you of home."

Nettie put her free arm around Grossmom and held her close.

"Oh, Grossmom," Nettie whispered. "I'll take good care of it."

"I knew you would. That's why I'm giving it to you." Grossmom planted a kiss on Nettie's cheek.

"Now put it in the box and when you get to America, hang it on the wall. I'm glad Ben found a place for you to live but you mustn't stay. You must go to America."

"I'm not sure I want to go now that we're back."

Grossmom sat down on the edge of the bed. "You must. I know it's hard. My mamma often told me how hard it was for her and Pappa to leave Prussia and come here to Russia at the turn of the century. They left everything they owned only to start all over again. When persecution threatened, our people have always left. They're a courageous people."

"But this is different. Pappa says they'll give the men something else to do."

"You can't be sure. This is your chance to make sure it won't happen. I'll do everything I can to persuade your mamma and pappa to let you go. They should go too. Johan will soon be old enough for the military lottery. They need to get him out of Russia."

She shook her head solemnly. "And when your pappa and mamma go, I'll go with them."

Nettie's eyes brightened. "Will you, really?"

"*Ya*, I'll go along."

Nettie put her arms around Grossmom and gave her a big hug. "That would make it easier for us."

Grossmom watched Nettie lay the plate among the soft things in the box then she left to help Mamma with supper.

*** 

When Ben came home with a wagon-load of lumber the next day, Nettie, with Eva in her arms, went out to meet him.

"Did you need that much?" she asked.

"Enough to make two bed frames and to hold the straw ticks. I'll have to build a table and benches, too."

"Too bad Penners sold their furniture. It would have been easier."

"Anyway, I brought ticking, a tea kettle, a frying pan and a one-hundred pound bag of flour. And look what else I bought."

He took out a long roll wrapped in brown paper and tied with string.

"Open it," he said.

"Out here?"

"No better place."

Nettie carefully untied the string and handed it to Ben. Then, while Nettie unrolled the wrapping, he looped the string around his two fingers and tied it in a knot then stuck it in his pocket.

Inside the wrapping, was a roll of blue and white checkered oil cloth -- enough to cover a table.

65

Nettie's eyes shone. "Oh, Ben, you shouldn't have."

Ben's blue eyes sparkled. "Knew you'd appreciate a bit of color in the kitchen. Matches your eyes."

"Nearly matches yours too."

Nettie stitched the ticking into three bags and helped Ben stuff them with straw. After packing their belongings into Ben's wagon, they climbed in and left for their new home.

Mamma waved her apron at them.

When Ben had carried all their things into the house, Nettie opened the lid of the immigrant box and took out the plate Grossmom had given her.

"Let's hang it tonight," she told Ben.

"Tonight?"

"It'll add a touch of color to our plain little house."

"All right then."

When Ben had fastened the holder to the wall and inserted the plate, they all stood back and admired the plate.

"You're right," Ben said. "It adds a nice touch and it'll remind us that we're going to America."

"Remind us of Grossmom and our ancestors too," Nettie added.

She turned abruptly to Andrew. "It's getting late. Off to your bed in the corner."

She picked Eva up, took off her clothes and put her to bed on their straw tick.

Later that evening, Ben sat down on the tick and took off his boots. He lay back and watched Nettie brush her hair.

"It's good to be in our own house again," he whispered so he wouldn't awaken Eva and Andrew, who were already asleep, Eva on Ben and Nettie's bed and Andrew on the floor in the corner.

"Yes, it is good," Nettie answered. "It's just the right size for us, even when the new baby arrives. Be better for Mamma and Pappa too."

"You're right, Nettie. These little houses weren't made for big families. But we won't stay long," he added. "Just 'til we leave for America."

Nettie nodded but already she wasn't so sure she wanted to leave. Just being here alone under one roof gave here all the satisfaction she needed.

"We'll have to watch our spending," Ben said. "We still have some things to buy. We need a cow and some chickens."

"Mamma said we can take back the hen we gave her when we left this spring. It's sitting on eggs and when they hatch and grow, we'll have chickens to fry and then some for eggs later on. Maybe they'll lend us a cow too or give us some milk."

"That'll help and we can buy a piglet to raise and butcher before we leave. Won't take much to feed it — just some acorns and some slop. We'll make it into *vorscht* for the journey."

Ben stretched out on the stuffed straw tick. "It'll all help but I'm hoping to have plenty of hauling. We have to pay back the loan for the team and wagon."

"And don't forget, Ben, Andrew and Eva will need new shoes and some other clothing. They're growing so fast."

Ben nodded. "You're right. Before we know it they'll be grown up. That's why I'd like to take Andrew with me when I haul wheat to Schepetowka next Friday."

"But he'll miss school."

"One day won't hurt him and we'll be back on Saturday. I think he'd like that."

"He would but he'll get too tired."

"Won't hurt him this once. Besides, he can sleep on the way." Ben paused. "Give me a chance to be with him. If I get much hauling, I'll be gone a lot."

"Well," Nettie said reluctantly, "if you think so."

"I do."

And so it was settled. Andrew would accompany Ben when he hauled wheat the next Friday.

***

The next morning, Nettie caught Andrew as they were leaving for church. "Your ears, Andrew, did you wash them? Let's see.
You can't go to church without washing them."

She grabbed him by the right ear and examined it.

"Ouch, Ma, you're hurting me."

Ignoring his protests, Nettie continued her examination.

"I knew it!" she said. She jerked Andrew back into the kitchen, where, despite yelps of pain, she scrubbed both ears with a cloth.

"There," she said when she had finished. "Next time we go to church remember to clean them yourself."

Nettie closed the door behind them then she and Andrew joined Ben and Eva waiting for them at the side of the house. She didn't bother to lock the door. There was no need to.

"Well, one thing's sure," Ben said as they walked to church, "we wouldn't be here for the services today if those thieves hadn't robbed us. We'd be on the ship. If we had services at all, they'd likely be in a bare room."

Nettie smiled. "And in America, we might not have such a fine building. I don't suppose they have such nice churches in America."

"No, at least not where our people are taking up homesteads. But take my word for it, Nettie, they'll build one as soon as they can. Worship of God always has been important to them."

Indeed, the people had built this building at great sacrifice. And, unlike the state churches, they had built it without a penny from the Tsar. They had willingly given of their limited means and had built it with their own hands. The pews and podium like the hand-turned altar balustrades were made of oak cut from their own trees. It was indeed a hallmark in their little community.

When they entered the church, Nettie slipped in next to Susan Wedel, who was seated in the section near the back where the young women usually sat.

Nettie and Susan had been best friends since childhood.

They attended the same school, the same church and they were married the same year. Their sons, Andrew and David, were born merely six weeks apart.

Like Nettie, Susan wore her long dark hair in a *chignon* at the back of her neck. She was plump and jolly and when she laughed, her whole body shook.

Ben and Andrew took seats across the aisle. The gray-bearded men were seated at the front. Their wives, dressed in black and wearing black bonnets of ribbons and lace, were seated across the aisle. The rest of the congregation occupied the rows in between, the men on one side and the women on the other.

When the bell in the belfry chimed, the song leader, carrying the congregation's only hymn book, stepped to the podium and announced the first hymn. He tapped the book with his tuning fork then hummed the tone and sang the first line. The congregation repeated the line in four-part harmony. The song leader sang the second line and again the congregation repeated that line. They continued this exchange throughout that hymn and several more. Then the choir sang.

Next, the leading elder, Abraham Schmidt, stepped to the podium and delivered a long sermon. Andrew squirmed restlessly but Eva fell asleep.

After the service but she and Ben were inundated with people asking questions. Susan, sizing up the situation, leaned over and invited Nettie and Ben for *faspa* that evening.

Late that afternoon when Ben and Nettie and the children arrived at the farm Abe managed for the nobleman, Abe and Susan met them in the yard. Abe and Ben took care of the horses and the two boys ran off to play. Susan led the way into the house.

Inside, Susan wrapped her ample arms around Nettie. "I'm so glad you're back," she said. "We heard what happened."

Then her eyes twinkled. "Actually, to tell you the truth, I'm glad it happened."

"Susan, don't tell anybody but I am glad to be back, too,"

Nettie whispered. "Ben wants to try again but I'm not so sure."

Susan chuckled and her body shook. "I don't blame you." Then her face grew sober. "What would you have done about the baby? What if it'd been born on the journey?"

"We could have handled it. After all, it wasn't our first child. I've had Andrew and Eva and the two that didn't live. Even so, I'm glad that I'm here with Mamma."

Susan nodded. "Yes, much better." She put her hands on her hips. "Well, I'm glad you're back. And I hope you don't try it again."

The door opened and Ben and Abe stepped into the kitchen.

"*Faspa* ready?" Abe wanted to know. "I'm starving."

Susan chuckled again. "Oh, Abe, you're always hungry. It'll be ready by the time you wash your hands."

At first the talk around the table centered around farming and gardening but the conversation soon turned to Ben and Nettie's return.

Susan poured more coffee. "We've heard all kinds of things but we don't know what's rumor and what isn't. Tell us what happened."

And so Ben, with additions and clarifications from Nettie, told the whole story.

"I've heard it's happened before," Abe said when Ben had finished. "And, with so many people packing the railroad stations, I'm sure it'll happen again. So many people leaving. I think it's a mistake."

Ben shook his head. "I don't agree. Things are getting bad."

"Just rumor, that's all. We feel perfectly safe even though we're not living in a *dorf*. Things aren't nearly as bad as they say. It's bound to happen in a railroad center like Oschonin. Crowds attract criminal types. Besides, it might be worse in America. All those Indians. And so many strangers. You won't know whom to trust."

Ben laid his half-eaten cookie on his plate.

"Abe, Nettie's uncle's been to America. He says they've pushed the Indians west to make room for civilization. Besides, our people settled in their own communities like they did here. They look after each other."

"Sounds good but who knows what's true. The American politicians want people to come to America and they'll lie to get them there."

"Can't be much worse than here. Russian politicians want to keep us here. Have you heard about the terrible things happening in St. Petersburg?"

"That's a long ways from here."

"But it could happen here."

Abe took another cookie. "Could but it's not likely."

"Well, I'd like to go when the big group leaves, if we can get the money, that is, and if Nettie will. Borrowed for the outfit but I'm hoping to get enough hauling to pay for it. We'll sell it when we leave and use that money."

"We're staying," Abe said. "The nobleman's been good to me and he'll give me work and a place to live for as long as I want. He'll likely keep me out of the army too."

Ben leaned forward, his eyes gleaming. "But just think! In America you can *own* land."

Abe shook his head. "We're staying."

The afternoon ended all too soon. "You must come again," Susan told Nettie as she hugged her goodbye. "Maybe Ben can drop you off sometime when he's taking freight by."

She chuckled. "We'll have a wonderful time gossiping."

# Chapter Ten

The following day, a government official rode into Ben and Nettie's yard. Ben saw him and went to meet him.

"I'm looking for Benjamin P. Richert," the official told him.

"You're speaking to him. What do you want?"

The official took a sheet of paper from his pocket. "We received your application for a passport but there's a problem."

"A problem? Didn't I fill in all the information?"

"Oh, yes you filled it all in. The problem is that we've already issued you a passport. Not only that but the passport and papers were used."

"But ..."

"Why is it that you are still here in Russia and are applying for another? Did you sell the other passport?"

Ben's mouth dropped open. "Oh, no! It was stolen?"

"Stolen? You should have reported it."

"But I did, as soon as it happened."

"We don't have a record of it."

"I reported it in Oschonin."

The official studied Ben's face. "In Oschonin? Are you sure?"

"Of course I'm sure," Ben roared. "Wouldn't I know whether or not I had reported it? Did it the same morning that they stole it."

The officer shook his head. "This demands investigation. We'll have to look into this before we can issue another passport. And, of course, you can't request a visa from America until then."

The official's eyes narrowed. "Stolen passports bring a lotta money. They're in great demand. It's very tempting to sell them. But I must warn you, if you sold yours, you will be severely penalized."

Ben's eyes flashed. "But I didn't sell it! My friends will back me up."

"Oh? Very good! That will help in our investigation." The officer took a pencil from his pocket. "And what are their addresses?"

Ben thought for a moment. "Actually, they're aboard the train to Antwerp on their way to America."

The officer grinned and put away his pencil. "Then, of course, we won't be able to question them, will we? Nevertheless, we'll look into it. You know, of course, that our government is reluctant to issue passports to people going to America, especially when they have already received a passport before. Like I said, how do we know that you didn't sell it to another family?"

Ben sputtered. "Check with the police in Oschonin," he said at last. "They'll tell you I reported it the morning it happened."

The official folded the paper and put it into his coat pocket. "We will make an investigation. But we charge a fee for that -- say ten *rubles*."

"But isn't that your job? Doesn't the government pay for that?"

The officer shook his head. "This is added responsibility. It's not covered by the Tsar. If you want us to look into it, you'll have to pay."

Ben stuck out his bearded chin. "I think I'll look into that."

"If you do, it'll take even longer."

Ben heaved a sigh of resignation and pulled out his new money purse. He chose a few coins and offered them to the officer.

The officer slowly shook his head. "Not really enough," he said.

Ben's eyes flashed. "That's all I have."

The officer took the coins and put them into his pocket. "Let me warn you," he said when he had pocketed them. "This will take some time. I wouldn't be in a hurry to go anywhere. Like I said, the Tsar frowns on people who apply for passports."

The official slowly shook his head. "No, the Tsar is not happy that people, especially your people, are leaving. He's sure to do something to stop them."

He mounted his horse and rode away. Ben leaned his pitchfork against the house and stalked into the kitchen, slamming the door behind him.

"One more reason to leave Russia," he thundered. "They'll bleed us to death."

* * *

"I'm picking up a load of wheat tomorrow," Ben told Nettie the next day. "Go right by Wedels. Want to go along?"

"Oh, I'd love to!"

"Then it's as good as done. We'll leave right after breakfast. Do you think Mamma will see Andrew off to school?"

"I'm sure she will."

When they drove into the Wedel yard the next morning, the dog barked lustily but no one appeared to greet them.

"Maybe they're not home." Nettie suggested.

"Got to be. Horses are out in the pasture. I'll go see if anyone's in the house."

He vaulted over the side of his wagon and fastened the horses to the hitching post. The dog stopped barking, wagged his tail then, sniffing at Ben's heels, he followed Ben to the door.

The door stood open and Ben looked in. He gasped when he saw the chaos in the room. Cupboard doors and drawers stood wide open, their contents scattered over the floor. A deadly silence filled the room.

Then Ben saw Abe and Susan's twisted bodies laying in one corner. Ben crossed the room and dropped to his knees beside them. Their faces were bruised and swollen and blood was seeping from their mouths.

Then Ben thought of Nettie and Eva waiting in the wagon. He quickly rose to his feet but before he could reach the door, he heard Nettie scream. She was standing in the doorway holding Eva.

"What's happened?"

"Something terrible!"

"Where are they?"

Ben nodded toward the corner. Nettie, with Eva still in her arms, rushed across the room and fell on her knees between them.

Then Ben heard muffled sounds coming from the next room. When he checked, he found David tied to a chair with a rag stuffed in his mouth. When David saw Ben, he sobbed with relief.

Ben took a knife from his pocket, flicked it open then slashed the ropes. When the ropes fell off, the sobbing boy ran to his parents' side. But the silent forms did not respond. Nettie put her arms around him and held him close.

Ben dropped to his knees and felt Abe's face. His skin was warm and he was still breathing. Ben sighed with relief. He wet some clean rags he found on the floor then he wiped Susan and Abe's faces.

Abe opened his eyes first. His eyes filled with terror when he saw Ben.

"It's Ben, Abe," Ben told him. "Ben Richert."

Abe's shoulders relaxed a little. He tried to raise himself but he was too weak.

"Susan?" he asked.

"She's right beside you."

Abe tried to turn his body to look at her but he couldn't.

"Is she ... is she all right?" he asked.

"Nettie's tending to her. I think she's beginning to come to."

"Robbers!" he gasped. "That's who did it. Looking for money. We don't have any but they didn't believe me."

75

By now Susan had also gained consciousness. She tried to get up but, like Abe, she was too weak.

"David?" she asked.

David flung his arms around her. "Right here, Mamma."

"Thank God!" Susan breathed then closed her eyes again.

Ben found medicine in the cupboard, poured some into the open wounds then bandaged them using strips from an old sheet. He helped them both into bed.

"I hate to leave but I've got to deliver my load," he said.

"Be all right," Abe muttered. "Done what they wanted to. Won't be back."

"I'll be here," Nettie said.

"I'm not sure I want you to stay. Abe isn't strong enough to protect you."

"Like Abe said, they've gotten what they're looking for. We'll be all right."

Ben hesitated. "I guess there's no other way. When I'm in town, I'll report it to the police."

But Ben knew nothing would be done. It was happening too often these days. The police couldn't keep up with these criminals, even if they wanted to.

Nettie and Eva stayed until Ben returned. By then, Abe and Susan were sitting up and color had returned to their cheeks.

After extracting a promise that they would take it easy a few days, Ben and Nettie started back to Karlswalde. The ride back was a quiet one.

"How can anyone be so wicked?" Nettie asked at last. "They might have killed them."

"It's happening all too often. Violence is erupting all over the country. The Tsar's enemies are foaming at the mouth. One of these days they're going to kill him."

"But St. Petersburg's far away."

Ben shook his head. "Closer than you think."

"Do you really think it will affect us?"

"Already has. Much of the violence is aimed at our people. Nettie, I'm more sure than ever that there'll be open persecution."

"But we live in *dorfs*. We can watch over each other. Abe and Susan lived all by themselves."

"That's true but I think we'll see it in our *dorfs* too."

"Do you think these are the same men who robbed you?"

Ben shook his head. "No, I don't think so. Schultz and Gorbansky rob immigrants. This is different. Probably young upstarts who see it as an easy way to get money."

Ben shuddered. It could have been Nettie and the children. He *had* to persuade Nettie to leave. They couldn't stay any longer. On their way home, Ben and Nettie stopped by to see Mamma and Pappa. Pappa was mending harnesses with the hide he and Ben had tanned the winter before. Ben told Pappa about the robbery.

"What's going to happen next?" Pappa exclaimed. "First the Koehn family back in January. Now this. It's not safe."

Pappa cut a strip of leather from the hide. "It's good we live so close to each other, all in rows. We can watch out for each other."

"But, Pappa," Ben protested. "It's happening everywhere. Nobody's safe."

Pappa nodded. "True, but we have to trust God."

"But we also have to help ourselves. I agree with Uncle Tobias. It's time to leave."

"But Elder Schmidt says it's better to stay."

Ben shook his head. "He's wrong. We'll be sorry if we do, very sorry."

He laid his hand on Pappa's shoulder. "Pappa, I think this is the beginning of persecution."

But Ben could see that Pappa did not agree.

# Chapter Eleven

Early the next Friday morning Ben and Andrew left for Schepetowka.

The next day Nettie uncovered the yeast she had mixed the night before and added butter and flour to make a huge batch of *zwieback*. After she had thoroughly kneaded it, she pinched off a small piece for Eva.

Eva played with the dough until it turned gray then rolled it into two balls and set one on top of the other to make a *zwieback*. But before she set the dough to rise, she took off the top ball and put it into her mouth.

She quickly spit it out.

Nettie looked at Eva in surprise then pinched off a piece of dough and tasted it. The dough was salty, way too salty.

What was she to do with it? If she made it into *zwieback*, no one would eat them. But she couldn't throw out the dough. Ben had said they mustn't waste money. Certainly, throwing away a whole batch of dough, would be wasting flour, not to speak of all the butter she put in.

Nettie had no choice. She buried the dough in the garden then stirred up another batch.

Nettie felt a little guilty burying the dough but she was relieved to know it was out of sight. But when she put Eva down for her nap, she glanced out the window. To her horror, the yeast had activated in the warm sun. The dough was mushrooming out of the ground. It was twice its original size.

She hurried out the door, picked up a sturdy stick and beat the mass of dough to its original size. An hour later it had again doubled. Once again she beat it down. All afternoon the dough kept billowing out of the ground. Nettie beat it down each time. Would it ever stop?

If it continued to rise, it would still be there when Ben and Andrew returned. Ben would see it and he'd know she had wasted money. She couldn't let him see it. She dug a little deeper and dumped the defiant lump into the hole.

When Nettie had filled the hole with dirt, she sat down to rest in the living room. She glanced up and her eyes caught Grossmom's plate hanging on the wall. Beautiful as it was, it seemed to be glaring at her, accusing her of wasting money, money they could have used to emigrate. Nettie turned away but she kept glancing back.

All the rest of the afternoon, Nettie kept a watchful eye for Ben's wagon. But to Nettie's relief, it was dark when Ben and Andrew finally drove into the yard. Both declared they were starved so they sat down immediately for a supper of fresh *zwieback* and milk. While they ate, Ben and Andrew told Nettie about their day and, to Nettie's relief, they didn't ask about hers.

But the next morning, when Nettie looked out the bedroom window, there was that familiar mushroom again. It seemed to be bigger than ever and growing before her eyes. Nettie gasped then burst into tears.

Ben, with Eva in his arms, rushed to her side.

Eva squealed with delight when she saw the dough.

"Ma's dough," she exclaimed as she pointed at the white mass emerging from the earth.

Ben frowned and gave Nettie a questioning look.

Ben roared with laughter when Nettie explained.

"Then you aren't angry with me?" Nettie asked in surprise. "I didn't mean to waste money."

Ben put his arm around Nettie. "Of course you didn't. And one time won't break us."

He released Nettie and set Eva on the floor.

"Now let's have some of those fresh *zwieback* before we go to church," he said.

# Chapter Twelve

"Ben! Ben! Wake up!"

Ben rolled over to face Nettie. "What is it?"

"The baby!" Nettie answered then doubled up in pain.

"But it's not time."

"I know. I'm afraid we'll lose this one too, like we did the other two."

"Shall I go get Mamma?"

"No. Wait."

"But ..."

"Maybe if I lie still, I won't lose the baby."

Nettie grimaced again. "Ben, hold my hand."

Ben put his arm around Nettie and held her close. It was almost more than Ben could bear. If only he could do something. The worst part of it was if the baby came now, it would all be in vain. The baby wouldn't live.

Ben waited until the contraction had subsided. "I better get Mamma. Will you be all right if I go?"

Nettie reached out a limp hand. "There's no other way."

Ben rose. "All right, then. I'll be back as soon as I can."

Ben soon returned with Mamma.

"Heat some water," Mamma told Ben then hurried into the bedroom.

Nettie was having another contraction. Mamma laid her hand on Nettie's forehead and waited.

When the contraction had subsided, Nettie looked up at Mamma with dark soulful eyes. "Oh, Mamma, what can I do? The baby's not supposed to come yet."

Mamma rubbed Nettie's back. "How long has it been?"

"A long time. I didn't wake Ben right away."

Mamma frowned. "Why didn't you send him sooner?"

"I was sure it would pass but, Mamma, it's getting worse."

Neither woman spoke until Nettie was comfortable again.

Mamma sent Ben for a warm, wet towel. When he returned, Mamma laid the towel on Nettie's back just as Mamma's mother and her mother before her had done. Then she gently massaged Nettie's swollen belly. Ben stood nearby to exchange warm towels for cold ones.

Twice, Mamma tried to send Ben from the room but except to stir up the fire and heat more water, he refused to leave Nettie's side.

It was morning before the baby was born. The baby was another boy. But the infant was too young to live.

Nettie held the tiny body close to her breast as hot tears raced down her cheeks. She touched the transparent eyelids, now tightly closed. They would never look into her face. Nettie grimaced as she drank the medicinal mixture Mamma handed her, then, exhausted, she handed the baby back to Mamma, turned on her side and slept.

Mamma wrapped the tiny infant in a piece of an old sheet while, Ben, choking back the tears, went out to dig a grave. He selected a spot in the cemetery next to the tiny mounds where they had buried the other two infants.

Then, before lowering his small son into the grave, he prayed committing the little one into the safekeeping of his Heavenly Father. And he prayed for strength for Nettie and himself as they suffered yet another disappointment.

"We'll see you again," he said aloud. "We'll meet you in heaven, you and your sister and brother."

Then Ben dug up a clump of purple violets and planted it at the head of the tiny grave. Each spring, when the violets bloomed, they would remind them of the little boy who had lived for such a short time.

As Ben stood looking at the tiny mound, he wondered who would keep off the weeds if they left. Mamma? She and Pappa had lost children of their own. Couldn't count on them. The purple violets would stand guard. And the Heavenly Father would look after their souls.

Reluctantly, Ben walked back to the house. Poor Nettie. She had always wanted lots of children. She was only seventeen when they were married. Now at twenty-six, she had already lost three children. They had been married nine years and had only two living children to show for it.

And this last one was all his fault, Ben told himself. If he hadn't insisted on leaving, their little son's life might have been spared. But now because of his stubbornness, Nettie had lost this baby too.

* * *

When Nettie awakened later that day, the impact of their loss hit her full force. Tears rolled down her cheeks. She had lost another precious infant. And it was all Ben's fault. If he hadn't insisted on leaving, their son would have lived.

Nettie turned to the wall and wept. Then someone patted her on the shoulder. She opened her eyes and saw Grossmom bending over her.

"Grossmom, how did you get here?"

"Ben brought me." Grossmom's eyes were also wet with tears.

"Nettie, dear, it's all right. Your baby's with Jesus and one day you'll see him again," she said in a soothing voice.

"But my arms feel so empty."

Grossmom nodded. "I know. I lost four babies myself and your mamma has lost some too. It hurts a lot."

"If Ben hadn't insisted, this might not have happened."

"And then again, it might have. You were at home when you lost the other two."

"I think it was the long journey to and from Oschonin,

especially in Hoffman's wagon. It was meant to haul freight, not people, especially not a woman with child."

Grossmom put her arms around Nettie and held her close. "We can't second-guess God. It may not help now but I believe He will give you more children. Perhaps the next one will live."

"But I want this one."

Grossmom nodded. "I know. That's the way it always is. But you'll see, even though the next one will never take this baby's place, it will comfort you."

She withdrew her arms then laid one hand on Nettie's shoulder again. "Let me pray with you. It is really God who can comfort. I know! Trust yourself into His care."

They both closed their eyes and Grossmom prayed for Nettie and Ben then entrusted the little one into the loving care of the Heavenly Father. "And give them another child," she added.

Nettie reached out and touched Grossmom's hand. "Do you really think I can ever be happy again, Grossmom?"

"Of course, but it will take time."

"And Ben. I feel like I never want him to touch me again."

"Ben loves you, *mein kindtlein*."

"But it was his fault."

"I understand how you feel, *mein kindtlein*. I'll pray that God will take away your bitterness. It can only hurt you."

"Pray hard, Grossmom. I feel like I can never be happy again."

Things just didn't seem the same to Nettie anymore. Nevertheless, the world went on. The vegetables in the garden nudged their heads through the black soil and the purple crocuses at the front of the house nodded their heads in the breeze. Across Main Street, the grass in the pasture turned green and the sturdy oaks surrounding the little *dorf* of Karlswalde put on their green clothes.

But Nettie did not notice. Although she had physically recovered, an overpowering melancholy engulfed her.

Nettie knew Ben still hoped to leave but they didn't talk about it anymore. Sometimes, when Ben didn't think Nettie noticed, he gave her a puzzled look. Nettie knew he didn't understand her. How could he? She didn't understand herself. Nettie was sure he could see she took no interest in life, that she just went through the motions.

Meanwhile, Ben continued to haul wheat.

And all the time talk about a mass exodus continued. One group from Heinrichsdorf was leaving in August and the group from Karlswalde was making plans to leave in November. Ben hoped he and Nettie could join the latter group.

Then gradually, Nettie began to take an interest in life again. And one thing she knew, she didn't want to leave Mamma and Pappa. She did not want to go to America. Ben could sense it too. He talked to her about it one night as they were preparing for bed.

Nettie had let down her long silky hair and was brushing the honey-colored tresses that reached nearly to her waist when Ben came into the room. He moved Eva to one side then lay down to watch Nettie.

"We haven't talked about America lately," Ben said.

"Ben, I've been thinking. Maybe we shouldn't go."

"Not go? But we've been planning on it. Even when those crooks took the money, we were determined not to let that stop us."

"I know, Ben, but it is awfully nice to be with family." Nettie frowned. "If only they hadn't passed that law."

Ben rose and blew out the candle then pulled Nettie to the bed beside him and held her in his arms.

"It isn't only that, Nettie. In America, we can own land, acres of it. We can get it by proving up on it. We'll never own land here. Oh, we can rent it, especially with everyone leaving. In America the land is free."

"Things are changing. Maybe that will change too."

Ben shook his head. "No, I don't think so. I think the Tsar will take the land our people leave behind and give it to others to farm. And don't forget there's the military law. If we don't leave, I may have to serve."

"Some say that God brought judgment on us when they took the papers and the money. Do you believe that?"

Ben pulled Nettie closer.

"No. Look at the hundreds who left on that ship. And the hundreds who left before them. All reports are that the people are prospering. No, I don't think God would have picked us out to punish us."

Ben put one hand on each of Nettie's cheeks and looked into her eyes. "But, Nettie, my love, if you don't want to go, we'll stay. I promise."

* * *

The next morning, Nettie hummed softly as she stirred the laundry boiling in the huge kettle suspended over the open fire in the yard. Before leaving that morning, Ben had filled the kettle with water and built a fire under it.

A sense of contentment that she hadn't experienced since her baby died settled over Nettie as she hung the clean shirts and socks on the line. Ben had promised not to leave Karlswalde against her will. The truth was she didn't want to go and now she had his assurance that they would not be leaving. The world looked brighter.

When the clothes had boiled long enough, Nettie fished them out with a long stick then rinsed them in a tub of clear water. She ran them through the wringer then hung them on lines to dry.

As she watched the clothes blowing in the breeze, she dreamed of the years ahead. They'd have lots of children, she told herself.

Life was good now that Ben had promised to remain in Russia.

# Chapter Thirteen

One day, while Ben was hauling wheat to Schepetowka, he met Joseph Hoffman. They pulled off the road to talk.

"Glad to see you took my advice and bought a team and wagon," Hoffman told Ben. "When you leaving for America?"

Ben stroked his beard. "I'm not sure we're going."

"Not going?" Joseph bellowed. "I was sure you'd leave with the big group. What changed your mind?"

"Nettie doesn't really want to go. She doesn't want to leave her parents."

"Maybe she'd change her mind if she heard Albert Graber."

"Albert Graber? Who's he?"

"Haven't you heard about him?"

Ben shook his head. "Never heard of him."

"Well, he's been to America and now he's back telling everyone how wonderful America is. He's drawing big crowds."

Joseph leaned forward then lowered his voice.

"The Russians don't like it. There's talk that the Tsar is going to put a stop to it just like they did to Johannes Wall. What they'll do, I don't know. But you ought to hear him before they shut him up."

"Are you sure he's honest? Heard his kind of men get money for each person that settles in America."

"Oh yes. I've heard that too but this man is one of your people. I think he really is trying to get you people to leave. Maybe he does get a *ruble* or two but I don't think that's his main reason for getting your people to leave."

Ben's eyes brightened with interest. "Where can I hear him?"

"I hear he's coming to Ostrog."

"When?"

Joseph shrugged. "Don't know. But you'll know when he's there. There'll be a crowd of people gathered around him."

Joseph loosened the lines he had tied to the wagon post.

"I'd better be going. Want to get another load on the wagon before the sun sets."

He snapped the reins and pulled onto the road then called back over his shoulder. "Don't miss your chance to hear him," he said.

Ben watched Joseph's wagon disappear into the dust then he continued on to Schepetowka with his load.

Just as Ben entered the road leading to the train station, he saw them. He was sure of it. There they were, Schultz and Gorbansky. As he might have guessed, they were standing in front of the saloon. The men looked up as he passed but Ben didn't think they recognized him. He'd deliver his load and then come back to confront them.

* * *

"That's him!" Gorbansky shouted when Ben had passed.

"Shut up! Want him to notice?"

"But it's him. I tell you it's him. It's Ben Richert, the man we stole the money from."

"Don't use that word! We didn't steal it. We just relieved him of his load."

"Well, whatever. He probably recognized us. Probably will turn around at the next corner."

"Don't be stupid! We'll just step back in the saloon."

"And get caught in there?"

"Watch and see."

Schultz opened the door and entered the saloon. Gorbansky followed.

The bartender recognized them.

"Have another?" he asked.

Schultz shook his head. "Don't have time. Hafta be going."

He pulled several *rubles* out of his pocket. "If someone asks about us, you haven't seen us. See?" he said in a hushed whisper.

The bartender winked and stuffed the *rubles* into his pocket. "Ain't seen neither of you."

Schultz and Gorbansky left the saloon and before untying their horses, they checked carefully to make sure Ben was not in sight. When they were satisfied, they hurried out of town.

Once out of town, Schultz slowed his horse to a trot and rode beside Gorbansky.

"Can't afford to keep running into Richert," he said. "It's not safe."

"So what'ya gonna do? Can't keep him from hauling grain."

"Ah, but we can. He's hauling wheat for the nobleman and I know the man who hires the haulers." He winked at Gorbansky.

"Yes, sir, that new wagon isn't going to do Richert much good. Wait and see."

***

By the time Ben reached the elevators near the train station, a long line of wagons had already formed. Ben took his place at the end of the line.

But when Ben returned to Main Street, the men had disappeared. Ben stomped into the saloon and approached the bartender.

"Can you tell me where Schultz and Gorbansky went?"

The bartender frowned. "Who?"

Ben's temper flared. "Schultz and Gorbansky. I saw them. Standing outside your door. Didn't they come in for a drink?"

"Two strangers came in about half hour ago. Had a couple of drinks and left. Don't think they're from these parts."

"Did anybody talk to them?"

The bartender shook his head. "Don't think so. Kept to themselves. What do ya want them for?"

"They're thieves, not only stole my money but our passport and visa, too."

"Stole them?"

"In Oschonin. We were on our way to America."

The bartender narrowed his eyes. "You sure it's them?"

"I'd know them anywhere."

"Oschonin's a long ways away. Why would they come here?"

"To find some other fool," Ben turned to leave. "Where's the government office?"

"Down the street a couple of buildings. Has a sign on the front."

Ben stomped out the door. But although the official took down the information, he didn't give Ben much hope.

"They were likely just passing through. Besides, if they took your papers, they've sold them a long time ago. That was last April, you said?"

Ben nodded.

"Did you report it when it happened?"

"That morning."

The official wrinkled his brow. "We don't have a record of it. Besides, I'm sure they're long gone now, especially if they happened to see you. Actually, you're not free of suspicion yourself. Passports bring good money. How do we know you didn't sell yours? I could arrest you on suspicion of theft."

Ben glared at the official. "Like I said, they're already checking this out in Oschonin. Had to pay *him* to do it."

The official nodded. "But, of course, it takes a lot of time to check these things out. Would you like for me to check it out from this end? I could do it for a few *rubles*."

Ben felt the color creeping up his neck. He turned and stalked out the door. Once out in the fresh air, his anger subsided and he could think more clearly. Actually, he was fortunate the official hadn't arrested him or at least detained him.

Things certainly had changed. Before, the officials had not exactly been friendly to his people but at least they tolerated them. Now Ben sensed a decided animosity. He could only believe it would get worse. Yes, it was time for him and Nettie to leave. But he had promised Nettie that they would not leave if she wanted to stay. How could he convince her?

Ben hauled a few more loads for the nobleman when suddenly the hauling ceased. Ben checked with the overseer in Ostrog.

The overseer seemed surprised. "Heard you didn't want hauling," he told Ben.

"Didn't want hauling? What made you think that?"

"Understood you stopped by to tell us."

"I told you I didn't want to haul anymore?"

"That's what I was told."

"Well, it's not so. I'll take all I can get."

"All right then, you can pick up a load tomorrow morning. There'll be as much work as you want."

On his way back, Ben saw a crowd of people gathered in the town square. A man, elevated a little higher than the people around him, was addressing the crowd in a loud voice. Even from this distance, Ben could hear him shout but could not hear what he was saying. Was this the man Hoffman was talking about? Was this Graber?

Ben drove his team as near to the crowd as he could then tied the horses to a hitching post. He worked his way to the front of the crowd.

"There's plenty of land to be had just for the taking," the man was saying. "Land like this, gently rolling, but without timber. No need to clear it before plowing. Good land too."

The man pointed his finger at Ben. "Young man," he said, "as sure as my name is Albert Graber, strong, young men like you can break up the sod in no time. In a few years you'll have a thriving farm of your own."

Ben moved a little closer.

Graber saw him and his face broke into a broad grin. "I talked to a farmer just before I came. He got a fair crop the first year. Then in the spring he noticed volunteer wheat coming through the ground. He decided not to seed but to let the volunteer wheat grow. When he harvested it the next fall, and after costs, he made four hundred and fifty dollars. Can you believe almost two hundred and fifty *rubles*?"

"But a lot of people have already gone," Ben said. "Are you sure there's land left?"

"Lots of it. It's a big country. Young man, you listen to me. I can put you in touch with the right people. You could leave on the next ship."

A murmur of wonder rippled through the crowd. All eyes were riveted on Graber. He knew how to control an audience, that was certain.

Graber's eyes focused on Ben again. "Don't want to go in the army, do you?"

Ben shook his head.

"Then you better go to America."

Ben stayed a little longer then left so he could reach home before dark. But he had heard enough. He could hardly wait to share his news with Nettie.

But that night Nettie had news of her own. "Ben, we're going to have another baby," she whispered when they were getting ready for bed.

Her eyes beamed. "I'm sure of it."

Ben tried hard to hide his disappointment. Was this the end of his dreams? Could he risk taking Nettie now that she was in the family way again? Could he ask her to endanger this baby's life? He managed a smile but his heart wasn't in it. He hoped Nettie didn't detect his disappointment. Nettie was made to have babies. She wanted lots of them.

Nettie did not notice his lack of enthusiasm. She was wrapped up in her own happiness.

A week later, on his way back from Schepetowka, Ben met Igor Savinsky. Igor had worked on the nobleman's land with Ben and his father when Ben was a teenager. Strong and eager, the handsome, dark-eyed young Russian had worked hard, pitching hay, heaving hundred pound sacks of grain or whatever else needed doing.

He quickly learned the innovative methods of farming Ben's people had introduced. Now he was using those same techniques on the few acres he rented. Ben had heard Igor's acreage was doing well and he believed it. He had seen Igor's team and wagon and it was a far cry from the crude wagons the Russians pulled behind their scruffy ponies. Igor drove a painted wagon nearly as nice as Pappa's and owned a team of sleek horses.

When Igor married, his wife, Elsa, had helped out when new babies were born to Ben's mother. Through the years, Ben ran into Igor now and then and they always enjoyed a good chat. Ben's father would never have understood friendship with a Russian. His people didn't mingle with other cultures. And so Ben and Igor met infrequently, and that by accident.

Sometimes, when Ben talked to Igor, he almost believed Igor had made a personal commitment to God. He couldn't ask Igor for it was clearly stated in Catherine the Great's manifesto that immigrants could not proselytize the Russians. Severe penalties would be swiftly meted out to those who violated that order.

Igor and Ben's conversation naturally turned to Albert Graber and the stir he was causing.

"Heard him the other day," Ben told Igor. "He's a powerful speaker."

"And did he persuade you to leave?" Igor wanted to know.

"Igor, the truth is, I'd like to."

"Then why don't you?"

"I might but Nettie is ... " He paused. "She's in the family way again. I'm not sure I should take her in that condition."

Igor took off his hat and ran his hand through his hair.

"There'd be mid-wives to help her. Graber sure makes America sound good but he better be careful," he said. "He's stirring up trouble. I heard the Tsar is plenty worried that he'll persuade more people to leave. You Hollanders are the best farmers in the country. I think the Tsar will do everything he can to make you stay."

Igor's face clouded over. "Ben, if you're going to America, I wouldn't wait too long. I have a feeling the Tsar'll make it hard or almost impossible to leave."

Ben nodded.

"And if you stay," Igor continued, "you'll have to serve in the army."

"Oh, I couldn't do that. Our people have never taken up arms."

"They have ways of forcing you to or putting you in prison. Wouldn't want that to happen, would you?"

"No, not that."

They talked a little longer then they parted company.

But a few days later just at suppertime, Igor arrived in the yard. Ben could hardly believe his eyes. Igor had never before initiated a visit.

"Can we talk somewhere" Igor asked Ben. "Alone?"

"Sure how about behind the hay stack?"

"That would do."

Ben grinned as he sat down behind the stack. "Kind of like old times," he said. "You and me sitting behind a hay stack swapping stories."

Igor ignored Ben's attempt at levity. "I hope I'm not causing trouble with your people," he said.

"Why should you?"

"You should figure that out. I'm Russian and you're German."

"Dutch," Ben corrected.

"Well, whatever. I came because I heard that the Tsar plans to arrest Albert Graber and put him in jail."

"Put him in jail? Whatever for?"

"For inciting unrest, causing disturbance."

"But Graber doesn't do anything but talk. What can they do? I hear he's an American citizen."

"Everywhere he goes he draws crowds."

"Nothing wrong with crowds, is there?"

"He's causing a lot of dissatisfaction. Four more families have already sold their crops in the fields and are leaving next month. They say as many as fifty more are considering leaving. And that's just around here."

"I suppose that could be a problem to the Tsar."

"It is. That's why I came. Could you get in touch with Graber and warn him. If you could get him to Poland, the Tsar couldn't touch him."

"But I don't know where he is."

"He's in Kopez."

"And you want me to go all that way to warn him? I don't really know him."

"But he's one of your people. If they put him in jail, I don't know what'll happen to him. It could affect your people. They're watching him. I know. I have it on good authority. They're just biding their time."

Ben's eyes studied Igor's face before he spoke. "Igor, you could be in big trouble for telling me and get arrested yourself. Why are you going to all this trouble? Why are you taking the risk?"

"I think you know the answer to that, Ben." Igor rose. "I've got to go now. But you will do something to help him, won't you?"

Ben hesitated then offered his hand. "Yes, Igor, I will."

Igor shook Ben's hand then turned to leave. Ben watched him turn out of the yard then, slowly, Ben made his way back into the house. How could he possibly let Graber know? He had a load of wheat to haul to Schepetowka and he needed the income. Still, if he didn't, what would happen to Graber?

In the end, Ben asked Pappa to take the load. As it happened, Pappa did not have a load to haul that day.

Ben left early the next morning. Why should he be giving up the chance to earn money? He certainly needed the money. Yet, if he could help Graber, it would all be worthwhile. If ever a man was sold on an idea, it was Graber. He certainly couldn't be lying. Lying would do him no good. No, Ben decided, He was genuine. He really believed their people would be better off in America.

When Ben reached Kopez, he learned that Tsarist officials had already arrested Graber and had put him in jail. There was no-thing Ben could do so he went home.

# Chapter Fourteen

A few days later, Igor drove into the yard again. "If you're not careful, you'll make this a habit," Ben told Igor.

Igor nodded. "I hope I'm not making trouble for you."

Ben shook his head. "No trouble. At least no one's said anything."

"I came to tell you that they let Graber go," Igor said.

"They did? How come?"

"Didn't explain, just deported him. I think it's because the Tsar doesn't want to irritate your people."

"Don't think it'll do any good. They'll leave anyway."

Igor's face grew serious. "Are you leaving with the others?"

"I had hoped to but Nettie doesn't want to go. I've sent for a passport but it hasn't come yet. They say the Tsar is making it harder to get out."

"They can't keep you, really."

"Ah, but they have strings attached. They say I sold our visa and passport."

Igor hesitated a moment before he spoke. "They hope you won't leave if they put on enough pressure."

"They may succeed too. Besides Nettie not wanting to go, it takes a lot of money to buy tickets."

Igor pulled some *rubles* out of his pocket. "Will this help?"

Ben looked at Igor with astonishment. "What's that supposed to be for?"

"Your tickets."

"But ..."

Igor shoved the coins into Ben's hand. "I know it's not enough but there's enough for a ticket for my sister, Sophia, and

96

then a little to help pay for yours."

"Is Sophia going?"

Igor nodded. "She'd like to."

"Do your parents approve?"

Igor shook his head. "They'd never approve. If she goes, she'll leave without their permission."

"How is she going to manage that?"

"You buy her ticket and I'll see to it that she gets on the train to Antwerp."

Ben studied Igor a moment. "You're going to help Sophia run away? Won't you get in trouble yourself?"

Igor shrugged. "There's no other way."

Ben looked at the money in his hand. "I can't take this. I could never pay you back."

"Let's say it's payment for taking Sophia with you. Besides that, she can help with the children, make it easier for Nettie."

"But ..."

"No buts about it."

Igor's voice softened. "I don't know if you've guessed that Sophia has embraced your faith."

"Do your parents know?"

"No! And, of course, it mustn't get out. You can be sure they'd stop her."

"I might have known. Toby would never marry her otherwise."

"No, Sophia made the decision some time ago, when she was working for Toby's parents. But she couldn't tell anyone except me and Elsa and, of course, Toby."

Ben nodded. "Toby and his parents could have been in big trouble with the government."

"Exactly. And that's why they didn't plan to be married until they reached America or at least not until they were on the ship."

"Makes sense."

"And, if you haven't already guessed," Igor continued. "Elsa and I have made that decision too. After working with your father, we started studying the Bible, secretly of course, and I saw that it's personal faith in Jesus that makes you a child of God. It's made a difference in my life. Elsa and I don't seem to have as many arguments."

Ben took Igor's hand and shook it. "I suspected as much."

"I must ask you to keep it to yourself. Not so much for me but for Elsa and the children. I wouldn't want anything to happen to them. Maybe some day ..." Igor's voice trailed off.

"Maybe you ought to go to America, too."

"I've considered it. But it means leaving our families. I can't ask Elsa to do that."

"I've been thinking of the same thing. Nettie doesn't want to go because she doesn't want to leave her family. I've been hoping she'd change her mind. Am I right to demand this of Nettie?"

"You have more at stake. And there's the military law to think about." Igor shifted. "I think they'll make it harder to immigrate. Go, Ben, go before it's impossible to leave. And take Sophia with you before they cancel her passport."

Ben fingered the money thoughtfully then put it into his money purse. "If only I could be sure Nettie would be happy. And if only the passport would come. Can't apply for a visa until then. It's June already and the ship leaves in November."

* * *

Then one day the family passport arrived. Ben opened the envelope and studied the precious document.

"Praise God," he whispered. But what would Nettie think?

The next day Ben applied for the visa. And although he knew an answer would be long in coming, every time he picked up wheat near Ostrog he checked to see if the precious document had arrived. Unfortunately, each time he inquired, the officials assessed a fee for the information.

One night as he and Nettie were preparing for bed, he took

out the leather pouch in which he kept their savings. Nettie had released her hair from its *chignon* and was brushing the long silky tresses. He watched her a moment. What a beautiful woman! He didn't deserve her. Involuntarily, he glanced at the small bulge below Nettie's waistline then quickly looked away. Could he ask her to do this in her condition?

"If my addition is right," he told Nettie, "we have about half the money we need to pay back the loan. If I keep hauling we'll have no trouble paying it off. We'll even have extra for some things for the house. Or, instead of buying things for the house, we could buy tickets to America, especially with the money Igor gave me. Which will it be?"

Ben held his breath as he waited for an answer. It seemed an eternity before Nettie spoke.

"Igor gave you money? Why didn't you tell me?"

"I, I guess I forgot."

"You were holding it from me! That's what you were doing. You've planned to go all along even if I don't want to!"

Ben touched her arm. "No, Nettie, you don't understand. I think we ought to go but I won't force you."

"You know I don't want to go and you told me we wouldn't go if I didn't want to. I don't want to leave Mamma and Pappa, especially with another little one coming."

Nettie laid the brush on the dresser top. "Still, I don't want them to put you in the army either."

Ben gathered Nettie into his arms. "It won't be the army now. When General Von Tolteben visited our *dorfs*, he told us it wouldn't be. It'll likely be the army workshops or the medical corps or even the forestry division."

"But you'd be away for seven years." Nettie brushed a tear from her eye. "I couldn't bear to be separated that long. Why just think, Andrew would be fifteen when you got back and Eva would be nine." She touched her abdomen. "This baby would be seven."

Ben remained silent for a moment. This was exactly what he had been thinking the past few weeks. How could he be separated from his family that long? And yet, that's precisely what they were asking their parents to do.

Ben pulled Nettie to the edge of the bed and the two sat there side by side. "Nettie, whatever you decide will be fine with me. The passports came ..."

"They came? Why didn't you tell me?"

"Didn't have a chance. Besides, I don't want to pressure you. Want to do what makes you happiest. If you want to go, we can, unless, of course, they deny us our visa."

"They wouldn't, would they?"

"I think in the end they would issue it but I'm sure they'd investigate our reason for applying for another one. And that could take time, more time than we have before the ship leaves with the others."

"How much time do we have, Ben?"

"The *ukaz* goes into effect in October and the ship leaves in November so we're taking a risk the way it is. My number could come up in October, before the ship leaves."

Nettie laid her head on Ben's shoulder. "Oh, Ben, why does it have to be so hard? What are we going to do?"

Ben put two fingers under Nettie's chin and raised her face to look into her eyes. "We'll do whatever you want to do."

"Ben, I don't know what I want. But now that we're back, I don't see how we can ever leave Mamma and Pappa again." Nettie said.

Ben released Nettie and put away the money bag. "We don't have to decide tonight. If we decide not to go, we'll only be out a few *rubles*."

Nettie nodded. "We still have time."

"Nettie, let's pray right now and ask the Lord to change Mamma's mind. Pappa told me once, on one of our hauling trips, that he thinks we all should go. God can change Mamma's mind like he changed Jonah's."

"And I'll ask Grossmom to pray with us. She wants to go! And she thinks we should all go."

They slipped to their knees and asked God for a miracle.

# Chapter Fifteen

After four days on the train and ten days on the ocean, Toby arrived in Philadelphia. Pennsylvania church representatives met the passengers and helped them with their entry.

A hundred years before, the pacifist, William Penn, who had established the colony named after him, had welcomed another group of Hollanders. Now these Hollanders were following his example.

In Philadelphia, the immigrants boarded a train for Kansas. Toby's heart ached as he watched the families board the train. Everyone else had a family but he was alone. If only Sophia could have come with him. Or even Ben and Nettie. Toby wished with all his heart that Ben and Nettie could have been there with him. How long would it be before they joined him? And Sophia, when would he see her again?

The final whistle blew. The train hissed then slowly pulled out of the station. Soon they were traveling across rich farmland at full speed.

Toby marveled at the vastness of the new land and the diversity of its terrain. Parts of it were thickly forested but there were also vast acres of farmland dotted with houses and barns. There were cities, large ones like Chicago, and small *dorfs* about the size of Karlswalde. This was America! What a land of variety it was!

After changing trains several times, they arrived in Newton, Kansas. But when Toby learned that most of the good land had been claimed and that there was land available in Dakota Territory, he caught a ride north to check it out.

Three weeks later they reached Yankton, a small bustling town on the Missouri River. But Toby was disappointed when he saw the trees. Was all the land tree-studded like the area from which he came? Would they have to grub them out just as his people were doing in Russia?

But his fears were quickly dispelled when the railroad agent showed them the unclaimed acres. Except for a few near rivers and lakes, there were no trees, only rolling grassland. As they rode through the grasslands, Toby dreamed of tilling that soil and, like his forefathers in Russia, turn them into a verdant garden.

"Can you imagine," the representative told them, "each of you as head of a household can file for a hundred and sixty acres, live on it for five years and the land is yours. You have reached the Promised Land!"

The men cheered. But Toby was puzzled.

He turned to Paul Kaufman."What exactly does he mean by 'head of a household?'" Does a man have to have a family?"

Kaufman nodded. "That's what he said."

"You mean a single man can't file for a homestead?"

"That's it."

"Then ..."

"Then, what?"

"I guess I don't qualify."

"You mean you don't have a wife?"

Toby shook his head.

Paul Kaufman's face took on a knowing look. He nudged Toby with his elbow. "Then you better find some young widow and marry her." Kaufman broke into coarse laughter.

But Toby could not see the humor of it. His hopes and dreams had been shattered. He could not file a claim until Sophia arrived. But when would she come? And what would he do in the mean-time? And what if she never came? Toby's heart sank.

Kaufman nudged Toby again. "What you gonna do now?"

Toby shrugged.

"Have you thought about hiring out to break sod? It's hard work but I can see you're up to it. It'd give you a chance to earn money while you're waiting for a homestead. Might even make a deal to stay with some of 'em."

"How would I break up sod?" Toby stretched out his huge hairy hands. "With my bare hands?"

"No, you'd have to have a team, a plow and a wagon. Tell you what. Heard one of our people is moving back to Kansas. Maybe you can buy his outfit -- if you pay him enough. Just made a deal with a man myself yesterday. Can't do much here without a team and wagon. Need a plow too."

"How can I find the man?"

"I'll take you there."

Kaufman moved closer and lowered his voice. "And, like I said, I'd look around for a woman. A fella' needs a woman to help with the work. It's like havin' a hired man, only you don't have to pay 'em."

Kaufman's eyes took on a knowing look. "You know what I mean?"

"I'm not interested in just any woman. My bride's coming. But I would like to meet the man with a wagon and plow."

"Well, then it's as good as done. But I still say you'd better keep your eyes out for a woman and take her when you have a chance. Aren't many single ones around. As a matter of fact, my sister lost her husband not long ago. Needs someone to help on her claim."

Kaufman moved closer. "I'll introduce you if you like," he whispered. "Better than breaking sod for someone else."

Toby merely shook his head.

The next day Toby bought the team, wagon and plow. He also arranged to board with the Henry Steinhardt family.

"You mean you can't file for a homestead if you're single?" Steinhardt asked him.

"That's what Kaufman said."

"Hm, never heard of that. But then everybody that comes has a family."

"Tell you what," he added. "You help break up my sod and you can board with us the year around. You can sleep in your wagon 'til it gets too cold and then you can sleep on our kitchen floor. Mind you, it won't be the best but it'll give you a place to stay and some board. My wife's a good cook, too."

The two men shook hands on the agreement.

Toby found it easy to fit into the Steinhardt family. The four Steinhardt children took away some of his loneliness.

Toby worked long hours and not only helped Steinhardt with his sod but was able to earn money breaking sod on a neighbor's land.

"I'm glad you agreed to work for me," Steinhardt told Toby one day. "You're a hard worker and in no time we'll get this land ready to plant."

Steinhardt hesitated before continuing. "There is one other thing you might consider."

"Oh?"

"Shouldn't tell you 'cause I'm undercutting myself."

Toby's dark blue eyes opened wide with curiosity. "What's that?"

"There's a young widow, name's Amelia Tieszen. Immigrated here two years ago, she and her husband. Her husband died and Amelia's all alone on the homestead."

Toby scowled. "Are you talking about Kaufman's sister?"

"You've heard of her?"

Toby nodded. "And you're suggesting marriage?"

"Well, yes. I don't think you could do better."

Toby shook his head. "Kaufman's already suggested that. But I couldn't do it. I'm betrothed to Sophia and when she comes, we'll be married."

"Didn't you tell me earlier that her father doesn't want her to come, that he's forbidden her to marry you?"

Toby nodded.

"Then how do you know she'll ever come? For all you know, her father will keep her there and in the meantime, you'll miss your chance of a homestead, and a wife."

"If you saw Sophia, you'd understand. Henry, she's beautiful. Has dark, gentle eyes with long dark lashes, dark shiny hair and a slender waist. Not only that, she's a God-fearing woman. I could never love anyone like I love her."

"Didn't you say she's a Russian?"

Toby nodded.

"You'd marry a Russian?"

"Sophia's a believer. She wants to join our way of living."

"Well, I don't know," Steinhardt said slowly. "It's better to marry your own kind. Our people have always held to that. Besides, what if she never comes?"

"She'll come."

Steinhardt hesitated before he spoke again. "There is such a thing as marriage for convenience. You want a homestead. Amelia has land and needs a man. Besides, she's not afraid of hard work. I'm surprised somebody hasn't snatched her up already. I suppose it's because she wouldn't marry just any man."

His face broke into a grin and his eyes narrowed. "She is nice looking, Toby," he said.

Toby turned the words over in his mind. "I couldn't do it," he said at last. "I couldn't be unfaithful to Sophia."

"Not even if you never filed for a homestead and never married? A man needs a woman, you know. And you're no exception."

"Not even if I never own a piece of land," Toby declared.

But the next Sunday, when Toby attended church services in the house where they were held, he met the young widow. As Henry had said, she was pretty, though not as beautiful as Sophia. In contrast to Sophia's dark complexion, Amelia had fair skin tanned by the sun, bronze-colored hair and gray eyes. She was pretty in her way. Actually, he could do worse. And if he could judge from her reactions when they were introduced, the widow was not totally disinterested herself.

Toby saw her again the next Sunday. She was sitting across the aisle on the women's side. If he turned his head ever so slightly, he could see her profile. Toby liked what he saw but he knew he shouldn't be thinking of her. He deliberately turned his attention to the preacher and willed himself to listen.

But the backless benches were uncomfortable and to make matters worse, the room was small and the air stuffy. Added to that was the fact that the sermon was long and boring. Toby glanced once more at Amelia.

Her skin glowed with health. Her chin was firm and her nose ended in an intriguing lift. Her bronze-colored hair was twisted into a coil at the back of her neck. Toby found himself wondering what it would look like falling loose over her shoulders.

Suddenly, he sat up straight. What was he doing dreaming about this stranger when even now dark-haired Sophia was making plans to meet him? Ashamed of himself, Toby turned his attention to the preacher again. But the preacher was about to close his message and Toby had missed most of it, long as it was.

After the service, Tina Steinhardt invited Amelia to dinner. And since Toby hadn't driven his team and wagon, Tina suggested he ride with Amelia. Toby found an unexpected pleasure from the suggestion but dismissed it by assuring himself he was helping a widow.

Toby helped Amelia into her wagon and she smiled her thanks from deep inside her broad-brimmed bonnet. She handed Toby the reins.

"Would you like to drive?" she asked.

As Toby took the reins, his hands touched hers and Toby felt an unexpected pleasure. Her hands were gloved now but when Steinhardt had introduced them, she had extended a brown, work-worn hand. A bonnet would protect her face from the sun but there was little to protect her hands. Clearly, Amelia was doing man's work there on the claim.

Toby frowned. A woman shouldn't have to do that!

"Sure was nice of Tina to invite me over," Amelia said when they had turned out of the yard. "Gets lonesome all alone on the homestead."

"How long have you been by yourself?"

"A little over a year."

"And you've been doing all the work yourself?"

"Pretty much. My husband had broken a number of acres so I worked that."

"I'm sorry."

"It was hard, very hard but I decided to stay."

"But that's too hard for a woman."

"I know. And I don't have much to show for it. I'm not farming many acres and the first crop wasn't good. I'm hoping this year's crop will be better."

"Isn't there anyone who can help you? Don't you have a family?"

"Well, there's my brother, Paul, but you know how it is. He's busy himself breaking the sod on his own land. He came after we did and still has a lot left."

"Haven't your neighbors helped?"

"They have but they can only do so much. They too have land of their own."

Amelia dropped her eyelids. "There have been men who'd like to marry me. They've offered to help but I can't take help without encouraging them."

"Of course not. I'll see if I can't get you help. If the neighbors all pitched in, they could get a lot done."

Amelia fluttered her long eye lashes. Toby did not fail to notice. "That is very kind of you, Mr. Beyer."

"Oh, please call me Toby. Everyone does."

"All right then, and you call me Amelia."

If it weren't for Sophia, I might consider Amelia. And it would give me a chance to have land of my own. The thought crept in unaware but Toby quickly shrugged it aside.

They turned into the Steinhardt yard, where Steinhardt met them. Toby helped Amelia out of the wagon then he and Steinhardt took the horses to the barn.

They entered the house just as Amelia unfolded the apron she had brought and tied it around her waist. Toby and

Steinhardt seated themselves at the far end of the room and immersed themselves in a German newspaper.

From where Toby and Steinhardt sat, they could see the two women preparing dinner. Their friendly chatter drifted across the room.

Steinhardt broke the silence. "Nice looking, isn't she?"

Toby's face felt hot. He ran his hand over his hair. Was it that obvious that he was watching Amelia? Hadn't he covered his occasional glances well behind the paper? Besides, wasn't Steinhardt reading the paper himself?

Toby straightened up in his chair. "I've been thinking that some of us in the community ought to help her with her claim."

"We've already done that. Helped her break up a number of acres and helped her seed. Didn't she tell you? She can't handle much more than what's been broken."

"Maybe I can help in between jobs."

Steinhardt nodded. "She'll need help when it comes time to harvest."

"I'll plan on it."

"Good! And there'll be others."

Tina interrupted their conversation to announce dinner. Steinhardt rose and led the way to the table.

Somehow, the food tasted better to Toby that day.

When Amelia was ready to leave that afternoon, Steinhardt and Toby both went out to hitch Amelia's team to the wagon.

"I'll get the horses," Steinhardt volunteered.

Toby was left alone with Amelia.

"This has been such a wonderful day," Amelia exclaimed as they waited. "Gets lonesome all alone there on the claim."

"Yes, I suppose. But at least you know how to cook. Don't know what I'd do if I had to cook."

Amelia fluttered her eye lashes again then her gray eyes looked up into Toby's dark ones.

"Not unusual for a man. I've been wondering why you haven't filed for a claim instead of staying on Steinhardt's place."

Toby hesitated before he answered. *Didn't she know?*

"Can't 'til I'm married."

"Only married people can file for a homestead? I didn't know that."

"That's what your brother, Paul, said."

"That's a bit strange. I mean when you think about it, I'm a single woman now, that is a widow, and I have a claim. You're a man. But you can't have one. Seems like you ought to have a claim."

"I know. That's the way I see it too."

Widow Tieszen touched Toby's sleeve. "You must come over for a meal some time. I like to cook but it's not much fun making things just for myself. Besides, I'm sure you could do with company your own age and someone that's not married."

She turned her lovely gray eyes on him again. "You will come, won't you?"

At that moment Steinhardt arrived with the horses. Steinhardt's eyes twinkled when he heard Amelia's invitation. Toby quickly busied himself with the harness.

Amelia stepped closer to Toby. "How about tomorrow evening about five?" she asked.

Acutely aware that Steinhardt was taking it all in, Toby nevertheless accepted her invitation.

"All right then. Five o'clock."

She offered her hand to Toby. "If you'll be so kind as to help me into the wagon."

Toby obliged. When Amelia was seated, she cracked the reins and was off.

"Nice woman!" Steinhardt said as they watched Amelia disappear in a cloud of dust.

Although he felt a little guilty, he couldn't help looking forward to dinner with Amelia.

# Chapter Sixteen

"Would you like to make a trip to Ostrog tomorrow?" Ben asked Nettie one Friday morning. "Have a load of freight to pick up and thought you might like to ride along."

Nettie's eyes gleamed. "Oh, that would be wonderful!" she exclaimed as she twisted her hair into a *chignon* then reached for a hairpin to fasten it. "I haven't been anywhere but church and Wedels. Be a nice change."

Ben smiled. "I was sure you'd like it. I've had a little more hauling so we can spare a little cash for some clothes."

"How wonderful! Maybe I could get some material for Eva. Why her dresses only come halfway down her legs. And Andrew is wearing high-water pants! You need new clothes too. Just look at those pants. Grossmom has sewn patch over patch to make them wearable."

"Yes, we don't want to start out for America in rags."

Nettie spun around, her hand still holding the *chignon* in place, her eyes filled with anger.

"What did you say?"

"I asked if you wanted to go with me to Ostrog."

Nettie's eyes still blazed. "Not that. What did you say after that?"

"You mean about going to America?"

"Yes! Had you planned this all along? Behind my back?"

Ben put his arms around Nettie but she pulled away.

"Had you?" she demanded.

"No, but I should have," he shouted, his quick temper flaring. "Can't you see what this would mean? We've been married for nigh unto ten years and what do we have to show for it?"

Nettie placed one hand on her hips and supported her hair with the other. "We did have a nice place with cows and chickens but we gave all of it up so we could fulfill your silly notion of going to America. We'd still have it if we hadn't gone."

"Could I help it that thieves robbed us?"

Nettie's eyes softened a little. "No, I'm sorry. It's not your fault. But, Ben, we can't leave Mamma and Pappa behind. We might never see them again. And Grossmom. She's seventy-eight. Grossmom is very dear to me. If we go, we'll never see her again."

"We don't know how much longer she'll live. When she dies, you won't see her again anyway, that is, until you get to heaven. Besides, do you want to live like your parents or mine before they died, working our fingers to the bone and still barely eking out a living? Pappa is fifty-one and Mamma is forty-seven. And what do they have to show for it? Surely, by now you've come to your senses."

Ben stalked out the door, slamming the door behind him. Eva woke up with a start. Nettie comforted her then finished pinning her hair. She tied on an apron then hurried to the kitchen to fix breakfast.

But Ben did not return for breakfast. Andrew barely touched his food. Nettie was sure he sensed something was wrong.

Ben was back by noon but he gave no explanation for his long absence. At noon he took his place at the table and concentrated on eating, his eyes avoiding Nettie's. Nettie sat sullenly beside him. Andrew sneaked glances at each of them and ate little. Even Eva seemed to sense something was wrong.

That night when Ben and Nettie retired, they still had not resolved their differences. As usual, Ben was ready first but he turned to the wall and did not watch Nettie brush her hair.

The discord notwithstanding, Ben and Nettie started for Ostrog the next morning. Andrew went to school and Eva stayed with Mamma and Pappa.

They rode the six miles in silence. In Ostrog, Ben tied up the

111

horses near the dry goods store then left to make arrangements for the freight.

Nettie made her purchases without much enthusiasm and carried the neatly tied packages to the wagon, where she waited for Ben.

Then someone touched her sleeve. "Please, *Frau* Richert, may I speak to you?"

Nettie turned to see a young woman looking up into her face. The woman had gentle brown eyes and shining dark hair. She was wearing a gray calico dress sprinkled with sprigs of tiny pink flowers. She was beautiful but there were shadows under her dark eyes and her young face seemed drawn and weary.

"Why, of course, will you come up on the wagon and sit down?"

The girl shook her head. "No, thank you. I'd just like to have a few words with you. I'm Sophia Savinsky."

Nettie gave her a broad smile. "Toby's betrothed?"

Sophia nodded.

"And how is Toby?"

"I have not heard, *Frau* Richert."

"But, of course."

Tears welled up in Sophia's dark eyes. "I miss him." She brushed away a tear. "Are you still planning to immigrate to America?"

Nettie hesitated a moment. "We're not sure. It's very hard to leave Pappa and Mamma and Grossmom."

Sophia nodded. "I know. If I went, I'd leave my mother and father too. But I know I miss Toby more than I would miss them. *Frau* Richert, I can't live without him."

"There's another ship leaving in November."

"But I can't go alone." Sophia sighed. "Actually, if I go, I'll have to go without my parents' permission. But, *Frau* Richert, I must go."

"You'd go without their permission?"

"I'll have to, especially because of Boris."

"Boris?"

"Boris Zamskov. He's been trying to court me."

"And you're betrothed to Toby."

"Exactly. Besides, I've made a personal commitment to Jesus. Igor and Elsa have too."

"And what do your parents say to that?"

"Oh, they don't know. We haven't told them. And you must keep it to yourself too. You see, they would be deeply hurt if they knew ... and angry. Anyway, if we could leave soon, I could leave before Boris becomes more insistent. There's a ship leaving in August, they say."

"Oh, but we can't go that soon." Nettie dropped her eyes. "I'm not sure we can go at all."

"Not go at all? But isn't that what Ben wants?"

Sophia's face suddenly came alive. "What about the military lottery? Are you going to let them draw his number and be separated from you for years, maybe forever? I'd miss Toby too much. These months have been torture."

"But ..." Nettie didn't finish for Ben came walking toward the wagon.

He doffed his hat and bowed when he saw Sophia.

"This is Sophia, Ben," Nettie explained.

Ben doffed his hat again.

"Have you heard from Toby?"

"I haven't heard," Sophia told Ben. "But I know he's lonesome and wants me to come. I was hoping you'd soon be leaving for America so I could go with you."

Ben gave Nettie a quick glance. "I'm afraid our plans aren't fully made," he said.

A tear rolled down Sophia's cheek. "Well, let me know, that is let Igor know, if you decide to go."

She turned and quickly walked away.

It was a quiet ride back to Karlswalde. When they were nearly home, Nettie reached over and touched Ben's hand.

"Ben," she said, "you really want to go, don't you?"

Ben took Nettie's hand in his. "Nettie, I'm sorry for getting angry. I did tell you we'd do what you wanted to do and I should have kept my word."

"I've changed my mind, Ben."

Ben's mouth fell open.

"You've what?" Ben tried hard not to look too happy. "You mean you want to go to America?"

"I'm not sure I *want* to go, but let's say I'm willing to go. I don't want to be separated from you like Sophia is from Toby."

"But I wouldn't go to America without you."

Nettie looked down at her lap and picked at the stitches in her skirt. "Oh, I know that but your number might get chosen in the military lottery and then we'd be separated. I guess Sophia helped me see how miserable I'd be."

Ben glanced at Nettie but she was still picking at her skirt. After a while, she looked up.

"You sure?" Ben asked.

Nettie nodded.

"Then we'll leave in November."

"Let's pray Mamma and Pappa will decide to leave, too."

# Chapter Seventeen

The following Sunday after the morning message, Elder Tobias Unruh came to the podium and announced that the loan from the Pennsylvania churches had come through.

"They've agreed to lend our *dorf* nine thousand dollars so those who want to can immigrate to America."

One of the older men said "Amen."

The rest of the people broke into whispered conversation.

Then Elder Schmidt stepped to the podium. "I must agree that the Pennsylvania churches have been very generous in offering us this loan but I still abide by my convictions. It would be unwise to leave. The Tsar has made certain concessions that we can accept. We do not know what lies ahead in America. It would be a mistake to leave."

Someone said "Amen."

The rest of the congregation launched into more whispered discussion.

Realizing it would be useless to continue the service, Elder Schmidt pronounced the benediction and dismissed the congregation.

But the members hadn't finished their discussion. They gathered in small clusters and heatedly debated the wisdom of immigration. But it was clear, now that money was available, most of the people wanted to leave.

The discussion continued at the Buller table, where Ben and Nettie and the children had joined Mamma and Pappa for Sunday dinner.

Pappa dropped a bombshell. "Mamma, now we can emigrate too."

Mamma nearly dropped the bowl of potatoes she was carrying to the table. "Have you lost your mind?"

She set the bowl on the table then flopped into her chair. A hairpin fell out of the coil at the back of her head but she did not bother to pick it up off the floor.

Grossmom sat quietly, a smug look on her face.

Pappa stroked his goatee. "I talked with your brother, Tobias, and he thinks now that the loan has gone through, anyone who wants to can go."

"And give all this up?" Mamma protested.

"Give what up? What do we really have? We've worked all our lives, Mamma, and what do we have to show for it?"

"This house and furniture, some cows and pigs and horses. That's more than we'd have in America."

"That's all we have. And the house isn't even ours. Belongs to the nobleman."

"I think we should all go," Grossmom put in.

Mamma looked at her in astonishment. "You're too old and we can't leave you behind."

"*Ach!*" Grossmom threw up her hands. "I'm only seventy-eight. I am plenty strong enough."

Ben and Nettie listened awestruck. Could this really be Pappa and Mamma discussing immigration? They had prayed for this but it was hard to believe it was happening.

But Mamma was practical. "And if everyone's going to America, who would buy our things?"

Pappa poured coffee into his saucer and slurped it noisily before speaking. "There is that to think about."

He took another sip of coffee. "But things are getting bad here. We're not safe even in our own homes."

"Not safe here in this house?" Mamma asked in astonishment. "Remember Abe and Susan?"

"Abe and Susan live all by themselves, no one to look after them. We live in a *dorf* and can look out for each other."

"The same thing happened last winter. The people they attacked were just a mile or two from Karlswalde," Pappa countered.

"They stop wagons on the road and take their money," Ben put in.

Pappa nodded. "And don't forget the Russians hate us with a passion. Ben's right. Persecution has already begun. Besides, don't forget Johan will soon be old enough for the lottery. Then what?"

That and that alone stopped Mamma.

When Ben and Nettie were alone, Ben put his arm around Nettie. "It looks like God is answering our prayers. You may not have to leave Mamma and Pappa after all."

# Chapter Eighteen

That afternoon, a wagon and a team of horses turned into the Savinsky yard. Sophia and her mother had just started clearing away the noon dishes.

Sophia's father pulled aside the curtain and peered through the window. "Well, if it isn't Boris Zamskov!" he exclaimed.

He turned to Sophia. "Sophia, I'm sure he's coming to see you."

"But why would he come to see me? I haven't given him any encouragement."

Sophia's dark eyes took on a knowing look. "Has he talked to you?"

His eyes did not meet hers. "Why should he talk to me?"

"Why do young men talk to fathers of eligible women?" Sophia narrowed her eyes. "Did he talk to you, Father?"

"Well, as a matter of fact, he did. Sophia, he is a nice young man. Has a good position and comes from a good Russian family. And the family is fairly well off. You couldn't do any better."

"I'm not looking for someone to marry. You know I love Toby."

"And I forbad you to keep company with him," Father roared.

His dark eyes blazed. "Have you forgotten? Besides, didn't he leave for America? He'll find someone else. Then what?"

Sophia's mother broke into the exchange of words. "Father, you better go out and greet him," she said.

She turned to Sophia. "I'll finish the dishes. You go if he wants to take you for a Sunday drive. Now be nice to the young man."

Resigned, Sophia turned and left the room to freshen up.

A few minutes later Boris was helping her into the wagon and soon they were on their way. Sophia, dressed in a brown dress with crocheted lace at her throat and her wrists, had to admit it was a lovely day for a ride and that it was good to be in the company of another young person. Actually, if she didn't love Toby, she might consider Boris. As Father had said, Boris was handsome.

"Sophia," Boris said after a while. He laid his large hand on hers but Sophia slipped it out of his grasp.

"Why have you avoided me? Am I that repulsive?"

Sophia gasped. "Oh, no!"

"Then why have you avoided me?" His dark eyes searched hers. "Can't you see that I'm interested in you? Haven't you noticed?"

"I have but I've given my promise to Toby Beyer."

"But he went to America."

Sophia nodded. "I hope to follow him."

"Without your parents' consent? Hasn't your father forbidden you to see him, let alone marry him?"

Sophia nodded again. "I'm hoping he'll change his mind."

"But it's against the law to intermarry with those Hollander people. And what would you do about your religion? It's against the law for them to force you to change to theirs."

"He wouldn't force me. Besides, with Toby already in America the Russians won't bother with him. They can't prosecute him."

"That's true but do you want to displease our church fathers and maybe even get excommunicated?"

Sophia considered it a minute. "I don't think they'd do that," she said at last. "I'm not that important."

Boris narrowed his eyes. "They could make an example of you."

His face brightened. "Let's change the subject. Sophia, I am considering you for my wife. I believe you are just what I need."

He laid his hand on Sophia's shoulder. "Yes, you are just what I need."

Sophia's eyes twinkled. "And what if you don't fit into my plans?"

"Even if you don't love me, you'd do well to consider my proposal. I'm, that is, the nobleman has recognized my abilities and given me a good position. I could give you things that most young men couldn't give you, certainly not that other young man."

Sophia slowly shook her head. "Boris, you don't understand. I love Toby. And someday I will become his wife."

"Well, then," Boris said impatiently, "if that's the way you feel. Mind you, you are not the only eligible young woman in the country."

"And I sincerely hope you find the right one."

Sophia reached over and snapped the reins. The horses lunged forward and Boris had all he could do to control them.

"I'm not through yet," he said when they reached Sophia's home. "I'm going to do all I can to change your mind. I think I can win you."

# Chapter Nineteen

Summer turned to autumn. Harvest passed and the wheat fields turned to yellow stubble. Giant oak trees and roadside bushes blazed with color, reds, yellows and brown. Nights were cool now. When it frosted, Ben and Nettie would butcher their piglet, now grown big and fat. They would make *vorscht* for the journey. This year they would not cure the hams as they had in the past. They couldn't take them with them and there would be no one to eat them. They would make them all into *vorscht*.

It was October and in a month Ben and Nettie and most of Karlswalde would be on their way to America. Unlike other summers, Nettie and Mamma did not can vegetables. What they couldn't eat would go to waste.

At home, Mamma still grumbled about leaving. Nevertheless, she continued her preparation. She and Nettie discussed what they should take along.

"Ben said I took too much last time," Nettie told Mamma. "It was too heavy. But we only had the immigrant box and the bedding."

Mamma pushed a hair pin back into the coil at the back of her head. "Tobias says that's all anyone is allowed to take. That's not much for a family."

"No, it isn't. But Ben says it's only four days on the train to Antwerp and then ten days on the ship. We'll have to buy the rest in America."

"Who knows if we can buy the things we need. If we locate in unsettled country, there may not be any shops."

"Mamma, we can't worry about that. If the ship company won't let us take any more, that's that. And we won't have to take food along. The food's included in the ticket price."

"I still intend to take *zwieback* and *vorscht*."

"Of course. We'll need them for the journey to Antwerp. Train food's expensive."

"I think we should take enough for the ocean journey too. We may not like the food they serve. We'll toast the *zwieback* so they'll keep but we can take some fresh ones too, especially for the train ride."

Now that the time for their departure was drawing near, Nettie was getting excited.

"I'm still afraid of the Indians, she told Ben one night."

Ben brushed her worries aside. "The American government is pushing them west," he told her. "We won't have to worry."

Still Nettie couldn't help being concerned.

Ben continued to haul wheat to Schepetowka but the nobleman did not pay much for hauling and the money did not add up very fast.

"When I get the team and horses paid for," he told Nettie, "we'll put all the money away for passage. I was sure we'd have it paid for by now but here it's October already and we've made only small payments."

"But I thought we could borrow for the passage."

"We can but I'd like to start out without debt. If there's any left, we can use it to buy equipment in the new land."

* * *

One day when he was hauling wheat, Ben met Igor Savinsky. They pulled their wagons onto the shoulder of the road.

"Glad I ran into you," Igor said. "Heard the Karlswalders are leaving next month. Are you going too?"

Ben nodded. "Yes, Nettie has agreed to go. And her parents too."

"Thank God! Still all right for Sophia to go with you?"

"Sure. Have things changed any between her and your

122

parents?"

Igor shook his head. "No, but I wish they had. Father's forbidden Sophia to go."

"And you're going to help her anyway?"

Igor nodded. "Boris Zamskov tried to court her but she'd like to leave before Father insists she marry him."

"Boris Zamskov? The nobleman's right-hand man?"

Igor nodded. "The same. But he's a pompous oaf and proud of his position. I'm not sure he'd make a good husband even if Sophia were interested. Father was very angry when he heard she had turned him down. I don't think Boris will give up so easily."

"Hm, sounds like she has good sense. I'll buy her ticket so maybe you can come by and get it. She's welcome to join us. How'll she get to the train station? We'd pick her up but I'm afraid your father would run us off the yard."

"He would. I'll come and get the ticket from you and I'll get her to the train. I'm not sure just how I'll manage but I'll get her there."

"The train leaves early," Ben told him.

Igor extended his hand. "I know. Until then, thanks." He hesitated a moment. "And may God bless you in the new land."

Ben took Igor's hand and pressed hard. "I wish you were coming too. You've been like a brother to me. Are you sure you don't need the money you gave me? I can borrow a little more from the American churches."

Igor shook his head. "No, I want to do it."

Ben's face relaxed. "I must admit the money will come in handy. The officers informed me that I have to give them more money before we can leave. I think they're sticking it in their own pockets but what can I do?"

"I'm sure they are but you'll have to pay it. And Ben, I'll miss you too. Pray for me. It won't be easy when they find out I helped Sophia run away."


* * *

Another problem arose. The three hundred and twenty-five who were leaving had sold their horses and wagons. They needed transportation to Oschonin, where they would catch the train to Antwerp. A few who were staying offered rides but others refused to help. Ben contacted Joseph Hoffman.

"So you've decided to leave," Joseph said. "It's about time. The people from Heinrichsdorf left in August and the Michaliners are leaving too. I wondered if you'd ever decide to make the break."

Hoffman pushed back his hat.

"Sometimes I think I ought to leave, too. But my business has been pretty good and I'd have to give it up. Course, if I had sons instead of daughters, I'd leave in a moment. I hope I won't be sorry. I'm afraid we Germans are in for persecution."

Hoffman stared in the distance as though weighing his own thoughts. "But I'll take the chance," he said at last.

He extended his hand to Ben. "I'll be there to load early in the morning. Get you to Oschonin at a decent time so you can get a decent bed." He gave Ben a knowing look.

Ben winced at the reminder.

"Did you ever catch the thieves?" Hoffman asked.

Ben shook his head. "Saw them in Schepetowka once but they disappeared before I could talk to them. But I'm going to keep an eye out for them, even in America. I'd know them if I saw them."

"I think I met Schultz not long ago."

"You met Schultz?"

Hoffman nodded. "In Ostrog."

"There're lots of Schultzes around."

"Sure, I know. It's an old name. The men in charge of German *dorfs* are called Schultz. Lots of people have that name. Guess everyone wants to be in charge. Anyway, I'm sure this is the man who stole your stuff. Used to represent the railroad. Kinda sneaky and hangs out with one of the men who works for the overseer."

"So that's it. Earlier this summer the overseer told me that someone had notified them I didn't want to haul anymore. Sure sounds like Schultz. Well I'm going to America and I hope I'm rid of him."

"Don't count on it. Men like that always turn up like a bad *kopek*."

"I'll watch for him when I get there. I'll make him sorry he ever tried anything."

* * *

Ben did not earn enough money to pay off his team and wagon. Instead, he sold the outfit at a loss and took money from the cache he and Nettie had laid by and paid off their creditor. Ben applied for a loan and received enough money to buy tickets. With what was left of Igor's gift, after buying Sophia's ticket, he had enough to pay the bribe to the official with just a little more to take to America.

Pappa also sold his team and wagon at a loss as well. Most of the Karlswalders were leaving and there was no market for the things they left behind. Even the Lutherans who took over the houses seemed not to need those possessions. The Hollanders would have to leave what they couldn't take and others would help themselves.

Those who planned to stay firmly declared their disapproval of the mass exodus. There were heated arguments but in the end those same people planned a farewell service for those who were leaving. Differences were forgotten as they embraced and promised to pray for each other. Tears flowed as they expressed their hope of seeing each other again in heaven.

The following day, Nettie sewed money into the lining of their coats while Ben stuffed Turkey Red Wheat into Eva's two dolls. After Nettie sewed up the seams, they packed one doll in the immigrant box. Eva would carry the other. Then they were ready to leave.

Joseph Hoffman arrived early the next morning. They loaded their immigrant box and bedding then took their places in the wagon. This time Pappa and Mamma and their children were leaving too.

Ben leaned back in the seat and pulled his coat more snugly around him. The ground was covered with snow and a sharp wind was blowing from the north. With mixed feelings, he watched Karlswalde fade into the distance. Here he had spent his childhood and courted Nettie, beautiful blue-eyed Nettie with honey-colored hair. Of all men on earth God must have blessed him the most, he concluded.

Ben was happy to be going to America but as he passed the old familiar landmarks, there was a sense of loss. It wasn't so much that they were leaving their possessions behind. Ben and Nettie had parted with their possessions earlier that spring when they made their first attempt to emigrate. It was a part of their lives they were leaving behind, thirty years of Ben's and twenty-six of Nettie's. He had lived here all his life. He knew most of the people and, hopefully, this time they were not coming back.

Mamma and Pappa were leaving much more behind, everything they had accumulated during their lifetime. At fifty-one, Pappa had fifty *rubles* and nothing more than the clothes on his family's back, the things in the immigrant box and a bundle of bedding. Ben and Nettie had even less.

Farther down the road, they passed Abe and Susan Wedel's farm.

"Isn't this the house where the people got robbed and beaten up?" Hoffman asked.

Ben nodded.

"Are they leaving with your group?"

Ben shook his head. "Abe thinks it was an isolated case and that they're perfectly safe."

"He's a fool!" Hoffman thundered. "It can only get worse!"

"That's what I told him." Ben sighed. "But he wouldn't believe me."

"He's got his head in the sand!"

Andrew patted Ben on the forearm. "Pa are we really going to get on the ship this time?"

"Why, of course. We're on our way now."

"But last time those thieves stole our tickets and papers. What if they do it again?"

"They wouldn't dare!" Ben roared.

"How are you going to stop 'em?"

"I'll watch for them and you can help."

Ben put his hand on Andrew's knee. "Now don't you worry about a thing!"

The two lapsed into silence. If only Abe and Susan were emigrating too. Would Abe and Susan suffer for their faith? Would they eventually give their lives? Ben and Nettie could only pray for them and leave them in God's hand.

Then they reached Oschonin. Ben's quick temper flared as he remembered his earlier visit here. Oschonin held the bitterest of memories for him.

Hoffman broke into his thoughts. "Here we are. Are you taking a room in the hotel?"

Ben shook his head. "Can't afford it."

"Probably better than getting robbed."

"It won't happen again!" Ben declared.

"Well, I'd be careful if I were you."

"There are three hundred and twenty-five of us. We'll look after each other."

"That might be but thieves thrive in crowds. They can do their dirty work and slip away through a crowd. They're slick."

"You don't have to tell me that! But I learned my lesson and I'll watch for them." Ben's face tightened. "If I see them, I'll make them give back every *kopeck* they stole."

"Well, good luck then."

Hoffman brought the wagon as close to the depot door as possible. Then he helped Ben unload Ben and Nettie's belongings.

Ben and Nettie found room to sleep on one of the depot

benches but they both slept fitfully. Nettie, five months pregnant, found it hard to sleep sitting up. She was over morning sickness and, God willing, they'd reach America before this baby was born. Why had God allowed this pregnancy? God knew she wanted more children but this trip would have been so much easier without it.

Early the next morning, with Uncle Tobias in charge, the people from Karlswalde boarded the train. But Sophia was nowhere in sight. Had she changed her mind? Or had her father stopped her? They boarded the train without her.

# Chapter Twenty

Sophia lay quietly listening to the sounds of the night. Outside, the hoot of an owl broke the silence as it took flight across the snow-covered fields. Inside and on the other side of the wall, Father snored loudly. And in Sophia's room, on the opposite side of the bed, her sister, Catherine, slept soundly. Was Mother sleeping too?

Sophia waited for more than an hour to make sure the family was asleep. Then, quietly, she slipped out of bed. She shuddered as her feet hit the icy floor. Catherine turned, raised her head and mumbled something incoherent. But she closed her eyes again and laid her head back on the pillow.

Sophia breathed a long sigh of relief. What if Catherine awoke? She'd ask Sophia where she was going. If they talked, they'd awaken Mother for sure. But would she ever see Catherine again?

In the pale light seeping through the window, Sophia slipped on the clothes she had laid out the night before. Then, after putting on her thick overcoat and furry hat, she dropped the little angel Toby had carved into her pocket then cautiously opened the bedroom door. She closed it softly behind her then picked her way among her three brothers rolled up in quilts on the kitchen floor.

Before opening the door she took a paper from her pocket and laid it on the table. She had written the note yesterday when she was alone.

Dear, Father and Mother, I am going to America to meet Toby. I also want to tell you that I have come to believe that Jesus died for my sins and that there is nothing more I need to do to have eternal life. I love you and always will and am sorry to hurt you in this way. Sophia.

The words were so final. Would Father and Mother understand? Would they believe her when she said that she loved them? How she wished that they would understand that they could not work for their salvation, that Jesus paid for all their sins.

A tear rolled down her cheek, then another and another. Sophia turned and walked back to the shelf. She reached up and fumbled for the Byzantine cross she knew was laying there beside the statue. When she found it, she held the small religious medal-lion for a moment.

She couldn't see the details of the precious family icon but she knew every line by memory. How many times had Mother taken it from the shelf and told them how their Mother's grandfather carried this very cross into battle?

"It shielded him from danger," Mother told her children over and over again, "and it will protect us."

Sophia held it reverently in one hand and traced the details with the other. It was handcrafted of gold and the edges were decorated with tiny gold balls. At the center, a circle of tiny balls surrounded  the mosaic of the guardian saint.

"Forgive me, Mother," Sophia whispered as she slipped the icon into her pocket. "Forgive me."

She took a step to the door then stopped and took the medal from her pocket. Should she take it?

She was going on a treacherous journey.   She had never been on a ship before, much less on the ocean. How deep was the ocean and how far was it to America? What if the ship sank? And, if she made it to America, could she be sure the Indians wouldn't massacre her? Would she find Toby?

She dropped the medal back into her pocket. But as she did so, her hand touched the angel. She grasped the angel and held it a moment. Toby said God sometimes used angels to watch over His children. He said God would watch over her too if she trusted Him.

Sophia took the Byzantine cross out of her pocket again. Maybe she didn't need this icon. She put it back in its place then retraced her steps to the door. She would trust God for His protection.

Sophia grasped the safety bar spanning the doorway and slid it from its place. The bar slipped from her hands and hit the floor with a thud. Sophia waited breathlessly. But her brothers did not even stir.

When her mother did not appear, Sophia opened the door and stepped into the night. She shuddered at the blast of cold air that met her. She turned and looked once more at the sleeping figures."

"I love you," she whispered. "And I'll miss you. Please understand."

She closed the door behind her.

Sophia took her mittens from her pockets and put them on then made her way through the snow to the end of the barn. There she picked up the quilt and the few personal things she had stashed there then made her way to the road. Igor would meet her at the crossroads.

* * *

The train whistle shrieked impatiently and the hissing became more intense. Then slowly the train began to move. Where was Sophia? Had Sophia's father somehow learned of her plans?

Then the door at the end of the coach opened and Sophia, her face white, stepped in. The train lurched and threw Sophia into a seat in front of Ben and Nettie. Then the train shrieked its final warning. Sophia shuddered. This was it. They were leaving Russia. Would she ever see her parents again?

Sophia buried her face in her hands and sobbed. Nettie slipped into the seat beside her and put her arm around the sobbing young woman. Neither spoke.

"Oh, Nettie," Sophia said at last, her brown eyes filled with tears, "was I right to leave Father and Mother?"

"What does your heart say?" Nettie whispered as she took a handkerchief from her pocket and offered it to Sophia.

"My heart says I can't live without Toby," she said when her tears had subsided.

"Then you've done the right thing."

When Sophia had given her eyes a final wipe, Nettie moved back to the seat beside Ben.

Eva, who had turned two over the summer,  did not take easily to the crowded confines of the train, nor to the many strangers around her. She eyed Sophia with suspicion.

Sophia took a clean white handkerchief from her pocket, rolled it several times then tied a knot, turning the handkerchief into a cloth kitten. Eva's eyes danced with delight. She reached out and warily touched the kitten.

Then, shyly, she moved a little closer and watched Sophia unroll the handkerchief and transform it into a hammock with two  rolls nesting inside.

"Babies," Sophia said as she held up the swaying homemade hammock between her hands.

Eva took a step closer and peered into the hammock then gingerly touched the rolls. She giggled with delight.

"More!" she shouted. A friendship had been forged.

So engrossed was Eva in her play that she dropped the doll she was carrying. Ben quickly slipped from his seat and picked it up. They couldn't afford to lose it.

Andrew, who had turned seven during the summer, gave Sophia and Eva a disinterested glance then made a third trip to the water cooler at the back of the car. Ben put a stop to that. After that, Andrew amused himself by walking up and down the aisle, trying to keep his balance. Soon other boys in the car fell in line. Then to Andrew's chagrin, Eva toddled after them. Andrew quickly lost interest and brought out his carved horses and wagon. Johan and the other boys joined him with their toys.

Then the door at the front of the car opened and two Russian officials, their uniforms bedecked with medals, stepped in. They spoke to the passengers near the door and reached for their passports. The passengers watched with fearful eye as the officials examined the first passport. Would they stop them now that they were so close to freedom? Would they find some excuse to send them all back?

One of the officials reached for Sophia's papers. He gave the papers the same routine examination then suddenly he scowled and showed the documents to the other official, obviously the superior official. The two huddled over the papers and discussed them at length. Sophia sat quietly, her hands tightly clasped and her dark eyes intent on the officials.

"How is it that you are part of this group?" the first official asked at last. "You are Russian, are you not?"

"Yes, I am, as you will see by my papers."

"Then why are you traveling with these people?"

"They've invited me to." Sophia's knuckles turned white.

"And does your father know about this?"

Sophia hesitated. She was sure her parents had already found her note. Had he reported it to the police? Could they still stop her even now when she was so close to the border? The car grew very silent and all eyes strained to see Sophia.

The official shuffled his feet. "Does he?"

"Yes," Sophia said at last.

"You are a mere child and he is allowing you to travel alone on a ship?"

Sophia looked up with innocent eyes. "But I am not alone."

"But these are not our people," the official snarled.

"I feel perfectly safe, sir."

The official snorted in disgust.

The superior officer grabbed the papers.

"We'll check this out," he snapped then stalked into the next car.

The other official reached for Ben's papers. Ben stroked his beard and watched him study the documents. Would there be trouble because this was their second passport?

The official studied the papers a long time, longer than necessary, it seemed. Then he handed the papers back to Ben and took the next passenger's documents.

The superior official had still not returned by the time the official finished checking the other documents in the car.

But he returned an hour later and handed Sophia's papers back to her.

"You may proceed but don't be surprised if we detain you at the border. The Tsar cannot have his citizens leaving."

He turned and strode out of the car.

# Part II

# The Dream Threatened

# November 24, 1874-

# January 9, 1875

# Chapter Twenty-one

Four days later the train arrived in Antwerp, Belgium's main seaport. Their ship, the S.S. Abbotsford, the same ship Ben and Nettie were to have taken in April, lay waiting in the harbor. The ship was sleek and long from stem to stern. A single smokestack between two tall masts rose from the deck. The wind tugged at the furled sails and whipped away the steady stream of smoke rising from the smokestack. A British flag, the Union Jack, fluttered in the breeze.

A sense of urgency hung in the air as deck hands scurried about to prepare for the journey. Some loaded the ship with supplies and cargo while members of the steward's staff stocked the ship with food.

Fifteen-hundred passengers would soon board the S.S. Abbotsford. Three hundred and twenty-five of those passengers were from Karlswalde. Rumor had it that the ship would be loaded beyond capacity. Everyone, it seemed was sailing to America.

Andrew stood motionless, his eyes glued to the beehive of activity. Grown man that he was, Ben also stood mesmerized.

"Is that really our ship, Pa?" Andrew wanted to know.

"Yes, Andrew."

"Why do they need sails when the ship runs with steam?"

"In case of an emergency."

"You mean the engines might stop running?"

Ben stroked Andrew's head. "Oh, nothing like that. They keep the engines in good condition. I'm sure they've checked them."

"It's hard to believe, Nettie," Ben said, "We'll soon board

that ship and be on our way to America!"

He put his arm around Nettie's thickening waist. "In ten days we'll be there. Do you realize that this child will be born in America. It will be an American citizen before we will?"

Nettie looked up and smiled.

* * *

But imposing as the ship might be, Sophia was not impressed. Her mind was not on the ship. Sophia had felt uneasy since the day the two Russian officers accosted her. Had the officials contacted her father?

"What if they stop me before I can board the ship?" she asked Ben.

"Don't think they can. It's out of their jurisdiction."

But Sophia still felt uneasy. If only she had taken the little Byzantine cross. She thrust her hand in her pocket and felt the little angel Toby had given to her.

"Trust God," Toby had said.

She prayed silently and asked God to help her.

Late that afternoon, a small steamboat transported the passengers from the landing-stage to the S.S. Abbotsford. One by one the passengers made their way up the narrow gangway, its base on the unsteady steamboat. One woman lost her balance and had she not gripped the rails, she would have slipped into the churning water below.

"I can't make it," Nettie said when she saw how the gangway heaved as the vessels rolled and pitched in the choppy water.

"Don't look down," Ben told her, himself a little queasy. "I'll go first with Eva. Andrew will follow. You're next then the others."

With that, Ben started up the gangway.

He turned slightly and called over his shoulder. "Come on, Son, hold on to my coat."

Andrew grabbed Ben's coat, then scrambled up with ease. But Nettie hesitated.

Then, tentatively, she took the first step, and mustering all her courage, climbed to the top. There, waiting hands reached out to help her.

An officer checked their tickets and another directed them to their quarters. The three hundred and twenty-five from Karlswalde, they learned, would occupy the steerage, the lowest part of the ship. There would still be room for many more immigrants.

Ben and Nettie followed the crowd down the companionway, where a cold breeze was sweeping down the stairs. But the breeze could not blow away the horrible stench that rose to meet them. The stench worsened as they stepped into the dimly-lit steerage.

Sophia started to follow Ben and Nettie but an official gave her a gentle shove in the opposite direction. Sophia froze. Was this a trick of the Russians? Would they send her back to Russia? Reluctantly, she followed the women ahead. But they were not getting off the ship, as Sophia supposed. They were going to another compartment. As Sophia soon found out, they were single women traveling without a companion. She would bunk with them.

The compartments were gloomy and cold and smelled faintly of the chlorate of lime and carbolic acid that had been used in a weak attempt to cover the other odors.

Two tiers of berths lined the two long sides of the compartment. Each tier had six wooden berths, each a foot and a half wide and six feet long, making a total of twenty-four berths in each compartment.

By the time Sophia reached the compartment, only the top berths were empty. Sophia climbed to the top and spread her quilt over the wooden board then stowed her bag of personal belongings against the board separating the two berths.

Her eyes filled with tears. This was not how she had imagined this trip. True, the Russians hadn't stopped her. She should be thankful. But if they had, she would not be sleeping on this uncomfortable berth tonight. Instead she would soon be home and sleeping in her own bed. How could she ever spend ten days in this putrid room? Already their body odors were mingling with the stench of the ship and the cleaning compounds.

No sooner had the immigrants reached their compartments when word came that everyone must report to the deck to be examined for infectious diseases.

"They say it's some ploy of the Russian government to keep us from leaving." Nettie told Ben, her eyes dark with worry. "Do you think they're right?"

Ben shook his head. "Uncle Tobias says it's normal, that they also inspected the committee when it went to America."

"What if Andrew or Eva are getting sick? Would they send us back?"

"I suppose they could but none of us have been sick. I think we'll pass."

Ben was right. Their family and Pappa and Mamma's all passed inspection. Sophia also passed.

One family, however, was removed from the ship.

When the medical officers finished their inspection, tugboats pulled the ship downstream. From there the ship moved forward under its own power and dropped anchor in the mouth of the river. They would enter the North Sea early the next morning.

"I'm really worried about Sophia," Nettie told Ben as they stood at the rail and watched the proceedings. "She doesn't know anyone in that compartment."

Ben shifted Eva to his other arm.

"I'm concerned too, but there's nothing we can do. Like I said, I ..."

Suddenly he thrust Eva into Nettie's arms and lunged into the crowd. He shoved his way through the passengers then grabbed one of the immigrants by the collar.

"Schultz!" he bellowed.

When the man saw Ben, the color drained from his face. But

he quickly gained control of himself.

"Let go!" he yelled, releasing a string of unprintable words. "My name's not Schultz."

He tried to free himself but Ben held a firm grip.

"You robbed me!" Ben shouted. "You took my money and tickets."

"You've gotta be crazy!" Schultz yanked his collar from Ben's grasp. Before Ben could stop him, Schultz had melted into the crowd.

Ben glared after him. All the old anger came rushing back. This was the man who had stopped them from leaving the first time. If Schultz hadn't stolen his papers and tickets, they'd be in America right now, living on their own land.

"I'll get you," Ben promised. "Now that I know you're on this ship, I'll watch for you."

With that, Ben returned to Nettie's side.

Nettie looked up with questioning eyes. "Ben, what's the matter? Why'd you leave so suddenly?"

Ben didn't answer at first.

"I saw him," he said at last. "He's on this ship."

"Who's on this ship?"

"Schultz, the man who robbed me."

Ben's eyes were still scanning the mass of people. "He's here and if I find him, I'll make him give back every *kopeck*."

"What'll you do, Pa?" Andrew wanted to know, his eyes round with excitement. "Will you beat him up?"

Nettie touched Ben's shoulder. "Now look what you've done. Why don't you forget about Schultz?"

"Never!"

Ben clenched his fist. "He's going to pay for this."

"What'll you do, Pa?"

Nettie put her arm around Andrew and drew him to her side. "I don't think Pa will do anything."

She turned again to Ben. "Don't let this possess you. It'll only hurt you. We're on our way. Just let it be."

"But he robbed me."

Ben smiled confidently. "Who knows, Nettie, but that God let us be on the same ship so that we could get our money back. I'll watch for him. And I'll find him. You'll see."

"I don't think God works that way."

Ben ignored Nettie. His eyes, were still scanning the mass of people. "He's here and if I find him, I'll make him pay for it."

"The Bible says, 'vengeance is mine; I will repay.' You'll only hurt yourself if you let this bitterness continue."

"We'll see, Nettie. We'll see."

* * *

That evening, the steward's staff lowered tables from the ceiling of the common room and loaded them with platters of boiled beef and huge rusty kettles of soup and porridge.

No sooner had the food arrived than a hungry mob swarmed the tables. The hungry passengers elbowed their way next to the tables and greedily helped themselves. Quickly assessing the situation, Ben, with Eva in his arms, pushed Nettie and Andrew forward.

"Ben, you can't be rude. Let's wait 'til they're through."

"If we wait, we'll never get anything to eat," Ben growled. "Come on. You've got to think of the children and the little one you're carrying."

But although Nettie took her place beside Ben, she made it clear she wasn't pleased.

Then a hairy arm brushed her cheek, plunged a filthy hand into one of the platters of meat, then rummaged around for a piece to his liking. When he found it, he gulped it down and reached for more. Nettie gasped.

Ben gave her a worried look. "Guess we'll have to eat *zwieback*," he told her. "Hope they last."

"They won't if that's all we eat."

In the end, they filled their bowls with porridge then moved away from the table and sat on the floor in a less crowded space.

"At least it's filling," Nettie said, "And nobody's stuck their hand in it. Ben, will we have to go through this at every meal?"

Ben merely grimaced.

At the door, they met Sophia. Andrew and Eva saw her first and ran to meet her.

"How do you get through this mob?" Sophia asked as she picked Eva up.

"Good question," Ben answered.

Nettie touched Sophia on the shoulder. "Sophia, it's not very appetizing. I hope you can take it better than I can."

"Well, I'm not very hungry. Maybe I'll wait 'til morning."

"You'll have to eat something," Nettie advised.

"If it's as bad as you say, I'd be better off not eating. My stomach's queasy anyway."

"The food isn't going to make it any better," Ben said. "Are your sleeping quarters all right?"

"All right but I was hoping we could all stay together. Instead, they made us single women sleep in separate quarters."

Ben nodded. "We heard. Our family's together and Pappa and Mamma and their children and, of course, Grossmom but there are other people there too."

"It's only ten days," Nettie put in.

"You're right," Ben said. "At least they've put all of our people in one section so it's not like we're with strangers. And in our compartment most speak *Plautdietsch*. Could be worse."

"If only it smelled better," Sophia said. "Smells like the ship needs a good cleaning. If they'd give me some soap and a brush, I'd scrub the compartment myself."

"And if the food was better." Nettie sighed. "We'll all be sighing for *borscht* by the time we reach America."

Together the little group left the commons and made their way back to their compartments. But Sophia couldn't bear the thought of her gloomy berth. Instead, she returned to the deck. A brisk wind was blowing from across the icy waters. Sophia pulled her coat more firmly around her.

On the shore, the glimmering lights of Antwerp winked at

142

her through the dark night. Above her, the glittering stars twinkled in the sky. Around her, restless waves lapped noisily at the ship. A pang of loneliness engulfed her. With all her heart, she wished Toby were here by her side and she were in his arms. Dear Toby, did he miss her as much as she missed him?

Reluctantly, Sophia turned her back to the sea and started for her berth. She nearly bumped into the man next to her.

Sophia looked up in surprise. "Oh, sorry!" she exclaimed. "I didn't know you were there."

"That's all right. Guess I wasn't watching like I should. It is a beautiful sight our here, isn't it?"

The man was tall and lanky with a frank, friendly smile.

"You were watching the shoreline too?"

Sophia nodded. "But I have to be going."

"Can't you stay a while longer?"

"No, that is, I need to get back."

"Well, then, I'll see you in the morning."

Sophia hurried to the companionway.

# Chapter Twenty-two

While Sophia was on the deck, Ben and Nettie were putting the children to bed. The S.S. Abbotsford would leave at eight the following morning. If Andrew were to see the ship sail out to sea, they would have to get him and Eva to bed early.

Nettie sighed. "Oh, Ben, don't you wish we could be alone? We always have the best talks."

"I know, Nettie. I'm so glad we found a house of our own after we went back in April. We may not have had the best accommodations but at least we were alone."

"I was satisfied."

Ben smiled. "Don't think I didn't appreciate that. I wish I could have given you better things. Maybe it will be better in America."

"Ben, I've been happy. You know that."

"Yes, and I have too. Like you said, it would be nicer if we had a room of our own, even if we had to share it with both children. But our tickets don't cover private rooms and, what's more, we couldn't afford them even if they were available. They say the ship is already overloaded."

Ben could have bit his tongue.

Nettie snapped to attention. "Overloaded? Is it safe, Ben?"

"Safe enough." Ben winced a little at the lie.

He couldn't tell her he had heard there weren't enough lifeboats. This he knew though, if they should need lifeboats, he'd see to it that Nettie and the children got on.

Ben put his arm around Nettie's waist. "It'll only be ten days."

Nettie smiled into his eyes. "I can hardly believe it."

144

Ben held her a little tighter. "Nor I. But it's true."

He kissed Nettie then climbed into his own berth above hers. Nettie lay Eva on the wooden slab and, still dressed, squeezed in beside her. When Eva was asleep, Nettie would move to her own berth. Right now, Eva needed her.

Ben was right, Nettie mused. God was good to give them another chance to emigrate. She closed her eyes and thanked God for his goodness then committed her little family into his hands. Eva fell asleep immediately. But no sooner had she fallen asleep when a child's scream shattered the silence. Eva stirred, whimpered, then snuggled closer to her mother.

But the screaming child had no intentions of quieting down. The screaming turned into wailing that would not stop. Soon other children joined the cacophony of noise. It was a long time before the compartment quieted down. But the silence was soon broken by the cries of another restless, frustrated child. Sleep did not come to Nettie until the early morning hours.

When Nettie awakened, she felt worn-out. But she wiped her face with a damp cloth then ran a brush through her blonde hair and coiled the hair at the back of her neck. In an attempt to smooth out the wrinkles, she ran her hands  the length of her dress. But the wrinkles would not disappear.

With a toss of her head, she roused Eva and joined Ben and Andrew, who were waiting for them at the door.

They reached the rail just in time to see the sailors pull up the anchor. Slowly the S.S. Abbotsford moved into the open sea. It picked up speed and soon it left the shores of Belgium and was steaming its way through the North Sea.

Only after the land disappeared from sight did the little family leave the rail and move toward the dining tables. But although the food looked even less appetizing than it had the night before, they managed to eat a little. The other two meals were no better.

Late that evening, the ship passed into the English Channel. They would follow this arm of the Atlantic Ocean to Land's End, the most western point of the English coastline. There they would enter the main body of the Atlantic.

* * *

Although Sophia went to the dining area for meals, she ate little. She spent most of the day in her room. In the evening she returned to the rail and looked up into the star-studded sky. Were those same stars looking down on Toby too?

Then someone brushed against her. To her surprise, it was the man she had met the evening before.

His eyes lit up in surprise.

"Oh, we meet again. You must enjoy the night air. I do."

Sophia nodded.

"It is a little crisp, but not like it would be in Russia," the man said. "Are you traveling alone?"

Sophia hesitated. They had not been introduced. Should she be speaking to a strange man? Still, everyone here, or many of them were from Russia and thus they weren't complete strangers. "Yes," she answered belatedly.

"And I suppose you're from Karlswalde. Everybody here seems to be from Karlswalde."

"Well, I'm not."

"Guess that's why I haven't seen you there. I'm sure I would have remembered you."

Sophia blushed then turned abruptly. "It's getting late."

The man laid his hand on her arm. "Stay just a little longer, won't you? I'm Peter Jansen. I'm from Ostrog."

Sophia's eyes lit up. "Ostrog?"

"You know the town?"

"Of course."

"Is that where you're from?"

"No, but my *dorf* isn't far away."

Peter looked hopeful. "Then maybe we *have* met."

"No I don't think so."

146

"What did you say your name was?"

"I didn't."

"No, I guess not. I only wondered if we had met."

"I don't think we have. But you might know my brother. His name is Igor Savinsky."

"Savinsky. Then you're not one of us, that is not one of our people."

"No, Russian."

"Russian? How did you come to be on this ship?"

"I'm on my way to meet my betrothed."

Peter's face fell. "You're betrothed?"

Sophia nodded. "Yes, he's one of your people."

"Then why did he leave without you?"

"I, that is, my father refused to let me go."

"Then why didn't he stay?"

"He already had his steamship ticket. I agreed to follow. And that's just what I'm doing."

His face dropped again.

"Not very wise of him," he said at last. "Doesn't he realize you're much too beautiful not to attract other men?"

"I, I really must be going."

Peter touched her sleeve again. "Wait. Can't we be friends anyway? Surely there isn't any harm in that."

"I really must go." Sophia turned and this time she walked swiftly toward the companionway.

Peter followed. "I'm going that way myself. Please, ..." Peter waited for Sophia to give him her name. But Sophia refused.

"Let me accompany you. It really isn't safe for a lady to be here alone on the deck."

"I'm sure I'll be all right."

But Peter would not be discouraged. He kept stride with her all the way back to her compartment then bade her goodnight and continued on his way.

\* \* \*

That night, just after midnight, an enormous jolt jarred the ship. Metal scraped against metal then the ship shuddered to a halt. Women and children screamed as the jolt nearly tossed them out of their berths.

Ben sat up with a start. Were the Russians attacking? Would they force them off the ship and into their own vessels? Would they take them back to Russia?

Ben looked into Nettie's berth. "You all right?" he asked.

"What is it?"

"Don't know but I'll go up to the deck and try to find out."

"It's the Russians," someone shouted from across the room. "They've come to take us back."

Ben slid from his berth and confronted the man. "You're scaring the women and children," Ben told him. "We don't know it's the Russians."

"They have to be warned," the man stubbornly maintained as he hurried to another compartment.

Then from the floor above came a jumble of noise: scurrying feet, shouting men and the rumble of heavy objects being shoved across the floor. Then followed the sound of rhythmic pumping and of swishing water.

Ben checked on Grossmom and Nettie's parents. Both Mamma and Grossmom, wide-eyed with fright, were huddled together on Grossmom's berth. Grossmom, wearing a dark blue dress and a woolen *babushka*, looked as fragile as a butterfly. Ben was sure a strong wind would have blown her away.

He put his arm around Grossmom and held her close. "It's going to be all right, Grossmom," he told her.

"What happened?" Grossmom asked.

"Sounds like the ship hit something."

"What would they hit here in the middle of the sea?"

"I don't know."

A women in the next berth leaped to her feet. "Shouldn't we get out of here?"

"Where'll we go?' Ben asked. "If the ship sinks, we wouldn't be any better off on the deck."

The woman burst into tears.

Ben laid his hand on her shoulder. "Let's sit down and wait for orders."

"But we'll all drown," she wailed.

The woman grabbed Mamma's arm. "Come! We've got to get out of here."

Ben shook his head. "Where will we go? We're as safe here as we'd be anywhere else on the ship. God will keep us safe."

The woman sat down again but it was clear she was not pleased.

"I think we should pray," Ben said at last.

They folded their hands and Ben committed them all to their heavenly Father.

When Ben had finished, he stood to his feet. "You stay here," he said. "I'm going to find out what's happened."

But when he reached the companionway, a steward stood in the entrance and would not allow Ben up the steps. The steward tried to explain what had happened but the man spoke only English and Ben could not understand him. Ben returned to Nettie and the children.

\* \* \*

Hours later Uncle Tobias came to their compartment and informed them that another ship, the S.S. Indus, had rammed the Abbotsford and damaged the starboard side. Water poured into one section but the crew temporarily stopped the leak and were pumping out the water.

"They're taking us to London so they can work on the ship," he told them. "We won't have to get off the ship. We'll just stay on board."

The S.S. Abbotsford limped into London and dropped anchor.

The following night two-year-old Katrina Fast, who slept in the berth next to Eva's, developed a high fever. Although her mother rocked her, Katrina would not be comforted. Few of the passengers in that compartment slept well that night.

The next night was no better, nor the next. And a few days later, the day the S.S. Abbotsford was to resume its journey, Katrina broke out with small red spots. Everyone believed it to be smallpox.

Nettie's heart pounded with fear. "Ben," she said, "Katrina's berth is next to Eva's. Just yesterday they played together. I'm sure she exposed Eva. What will we do if she gets smallpox too?"

Ben put his arm around Nettie. "Now, now, we don't know that it's smallpox."

"Mamma said it was and everyone agrees. Remember the little Dirks boy who died from it? And Anna Reimer? Those scars all over her face are from smallpox. Oh, Ben, what are we going to do if that happens to our pretty little girl?"

Ben stroked his beard. Nettie was right. If Eva contracted smallpox, she could die. In fact, she was likely to die. Smallpox was a deadly disease. Could Nettie survive the loss of yet another child? She had lost too many babies already.

Besides, he wouldn't want his little girl to have scars all over her face. And, certainly he wouldn't want her to die. And what about Andrew and Nettie? Smallpox was no respecter of age. And with Nettie with child, she could be in real danger.

When the doctor examined little Katrina, he confirmed their worst fears. Katrina, indeed, had smallpox.

At breakfast, they heard more discouraging news. Many more passengers were ill.

That night, Mamma awakened Ben and Nettie. "It's Grossmom," Mamma whispered. "She has a high fever. Ben, can you get some water to cool her down? And maybe you can help me with her, Nettie."

Ben went for the water and when he returned, Nettie and Mamma dipped cloths into the water then laid them on

150

Grossmom's forehead. When the cloths had warmed, they replaced them with cold ones.

Mamma and Nettie continued their vigil all night. Once or twice Grossmom roused.

"He's taken us out of Russia," she said in halting words. "God is good." She lapsed into silence again.

All the while, memories of Grossmom flooded Nettie's mind. When Grossvatter was still living, they lived only a few houses away. Sometimes when Nettie was no older than Andrew, Mamma would send her to Grossmom's with freshly baked bread. Grossmom would put away the bread then reach into the cupboard and take out a peppermint for Nettie.

Grossmom understood Nettie. Unlike other grandparents Nettie knew, Grossmom thought young. She always seemed to agree with Nettie's point of view.

When Grossvatter died, Grossmom came to live with them. That was just before she and Ben were married. Grossmom liked Ben from the start and the feeling was mutual.

Nettie dipped another cloth into the water, twisted it then handed it to Mamma.

It was Grossmom who had insisted that Ben and Nettie emigrate the first time. Later, she insisted they all leave. Now Grossmom was near death. She would never see the new land.

Grossmom slipped away in the early morning hours. Ben went in search of Uncle Tobias. Soon two sailors arrived and carried the body away.

After breakfast, the Karlswalders gathered in the common room to sing hymns and hear Uncle Tobias read words of comfort from Scripture. Then they moved to the deck and watched the men take the wooden box containing Grossmom's body out of the hold and down the gangplank where it was loaded into a wagon. The wagon slowly moved away out of sight. Grossmom's body would be buried in English soil. They watched until the wagon had disappeared from sight.

Then Nettie burst into tears.

"Oh, Ben," Nettie sobbed. "There'll be no one to see about

her grave. No one to put flowers there. She'll be all alone."

Ben put his strong arms around Nettie. "Grossmom's with Jesus," he said. "It's only her body they're burying."

"But it seems so lonely -- here all alone in England."

Ben put his arms around Nettie and they both stood silently, mourning Grossmom's passing.

With sad hearts, they returned to their compartment.

Two children died later that night. Like Grossmom, they were buried in English soil.

Although the S.S. Abbotsford was scheduled to leave that morning, it remained in port. Whole compartments were evacuated and turned into medical wards and British medical authorities came on board to examine the passengers. They assigned those with symptoms of smallpox to medical wards. The others were vaccinated.

"Persecution!" one of the passengers whispered as he passed Ben, who was standing in line with Nettie and the children, waiting to be vaccinated.

"It's come to this," the passenger continued. "The Russians have tricked us. They got us on this ship so they could persecute us."

He shook his head despondently and continued on his way, voicing his suspicions to others in the line.

"Why don't they tell us what's going on?" Nettie asked.

Ben shrugged. "Maybe they have. They speak English and of course none of us understand it. We'll have to learn it though. That's the language they speak in America."

"You mean we'll never be able to speak *Plautdietsch* again?"

"I don't think they could stop us from using it in our homes any more than the Tsar could make us speak Russian. But we'll have to learn English to do business."

Nettie released a long sigh. "That's a relief. I could never learn English but since I won't have to do business, I won't have to."

But the trouble was not over. Officials informed Uncle Tobias that their ship would be quarantined and would have to leave London.

Late that afternoon the S.S. Abbotsford pulled out of port and dropped anchor in the Thames River. It was a grim day and the sheets of rain pummeling the ship only added to the gloom.

Confined to their compartment in the steerage, Ben and Nettie waited in silence.

Ben broke the silence. "How long does it take to get over smallpox?" he asked.

"Two weeks, I think. Unless there are complications. Or they die."

"It only takes ten days to get from Antwerp to America! Maybe we'll get there before anyone else breaks out."

Nettie's eyes clouded over. "But what if one of us gets it on the way?"

"Don't think we have to worry." But Ben wished he felt as sure as his words.

"Do you think they'll make the ship stay here until they're sure no one else will get sick?"

Ben stroked his beard. "Could be but I'd think everyone who has been exposed has already come down with small pox."

Then a boat pulled up and took the sick patients to another ship.

"The healthy passengers will remain on the Abbotsford," Elder Unruh explained, "I and two other brethren will transfer to the hospital ship."

Benjamin Buller and Peter Unruh would take charge on the Abbotsford.

"Ben, what if Eva breaks out with smallpox?" Nettie asked when the ship was moving again. "Will they send us back?"

Ben stroked his beard. "They vaccinated her."

"But how do we know it'll work? I never heard of vaccinating in Russia."

"I wouldn't be surprised if the ruling class wasn't vaccinated. Uncle Tobias says the English have used the serum since the turn of the century."

"But how do we know Eva wasn't treated too late, that she'd

already been exposed?"

Ben tilted Nettie's chin upwards and looked into her eyes.

"We don't, of course. All we can do is trust our heavenly Father. Worrying isn't going to help. But trusting God will. Remember how He changed Mamma's mind and caused her to agree to leave?"

"You're right, of course." But Nettie couldn't help being concerned.

Ben was worried too. But he couldn't let Nettie know. Would they ever reach America? Would they ever see the new land?

# Chapter Twenty-three

The S.S. Abbotsford plowed steadily through the choppy waters of the English Channel. At Land's End, the most western point of England, it entered the main body of the Atlantic Ocean and made it's way along the southwestern coast of Ireland.

Before retiring for the night, Ben and Nettie took the children to the deck for a breath of fresh air. But the deck was far from pleasant. A stiff wind was whipping icy rain across the deck. They pulled their coats tightly around themselves then turned their backs to the driving rain.

"We're on our way at last," Ben said. "We've had a lot of trouble but now we can look forward to a peaceful journey. So far none of us has broken out with smallpox and the ship's seaworthy again. We can relax and enjoy the journey."

"Ben, that collision scared me. And then when Katrina came down with smallpox and we had to wait wondering what they'd do with us. "

"That's behind us. We'll soon be in America."

They did not remain long on the deck for the wind and the rain increased. They returned to their compartment.

By midnight, the storm became even worse, whipping the ocean into mountainous peaks. The steamer pitched and rolled as it plunged into each mountain of water.

Suddenly, without warning, the wind changed directions. The ship lurched, tossing the passengers about in their berths.

Ben retched violently. Others were vomiting too. Pappa and Johan were leaning over the side of their bunks.

Heavy footsteps clattered above them. Men shouted. Doors slammed as the crew battened down the hatches and screwed the ports in place.

Ben looked up into Nettie's berth. "You all right?" he asked.

Nettie, with Eva clutched in her arms, looked at him with eyes wide with terror.

"What's wrong?" she asked. "Is it, ... is it going to sink?"

"These ships are built like locomotives," Ben said with a confidence he didn't feel. "They're made to weather storms."

He swung his legs over the side of his berth.

"Guess I'll see what's happening."

By now old women were weeping and mumbling prayers while wide-eyed children sat up in their berths and whimpered piteously. Now and then someone shrieked for help from God.

Ben shoved himself out of his berth and nearly slid across the room as his feet hit the slimy floor. Just in time, he grasped a corner bunk post. Then he carefully picked his way across the floor.

But he soon returned. "They've closed off the companionway," he told Nettie.

"Did you see Mamma and the rest? Are they all right?"

"Far as I can tell. Didn't stop to check. It's too hard to walk on these floors. They're pretty slippery."

"And Pappa?"

"He was retching terribly."

"Oh, Ben, I'm so frightened."

"God's brought us this far. He'll take care of us. Shall we ask him to?"

They clasped hands and Ben prayed. After he prayed, they both felt better.

But with the ports and hatches closed day after day, the air soon became stifling. The stench became nearly unbearable. And no one cleaned the floors.

Meals were served spasmodically. Ben went to the table once to bring back food for his family but the food was undercooked and their sensitive stomachs couldn't tolerate it.

That night, Ben had hardly closed his eyes when Nettie called to him.

"Ben, I don't feel good," she whispered.

"It's this storm," he told her. "Makes everybody nauseous. Lay down and rest."

"It's not that, Ben. It's different. I... I think the baby's coming."

Ben jerked to attention. "No! You must be mistaken!"

"I don't think so. It's like the other times. And it's too early. Oh, Ben, we'll lose this baby too. Call Mamma."

But Mamma could not prevent the miscarriage. Once again, the baby, another boy, was too young to live.

"What are we going to do, Ben?" Nettie wanted to know. "There's no land to bury him in."

"I think they bury them in the sea."

"I couldn't bear that."

"Nothing else we can do."

Nettie's eyes brightened. "Ben, could we wrap him in a quilt and take him with us?"

"I don't think it would work."

"It might if we didn't tell anybody and it won't be very long."

Ben put his hand on Nettie's shoulder. "I know how you feel but our baby has died and what would we do when we reached America?"

"We could bury him there."

"No, Nettie, I don't think it would work. If the officials found out, they would make us give him up. They'd bury him at sea. It's better if we tell them now. I'll just wrap him in a blanket and put him on an empty berth. "

If only Uncle Tobias had come with them instead of remaining with the hospital ship.

"I'll get Elder Buller," Ben told Nettie. "He'll know what to do."

Ben soon returned with Elder Buller. "I'll notify the officials," Elder Buller told them.

He took off his hat. "This calls for prayer. Shall we pray?"

Elder Buller prayed a simple prayer then shook hands with each of them.

"I'll find someone," he told them before he left.

It wasn't until late that afternoon that one of the staff came and carried the tiny form away. They would keep it in the hold until the storm passed. Then they would lower it into the sea.

Nettie broke down and cried.

Then suddenly, the storm hit with increased fury. Nettie, wan and listless, spent her days in her berth. Johan played with Andrew while the four girls entertained Eva. Mamma kept a close eye on Nettie and sometimes Sophia came in to check on Nettie or to play with the children. Ben spent as much time as he could with Nettie but she barely acknowledged his visits.

Then, one day when Ben looked into Nettie's bunk, she reached out her hand to him. "Do you know what day this is?"

"I'm not sure. Tuesday, maybe."

"I don't mean the day of the week. What's the date?"

"As a matter of fact, I don't know but maybe someone has a calendar. I'll check and see."

When Ben returned, Nettie looked at him expectantly. "It's the day before Christmas, isn't it?"

Ben nodded.

"What about the children? We don't have any presents for them."

"That can't be helped. Nothing we can do."

"Couldn't we have some kind of a celebration? For the children?"

"Eva's too young. She doesn't remember Christmas."

"But Andrew does. He'll remember how he and Eva set plates on the table and then, in the morning, they found the presents we put on them. Remember how pleased he was last Christmas when we gave him the team and wagon you carved? Wasn't it fun surprising him? And remember how we strung streamers across the ceiling? And lit candles?"

"I remember. But we don't have streamers and if we had plates, there's nothing to put on them."

"But can't we do something special for the children?"

"We could sing."

Nettie's eyes brightened. "And you could tell them how Jesus was born in a manager. Would you, Ben?"

Ben nodded. "Sure. Would you like to come down and sit on Mamma's bed?"

"I don't think so. I don't feel up to it. But I'll listen. I can hear you from up here. And why don't you ask Sophia to join us. I'm sure she'd enjoy it."

Ben went for Sophia and after they returned, they all sang. Soon others in the compartment joined them and for a while they forgot the storm.

In the middle of the night, Nettie woke up to a silent world. Though the ship was still tossing, it was silent, deadly silent.

"Ben, do you hear that?"

"Hear what?"

"That's just it. There's no sound. Why? Why is it so quiet?"

Ben shrugged. "I don't know unless ..." he paused, "unless the engines have stopped."

"Could it be?"

"I don't know. I suppose they could have."

"If the engine's have stopped, will they use the sails?"

"Don't think they can in the storm. Maybe God doesn't mean for us to go to America."

Nettie jerked to attention. "What do you mean by that?"

Ben leaned his head against Nettie's bunk and sobbed.

Nettie stroked his hair but she didn't know how to handle this. It was Ben who was always her tower of strength. Now she had to be the strong one.

"Ben, we've got to have hope."

"Hope in what? This trip was doomed from the start. The trouble started when Schultz and Gorbansky stole me blind. I'd like to get even with them."

"Ben, don't! God will take care of them."

"I don't think God pays any attention to us."

"How can you say that?"

"Think about it. First I get robbed. Then the collision. Then smallpox. Grossmom dies. The storm. The baby. And now this."

"But, Ben, God knows. And He cares even when things look gloomy. The Bible says, 'Casting all your cares upon Him for He careth for you.' We've got to trust Him. Let's pray and ask him to help us."

Ben looked up at Nettie. "I can't, Nettie. I just can't."

"Then I'll pray."

When she had prayed, Ben raised his head and planted a kiss on Nettie's lips. "I feel a lot better," he declared.

* * *

The storm also awakened Sophia and the other women in her compartment. Some were vomiting. Some were screaming. Others were softly crying.

Miserable with fright and nausea, Sophia fumbled in her coat pocket for the Byzantine cross. But it wasn't there. Then she remembered she had put it back on the shelf. If only she had taken it with her. How often had she seen Mamma use it when she was afraid.

Then she reached in her other pocket and found the little angel Toby had carved for her. Desperately, she clutched it to her breast and mumbled all the prayers she could remember. But her prayers gave her no peace. Terror and loneliness still engulfed her. She wished she had never come. Father was right, she told herself. She should have listened to him.

Sophia clasped the angel more tightly and recited more prayers. If only Toby were here.

Suddenly she remembered that Toby had told her that this little angel could not bring help. It was just an inanimate object. It was God who could help her and she needed to pray to Him. The angel could only remind her of God's watchful care. God was there, waiting to hear his people ask for help. At the time, his words made sense. And they made sense now.

Hadn't God answered when she and Toby had asked God to

allow her to immigrate to America? Even when Father had refused to let her leave, God showed them a way. Toby was right. She could ask God for things just as she had asked her father for things when she was a small child. Sophia slipped the angel back into her pocket again.

But the storm continued for three more days.

Then Nettie lost her baby and Sophia helped take care of the children and spent time with Nettie.

Then, to her surprise, Ben appeared in the doorway and invited her to spend Christmas day with them. The singing cheered her and she slept more soundly that night.

Still, the storm would not let up.

# Chapter Twenty-four

In Dakota Territory, Amelia Tieszen invited Toby to have Christmas dinner with her. As he stepped into her kitchen, the tantalizing aroma of chicken greeted him. An overpowering feeling of homesickness swept over him. Was his family even now gathered around Grandmother's table feasting on stuffed goose and pie?

Amelia greeted him with a broad smile and drew him into the room. She reached for his coat. "You must be freezing! Here, stand next to the fire."

She pulled him next to the pot-bellied stove.

Toby held his hands out to the heat. "I must admit this fire feels wonderful," he said.

Amelia pointed to a nearby chair. "Pull it next to the stove," she said, "while I finish dinner."

Toby seated himself then watched Amelia work. Amelia was wearing a beige dress with tiny bronze-colored flowers that matched the color of her hair. Her long hair was wound in a coil at the back of her neck. A white lace-trimmed apron was tied around her waist.

The table, covered with a starched white cloth, was set for two.

"I hope you aren't disappointed it's chicken. I didn't think we could eat a whole goose."

"If it tastes as good as it smells, I'll never know the difference."

"It will. But I hope you're not disappointed you aren't eating with Steinhardts."

Toby raised his eyebrows. "Oh but they intended for you to

join them. Didn't you know? Didn't Tina mention it?"

Amelia was the picture of pure innocence. "Really? She didn't say a word."

Toby wrinkled his brow. "That's strange. She was surprised I was coming here. Said she couldn't see why you didn't come."

"I was surprised myself, and a little hurt I might add, that she hadn't invited me." Amelia tossed back her head. "But then, I figured maybe she invited another family and that there wasn't room."

"She had, but you know Tina. There's always room for one more at her table. She must have forgotten to ask you."

"Yes. Well I'm almost glad she forgot." Amelia tossed Toby a coy glance. "It's awfully nice just the two of us. It can be noisy in their small house, what with the children."

She took the chicken out of the oven and carved it.

"You sit over here," she told him after she set the food on the table. She touched the back of one of the chairs, "I'll sit across from you."

She waited while Toby took his place then seated herself and looked up at him again with her soulful eyes.

"Will you ask the blessing, Toby?"

They bowed their heads and Toby prayed.

"It's so good to have a man say the prayers at my table again," Amelia said when he finished. "It does get awfully lonesome around here."

She straightened herself in her chair. "But we mustn't think of sad things. We'll just enjoy ourselves."

Amelia picked up the platter of sliced roast chicken and passed it to Toby. When he had helped himself, she handed him the bowl of stuffing.

"Looks like the kind my mamma makes," he said as he took a generous portion. "Has raisins in too."

"Really? Now isn't that a coincidence? But then, of course, our families are the same kind of people. People with the same background get along better."

She gave him a knowing look then passed the potatoes and

then the gravy.

Toby ate heartily and when they finished the main meal, Amelia brought on a raisin pie. After eating two pieces, Toby pushed back his plate and declared he could eat no more.

Amelia tossed him a pleased smile. "Now you just sit down on the settee while I clear away the food. I'll do the dishes after you leave. It'll help pass away the time."

After she put away the food, she took off her apron and seated herself at the far end of the settee.

"Isn't it strange that we never met in Russia? Our *dorfs* weren't that far apart. But then, of course, I only had eyes for Reuben, though there were others I could have married."

She fluttered her eyes.

"Of course." Toby gave her an admiring look. "I'm surprised I didn't run into your husband."

"Actually, we left for America shortly after we were married. We were one of the first to leave."

Amelia looked down at her hands.

"We had such high hopes. Reuben had saved a little money to buy machinery and a few comforts of life like this settee and the stove. And then the accident happened. The runaway horse tipped the wagon and the wagon fell on top of him. He didn't have a chance."

"It must have been a terrible shock."

"It was and, of course, I miss him very much. Proving up on the land is too hard for a woman. But I don't want to go back to Russia or move to town and work as a maid. Reuben wouldn't have wanted me to. He would have wanted me to marry again. In fact, several men have suggested marriage."

"Then maybe you should marry one of them."

Amelia slowly shook her head. "No, I just haven't been interested, that is, until you came."

Despite himself, Toby was pleased. Amelia moved a little closer and fluttered her eyes again.

"This must sound awfully bold, Toby, and awfully sudden but I'm sure you understand. Time is important. I could give you a good start here on this claim. We'd soon have a very nice farm."

Amelia paused then reached over and laid her hand on his hairy arm. "How does that sound to you?" she asked, her hand still on his arm.

Toby wanted to take Amelia in his arms.

As though she read his thoughts, Amelia moved a little closer. Her soft body was touching his now. Toby reached around her slender shoulders and drew her even closer. He bent to kiss her. Then he remembered Sophia.

How could he do this to Sophia? Still, this was the twenty-fifth day of December. Sophia should have arrived long before this. Had Sophia's father kept her from coming? Or had Sophia married someone else?

Maybe she had married one of her own people. Sophia was a beautiful woman. She'd have many suitors. Maybe Boris persuaded her to marry him. Sophia said he was showing signs of interest.

But he couldn't bear to think of that. The fact was, there wasn't another woman in the world like Sophia.

And, as far as he knew, Ben and Nettie had not yet arrived. Earning money for tickets would take time. Maybe they hadn't even left Russia yet. No, he'd have to give Sophia a little more time.

Toby stood up. "I'm sorry, Amelia, I got carried away. I'm betrothed to another woman. I can't do this to her."

Amelia also rose and she stood very close. Her beautiful gray eyes looked into his. "I know. I've heard about her. But do you think she'll ever come? It's been months."

"Perhaps they were delayed. I have to wait a little longer."

Amelia's eyes blazed with sudden anger. "And you'd give up all this waiting for a woman, a Russian woman yet? How foolish can you get?"

"But I promised her."

Amelia's gray eyes softened again. She put her hand on Toby's shoulder. "I know how you feel. It's first love. I know all about it. But it'll pass. You'll see. But, frankly, I can't wait much longer. There isn't time for a long courtship. Like I said, I can't keep up all the hard work. Besides, there are plenty of men who would jump at the chance."

"Then I'll have to take my chances. I can't do this to Sophia."

# Chapter Twenty-five

The engines remained silent the second day and the third. Although the wind was not blowing as hard, the water was still rough.

"Can't they do something?" Nettie asked Ben.

Ben shrugged. "Probably working on it."

"Then why does it take so long?"

"Who knows?"

"Is the ship making any progress at all?"

"As far as I can tell, we're just drifting."

"Why don't they use the sails?"

"Too much wind."

Nettie grasped Ben's arm. "Are we ever going to make it to America?"

Ben embraced Nettie. "I don't know. That's all I can say."

He rose to his feet. "I'll talk to some of the men and see if I can find out what's going on."

Ben returned shortly. "They say a bearing's gone out and the steering mechanism won't work. They need parts."

Nettie's eyes opened wide. "How are they going to get them way out here in the middle of the ocean?"

"They hope a ship will come along and tow us."

"Oh, Ben, let's pray one will."

Nettie touched Ben's arm. "You know it wouldn't be so bad if we weren't so dirty. Didn't expect to be on this journey this long. Don't have any clean clothes and we can't wash them. Haven't washed my hair since we left home. And this place is filthy."

Nettie leaned against Ben's shoulder and began to cry. Ben

laid his cheek on her head and stroked her blonde hair.

"I don't mean to complain but it all seems so terrible. Sometimes I wish we had stayed in Karlswalde and taken our chances with the draft lottery."

Ben took Nettie in his arms. "I know just how you feel. You well know I've been discouraged too. And it's even worse for you. Let's just throw ourselves on the mercies of our God."

At noon, Sophia met them at the table then stopped by Nettie's compartment to talk. But her presence did not cheer them. An air of gloom had settled over her too.

After four days, the crew no longer served meals. Instead, they set out tins of canned goods and open bags of dried fruit at irregular intervals. Rumor had it that they were running out of food and water.

The compartments did take on a semblance of cleanliness as the crew, having been bribed by the captain with jugs of ale, made a pretense of cleaning.

On the eighth day, officers ordered the passengers to assemble on the deck to receive instructions for abandoning the ship. Women and children would be the first to use the lifeboats.

Ben rushed to Nettie's side and shepherded his little family toward the door.

"Come on," he told them. "No time to waste." He glanced over his shoulder to make sure Pappa and Mamma and their children were coming too.

"What about Sophia?" Nettie asked.

"No time to check," Ben answered.

But Ben was not prepared for the mob on deck. They were shoving their way to the rail. With his family in tow, Ben elbowed his way through the crowd. They reached the rail just as the deck hands released the falls to a lifeboat filled with women and children. They watched the boat plummet down the side of the ship.

Ben shoved Nettie and the children to the front of the line. But the officer in charge shook his head and gestured for them to stand back. Ben watched helplessly. The rumor was true, then.

There weren't enough lifeboats. It was too late. Nettie and the children would have to remain on the ship.

* * *

Sophia and the other single women in her compartment also heard the order to report to the deck. They rushed up the companionway and when they reached the deck, Sophia looked for Ben and Nettie but she could not find them in the crowd.

"How are we ever going to get to the lifeboats through this crowd?" Sophia asked the woman next to her.

"Don't see what's the hurry," the woman answered. "There'll be room for everyone. They're required to have enough lifeboats."

Then a man gave Sophia a shove as he elbowed his way to the rail. Had it not been for Peter Jansen standing behind her, she would have fallen. Peter helped her next to the rail.

Strong hands grabbed her and helped her into the boat. She had barely squeezed herself between two women when the boat began to descend.

The lifeboat had dropped only a few feet when an unexpected gust of wind caught it and hurled it against the side of the ship. Despite the efforts of the two sailors aboard, it dropped too quickly and hit the water, splashing the passengers with icy water. When the sailor unhooked the falls and set the boat adrift, the boat tipped precariously nearly spilling its passengers.

The boat righted itself but then it soared upward, over an enormous wave, rolled crazily, then righted itself and swooped over yet another wave. The passengers screamed as they clutched the sides of the boat. Sophia leaned over and retched horribly.

The boat lurched again as it hit yet another wave, soared upward then suddenly dropped again. Now the S.S. Abbotsford was nowhere in sight. Had the waves carried them so far in such a short time?

Then the boat rode up the next mountain of water. As it reached the crest, the S.S. Abbotsford again came into view. Then another unexpected gust of wind hurled the waves from a different angle. No one could predict which way the boat would go.

All the boats were now foundering in the boiling waters. Sophia's boat nearly collided with one.

Sophia found herself repeating memorized prayers but stopped before finishing the first prayer.

"Help me," she whispered in simple but halting words. "Keep me safe."

She felt a little better.

* * *

When the lifeboat left the ship, Ben spun around away from the rail.

"Murderers!" he thundered. "Cold-blooded murderers!"

Nettie tugged at Ben's shirt sleeve. "Ben! People are staring."

"Let them! They're stuck just like we are!"

"But the children."

Ben glanced at Andrew and Eva and softened his voice.

"There ought to be a law. The government ought to make sure the ships have enough lifeboats."

"But didn't you say the ship was overloaded?"

"Then they should have added more lifeboats!"

He swept his arm in a semicircle. "Look at 'em. Old people, young people and children. All gonna drown just because they don't have enough lifeboats."

Mamma, standing nearby, nodded. "I knew we shouldn't have come. I knew something terrible was going to happen."

"Now, Mamma, calm down." Pappa said. "We're safe for now."

"At least we're all here together," Nettie said, " you and us and ... Nettie stopped. "Sophia. Where is she? We haven't even checked on her."

"She's in that lifeboat," said a voice behind them.

Ben and Nettie turned to see who had spoken. .

"Are you sure it was Sophia?" Nettie asked.

"The same."

Peter offered Ben his hand.

"I'm Peter Jansen. Helped her on myself."

"Praise God. Thank you, Peter."

"Yes, thank you," Nettie put in.

"You don't have to thank me," Peter said. "I'm only glad there was room for her. But seeing that rough water, I'm not so sure she's any better off. I hope they sent food and water with them. But who knows how long the food will last. We may be better off than they."

Ben glanced at the lifeboats then looked at the British Union Jack hanging upside down, a sure sign the ship was in distress.

"All of us are in trouble."

Nettie's eyes grew wide with terror. "What are we going to do?"

"Nothing we can do but go back to our compartments or stay out here on the deck," Ben said. "I only wish you and the children could have gotten into a lifeboat."

"Is the ship really sinking?"

"Doesn't look good, Nettie. Unless we're rescued, there's no hope. They say the engines can't be fixed out here on the ocean. They need parts."

Ben couldn't tell her that the real danger lay in the fact that they were running out of food. And, even worse, water. Unless another ship rescued them, they would all die.

"Oh, Ben, why, after God gave us a second chance? Why is He letting us die out here in the water?"

Ben put his arm around Nettie. *Why, indeed.* Nettie's face turned ashen. It was merely a matter of days since she had lost the baby. She should be in bed, resting.

171

"I don't understand it myself. Doesn't seem fair. They shouldn't have started out without enough boats," Ben declared.

"What about Andrew and Eva? It doesn't seem fair that they should die so young. They're innocent children."

Ben stroked his beard and glanced at Andrew and Eva who were at the rail, watching the lifeboats.

Pappa laid his hand on Nettie's shoulder. "Innocent children always have suffered with adults," he said. "It's something that's hard to understand."

"A lotta things are hard to understand," Ben said. "Why did God let this happen when He got us this far?"

"That's exactly what I've been thinking," Nettie said.

"Nettie, don't forget that bad things do happen to good people," Pappa told her.

He turned to Ben. "I know you're angry because there wasn't room on the lifeboat for Nettie and the children. There wasn't room for Mamma and our children either. Bad things happened to our ancestors too. Think what they've suffered down through the centuries. We have to trust God as they did."

"You're right, Pappa," Ben said, "My temper got in the way. But it is hard to accept when it's happening to you."

The two families spent most of the morning on deck.

"Can't figure out," Ben said as they stood at the rail and watched the lifeboats, "why we haven't seen Schultz. I saw him that first day but haven't seen him since."

"He must be afraid of you and is keeping out of your way," Nettie suggested.

"He's wise," Ben answered, the old anger rising in him.

Halfway through the morning, Elder Buller informed them that he was holding a prayer meeting in the common room right after the noon meal.

Ben and Nettie did not eat lunch at the dining tables that day. Instead, they returned to their compartment for *zwieback*.

"They're almost gone," Nettie said. "Then what?"

Ben shrugged, his face grim.

Nettie put the remains of their meal away then they went to

the common room where Elder Buller was waiting.

"I have good news," Elder Buller told the group. "The reason they stopped loading passengers in lifeboats was not because they ran out of lifeboats but because someone saw smoke on the horizon. They couldn't be absolutely sure it was a ship so they waited to announce it. Now they have clearly seen the ship through their telescope. They're hoping the ship will tow us to the nearest port."

"Thank God," Ben said aloud.

"Yes, we'll take time to thank Him in just a moment. We do have one matter to pray for. We need to pray for the women and children on the lifeboats. Although this storm is over, the water is still dangerous. The boats could upset and dump the passengers into the sea. We need to pray for their safety."

He looked at Ben. "Ben, will you pray?"

Ben prayed and he prayed especially for Sophia. He had seen the waves pummel the little boats and he could well believe they were in danger.

"Take care of our sisters and the children," he finished, "and help them to trust you for their safety."

When the group disbanded, Ben and Nettie and the children returned to the deck to watch for the ship.

Gradually the dark object on the horizon turned into the shape of a ship. A roar rose from the deck. The ship moved steadily nearer and soon they could read its name painted on the side of the ship. It was the S.S. Pennsylvania. Help was coming.

As the ocean liner drew near the S.S. Abbotsford, it cut its speed and slowly positioned itself between the prevailing wind and the lifeboats. Then a deck hand from the Pennsylvania dropped a rope to the nearest lifeboat. One of the two sailors in the boat reached for the rope but as he did so, the lifeboat plunged over an enormous wave. The rope swung out of his reach. The boat tipped and almost upset. Then it righted itself again. But it drifted farther from the ship.

The deck hand pulled the rope in then threw it out again. This time the rope fell across the life boat. But the rope had barely been tied when a wave lifted the lifeboat and dropped it into a valley of water. Would the rope hold?

It did and the deck hands grasped it and pulled the life boat out of the boiling water and to the lee of the ship. The boat rose and then fell into the trough. After many failed attempts, the sailor hooked a rope to the other end of the boat.

But the boat was still in danger. One of the ropes could unhook and leave the boat dangling on only one rope. If it did, the passengers likely would be jettisoned into the water.

But the experienced deck hands knew their jobs. They kept the ropes taut until the boat reached the crest of the wave. As the boat began to drop over the crest, they pulled on the ropes and the wave passed harmlessly under the life boat.

The deck hands then hauled the boat upward and swung it onto the deck. Strong arms helped the frightened passengers out then the deck hand threw the rope to the next boat.

It was dusk before all the lifeboats had been rescued. And just in time. Another storm was brewing in the west.

With darkness descending, they could not see well enough to pass a cable to the Abbotsford. They would have to try again the next morning. Now the Pennsylvania positioned itself between the storm and the Abbotsford, taking the full fury of the storm when it hit shortly after dark. The next morning, as soon as it was light, they attempted to pass the cable.

The S.S. Pennsylvania had just pulled close enough to fasten the cable when a high mountain of water slammed the rescue ship into the Abbotsford.

Ben's heart jumped. Terror erupted among the passengers. Was history repeating itself? Would the Pennsylvania be too damaged to tow the Abbotsford into port?

But the damage was minor and the crew successfully secured the cable. In the morning, they would tow the ship to Queenstown, Ireland. That night Ben and Nettie slept.

But before Sophia retired, she stepped out on the deck again. Somewhere, across that water, Toby was waiting for her. How she wished she could hear from him.

# Chapter Twenty-six

When the ship reached Queenstown, a close inspection confirmed their earlier conclusions. The bearings had gone out and the propeller shaft had broken.

Because no one knew how long it would take to make the needed repairs, officials transferred the passengers to the railroad. They took the train to Dublin, where they boarded a ferry to Liverpool, England. There they boarded the S.S. Kenilworth. On New Year's Day they once more put out to sea.

Nine days later, on January 9, 1875, the ship turned up the Delaware River and docked in Philadelphia. The journey that should have taken less than two weeks had taken nearly two months.

Ben and Nettie and the children stood on the deck and watched the ship move toward land. It was cold and to shield them from the sharp wind, they pulled their coats more tightly around them.

"What about the Indians?"

"We don't have to worry. This is Philadelphia. Indians don't live in the city."

"But we're not staying in Philadelphia, are we?"

"Oh no. We're moving on. All the land here in Pennsylvania is settled. We're going to a place called Kansas. Toby will be there waiting for us."

"And how long will that take?"

"If America is as big as Russia, it could take a couple of weeks. We have to change trains several times, they say."

"Then how do we know Indians won't attack us along the way?"

Ben considered that for a minute. "As I understand it, the East is settled. Has been for a long time. And the government's pushed the Indians west. It must be safe to travel or they wouldn't let us go."

Nettie sighed. "And if we all live in *dorfs*, we can look after each other."

"We won't live in *dorfs*," Ben said quietly.

"Not live in *dorfs*?"

"We have to live on the land to claim it."

"You mean we'll have to live all alone in a strange place and with Indians around?"

"God brought us this far and He'll take care of us there."

"I know but I still can't help thinking about it."

\* \* \*

Nearby, Sophia and Peter were also watching the ship approach land. But Sophia was not thinking of Peter. She was thinking of Toby. Soon she would see him again!

Peter broke into her thoughts. "Looks like we're almost there, Sophia. We've reached America. What do you think?"

"I was wondering if it's all like that. Tall buildings and crowded like any other city. Why it looks like London. I expected wide open spaces and farms."

"There are, farther west. Have you decided what you're going to do?"

"Do? Why I'm going to go meet Toby, of course."

"But are you sure Toby is still waiting for you? It's been a long time."

Peter was right. Toby *had* been gone a long time. And she had been on the journey a long time herself, much longer than either of them had expected. Perhaps Toby had grown tired of waiting. Perhaps he had given up on her. Maybe he had married someone else.

Sophia slipped her hand into her pocket and fingered the little carving Toby had made for her. Surely Toby would not marry anyone but her.

"I was hoping you'd change your mind," Peter continued. "I'm thinking of staying here in Philadelphia to earn money before going west."

Peter put his arm around Sophia and Sophia did not withdraw. "It's going to be awfully lonesome all alone. I have some money saved, enough to take care of myself for a while. Enough for a wife, too. Will you stay? I'll take good care of you."

Sophia did not immediately answer. She couldn't think of a more thoughtful person than Peter. What would she have done without him? Ben had all he could do to take care of Nettie and the children, not to speak of his extended family. Yes, Peter had been very good to her. She was sure he'd make a good husband. But she had promised herself to Toby? How could she be disloyal to him?

"To tell the truth, Sophia, I've grown very fond of you," Peter said when she didn't answer. "I ... I wish you wouldn't go west."

"You've been very kind to me."

"Sophia, I hope you've noticed that it's more than kindness that I've shown. I love you. Will you marry me?"

Sophia looked down at the bag she was carrying, her long dark lashes resting on her smooth cheeks. "Toby's expecting me. I can't disappoint him."

Peter's eyes filled with disappointment. "Then that's your answer?"

Sophia nodded without looking up.

"Well, then there's not much more to say, is there?"

He held out his hand and Sophia took it. "I wish you much happiness. I won't soon forget you."

Peter walked away.

With a heavy heart, Sophia joined Ben and Nettie and the children standing at the rail. She'd miss Peter. He had been very good to her during the journey. Had she made a mistake by rejecting him? How did she know Toby was still waiting for her?

Ben and Nettie seemed to understand her need for silence and stood quietly watching the pilot boats as they moved forward to guide the ship.

Ben put his arm around Nettie. "We're here. We're in America."

"How'll we know where to go when we leave the ship?"

"Didn't I tell you? Some of the men from the Pennsylvania Mennonite churches are meeting us. Good of them."

Nettie frowned. "Will they expect us after all this time?"

"If they're not there, we'll send a messenger or a telegram."

Nettie looked down at her soiled coat. "What'll they think of our dirty clothes? Ben, I've worn these clothes for weeks. And the children, they look like little urchins. Eva's dress doesn't reach the top of her shoes anymore."

Ben grinned. "If it makes you feel any better, I've worn my clothes just as long."

His blue eyes grew sober again. "I can understand how you feel, Nettie. Cleanliness has always been important to you. These weeks surrounded with filth haven't been easy. No fresh water to wash clothes. No extra clothes. But soon you can wash and if there's enough money, we'll buy material for new clothes."

Nettie nodded. "I can hardly wait. Still, I can't help wondering what they'll think when they see us."

"They'll understand when they hear how long our journey has been."

"But they won't know until we tell them."

Andrew's shouts cut short their conversation. "Look! Look!" he shouted, pointing at a small boat. "It's coming to the ship."

They watched the boat pull up to the ship. Officious-looking men, obviously doctors, carried satchels aboard. Then they examined each passenger for infectious diseases.

Nettie's blue eyes widened. "Ben, could they still send us back? That is, if someone's sick, would they send them back after all that?"

"I suppose they could. It's like London. They don't want us

to bring in disease."

Nettie's eyes filled with terror. She grabbed Ben's sleeve. "What if Eva has smallpox? She played with Katrina."

Ben put his arm around Nettie. "I don't think we have anything to worry about. If she was going to get sick, she'd have gotten sick long before this."

But Ben wished he could be sure. Without a doubt, the Americans would examine them very carefully. Any sign of smallpox, and they wouldn't let them off the ship. He'd heard they'd sent some back before. If Eva were sick, would they force them to return to Russia?

But Eva passed inspection as did all the other passengers. The steamship proceeded to the dock.

"Thank God," Nettie breathed.

Ben extended his arm toward the horizon. His blue eyes beamed with delight. "Do you know what this means? We're in America."

Nettie nodded. "If only Grossmom were here. She wanted to come so badly."

"Actually, I think what she really wanted was for her family to come."

"I think you're right, Ben, and now, of course, she's with Jesus."

"Yes, she's much better off. And we are too. We won't have to worry about the draft lottery. We can worship God without interference. And, Nettie, we'll have land of our own."

# Chapter Twenty-seven

Meanwhile in Dakota Territory, Amelia was thinking of Toby too. She hadn't seen him in several weeks. The fact was she hadn't seen anyone for a long time. There had been one snowstorm after another. And now one of her cows was sick.

But today was a beautiful day. It was cold and there were several feet of snow on the ground but the sun was shining. She felt better already.

Besides, she had waited long enough. Amelia meant to have Toby as her husband. She had to act quickly. There was no telling when that Russian woman might turn up.

The cow wasn't too sick, she had to admit, but it furnished a good excuse.

Amelia put on the bronze-flowered dress she had worn on Christmas day. Toby had liked it, of that she was sure. Then she hitched her horse to the wagon and started on her way. Surely Toby would be home today.

Amelia was right. Toby came out to meet her as she drove into the Steinhardt yard. He smiled broadly.

"Well, look who's here." Toby reached up to help her out of the wagon. "Wait and I'll blanket your horse."

Amelia shook her head. "Can't stay. I have a sick cow and I wondered if you'd come look at her."

"Of course. Wait 'til I put on more clothing."

Toby soon returned wearing heavy clothes.

"Why don't you ride with me?" Amelia asked. "Then you won't have to hitch up your horse."

"I'd better take my own rig," Toby said, "then you won't have to take me back."

Amelia frowned. He'd be more likely to stay longer if he rode with her. She'd be able to control that. Toby wasn't going to be easy to manage, she decided. Still, she liked a man who knew what he wanted. As she saw it, she'd have to make him see that it was her he wanted.

Toby and his horse and wagon soon pulled up next to Amelia's. He motioned for Amelia to lead.

When they reached Amelia's yard, they covered Ben's horse with a blanket and put Amelia's in the barn.

"Poor Bossie," Amelia cooed as she stroked the cow's forehead.

"See how glazed her eyes are?" she said. "I know she's not feeling good."

Toby nodded then ran his hand over the cow's neck and over her belly. "Been this way long?"

"I didn't think she looked too good when I milked her last night. Then this morning she looked pretty bad. That's when I decided to ask you to come."

Toby nodded. "Not much we can do except maybe give her some of this." He picked up the bottle of dark liquid he had brought with him and forced the liquid down the cow's throat.

"What's that you gave her?"

"Some medicine we used to mix up for the nobleman's cattle. Often did the trick. Hope it'll work on her. I'll come by tonight and check," he said as he put the cork back into the bottle.

Amelia smiled her best smile. "Would you? I'd be ever so grateful. I've never tended a sick animal before."

"That's what neighbors are for." Toby opened the barn door and started for his horse.

But Amelia had other plans. "Can't you come in for a cup of coffee?" she asked. "And a cookie?"

Toby hesitated a moment. "A cup of coffee does sound good. And the cookie sounds even better."

Toby followed Amelia into her kitchen.

"Just hang your coat over there on the peg," Amelia said as she stirred the fire. "The coffee's still hot."

She placed several cookies on a plate then poured them each a steaming mug of coffee. Toby helped himself to a cookie.

Amelia pushed the plate more closely. "Here have another. Take two."

Toby took two more. "These are good."

"You'll have to take some home," Amelia told him. "I baked a big batch. Never'll eat them all myself."

Amelia's gray eyes filled with frank admiration. "It was good of you to come. But then, of course, I knew you would. You're so helpful."

"Just the neighborly thing to do." Still, Toby's words belied his feelings. Amelia was a woman who appreciated a man.

"You seem to know how to do so many things."

So Amelia had noticed. He did know quite a bit about farming and raising cattle. Had learned them working on the nobleman's farm. They'd not only raised cattle but also hogs. And they'd sown wheat and cut hay. Yes, sir, Toby told himself, he had learned a lot and now that training was being recognized. Some women wouldn't have noticed.

When Toby had finished his coffee and eaten two more cookies, he took his leave with a dozen cookies wrapped in newspaper in his hand.

"I'll see you this evening," he said as he stepped through the door. Toby's step was a little lighter and he couldn't help but look forward to this evening when he would see Amelia again.

The fact was Amelia was not the beauty that Sophia was but she was attractive. Amelia leaned toward plumpness whereas Sophia was thin and willowy. Amelia had gray eyes that reflected her changing emotions. Sophia had brown eyes, tender and compassionate. Sophia had striking dark hair that was different from most of the Hollanders. It complimented his own dark hair. Amelia's reddish hair blended into the blonde hair of his people and was an interesting contrast to his.

But Amelia was here in Dakota Territory. And she was available. She had made that clear. Toby wasn't sure he liked women to be that bold. But at least he knew where she stood.

At night, though, when he was alone, Toby felt guilty. He had promised to love Sophia for the rest of his days. This was January. Eight months had passed since he kissed her goodbye. In all that time he had not heard from her. If only he had some way of communicating with her. Why hadn't she come? Was she still in Russia? Where were Ben and Nettie? Why hadn't they come as Ben had promised? If only he know whether or not Sophia was still planning to come. If he knew she were coming, he'd wait as long as it took.

He and Henry Steinhardt talked it over before dinner one day. Toby and Henry were waiting for Tina to finish her preparations.

"Toby, why don't you marry Amelia? Life here on the prairie is hard enough with a wife but it's doubly hard without one."

Toby said nothing.

"I don't know what I'd do if I didn't have Tina here to have food on the table when I come in dead tired," Henry continued. "Don't know how I'd get my clothes washed or keep the house looking halfway decent. Besides, women can help out on the farm, milking and feeding the livestock. They can even help with the harvest. It's just like a hired hand only you don't have to pay her."

"I know but there's Sophia."

"It's been nearly a year."

"Eight months," corrected Toby.

"Well, whatever. But with Amelia, you have a head start on the other homesteaders. Amelia's not bad to look at and ..."

Toby flushed. What Henry was saying was exactly what he had been thinking.

"As a matter of fact, I've been wanting to talk to you about Amelia. Amelia's good company, a little forward. Speaks her mind. But at least I know where I stand. And then she does have a quick temper."

Henry grinned. "Nice making up, huh?"

Toby flushed again then ran his hand through his dark hair.

"She *has* made it clear that she's interested in me and that there are other men who are interested in her. I'm not sure I like a woman to be that forward. Would I be unfair to Sophia if I married Amelia and would Amelia and I get along?"

"You can't be sure Sophia will come. As far as getting along, I think you'd handle things."

* * *

Amelia invited Toby over for dinner the next Sunday. After they had finished eating and Amelia cleared away the remains, she sat down beside Toby on the settee. Toby felt comfortably full and content.

Before Toby knew what had happened, Amelia was sitting very close to him. She looked up at him with her beautiful gray eyes.

"Did you enjoy the dinner?" she asked.

"But, of course. It was a very good dinner."

"Better than Tina's?"

Toby nodded.

Amelia moved closer and her face took on a sly look. Toby could feel her body touching his. She reached up and touched his cheek.

"You know you could eat like this every day if we were married."

Amelia smiled then laid her hand on Toby's and stroked it.

"You have such strong hands," she said. She gave Toby an admiring look.

Toby's heart beat rapidly. Her hand looked so small. He was very conscious of her nearness. Then, as though he couldn't help himself, he put his arm around her and kissed her.

"I've been meaning to talk to you," he said when the kiss had ended.

Amelia did not wait any longer. "I knew you felt that way. I'll make you a wonderful wife."

Toby rose to his feet.

"Amelia, I'm sorry but I'm not ready for marriage yet. I, I have to think."

Toby drove home that afternoon with mixed feelings. Could he be happy married to Amelia knowing that Sophia was out there somewhere?

# Chapter Twenty-eight

At last, after long months of snow and cold weather in Dakota Territory, February arrived. Although it was still cold and there were still snowdrifts on the ground, there was hope that warmer days were coming. The winter had been severe. One blizzard had hardly passed when another came. The roads drifted shut and for weeks on end, they were virtually impassable.

Toby was thankful he had parked his wagon on Steinhardts' yard. With the extra quilts Amelia had given him, his bed on the floor was warm. During the day, when the weather would not permit Toby to be outside, he spent his time in the Steinhardts' house, playing games with the children.

Several times, despite the drifted roads, Toby made his way through the snow to Amelia's farm. Although Amelia was managing on her own, Toby did what he could to make life easier for her.

Toby found himself looking forward to these visits. Amelia was still pursuing him and Toby couldn't help finding pleasure in her attention. Toby had almost given up on Sophia. It was now nearly a year since she and Toby had said goodbye. Why hadn't she come? Had her father prevented it? For that matter, why hadn't Ben and Nettie arrived? No one seemed to know.

Then, before Toby really realized what was happening, Amelia began planning a wedding.

"We'll have it here in my house since we still don't have a proper church building," she told Toby. "I'm sure my brother's wife will help cook the meal. And maybe Tina. We'll have ham and *zwieback*, and of course, *plummemoosse*. I might even bake a wedding cake. Shall we set it for June?"

Toby agreed but a few days later he came to see Amelia with news. "Elder Wiebe is coming from Kansas next week. Wouldn't it be nice to have him marry us?"

"How long is he staying?"

"Just a few days. We'd have to have the wedding next week."

Amelia's face dropped. "Next week?"

"That doesn't leave much time for planning. I couldn't possibly get ready that soon. Couldn't we arrange to have another preacher?"

"We could but  Elder Wiebe is special."

"But my dress isn't finished!"

"Couldn't you wear one of your other dresses?"

"For the wedding? I so wanted our wedding to be special."

"It will, especially if Elder Wiebe performs it," Toby said with a hint of impatience.

"Toby, you don't understand. Women like to have nice weddings and since I'm bringing the money to the wedding, I think I should have what I want."

Toby put his arm around Amelia. "I agree and I understand that I'm not the one bringing money to our marriage, nor even land. I'm grateful to you for all that. But, after all, you've been married before and have already had a nice wedding."

Amelia dropped her eyes. Her dark lashes lay seductively on her pink cheeks. Toby reached up and stroked her cheek.

Amelia spoke at last. "Well, yes, I did have a nice wedding, but a nice wedding now will make up for the sorrow I went through."

"I'm hoping to make up for some of that. I'm hoping our marriage will be so wonderful that you'll forget all about what you went through."

"I'm not sure I want to forget all of it. After all, we did have a good marriage."

"Of course, but this is now and that's in the past. Let's look to the future." Toby tilted Amelia's face upward and looked into her eyes. "I couldn't bear to have you look back all the time."

"Then let's do it my way."

Toby did not speak for a long time. Was this the way life would be after they were married?

"All right," he said at last, "we'll do it your way."

But the next day Amelia's wagon came lumbering into the Steinhardt yard. Toby came out to take care of her horses.

"What a surprise!"

He reached up to take the reins.

"Can't stay long. Too much to do. I just wanted to tell you that I've been thinking it over and I've decided we can have our wedding next week."

Toby's dark eyes lit up with excitement. "You mean it?"

"Of course. Can we set a definite day so we can make plans for the food?"

"I think we could. Come, let's talk to Henry."

When Amelia left an hour later, the date had been set. They would be married ten days later, on Sunday afternoon.

Toby felt a surge of excitement. In ten days he would be a married man. It wouldn't be Sophia but Amelia would do very well. Amelia was a little bossy and she did have a temper but he could cope with that. There weren't many single women out here on the prairie.

Besides, now that they were being married in March, there would be time to file for a claim. At last he would have land of his own.

But shortly after the wedding, someone informed Toby that the Homestead Act actually allowed a single person to claim land providing that person was twenty-one years old. Toby had been twenty-one when he arrived in Dakota Territory. He could have filed for a claim on his own. Had Paul Kaufman lied to him just so Toby would marry his sister?

A little later, word reached Dakota that, after a long and treacherous journey, immigrants from Karlswalde had arrived in Kansas. From Kansas some had moved to Iowa. Were Ben and Nettie in that group? Was Sophia with them? For the first time, Toby felt doubts about his marriage to Amelia.

# Part Three

# Iowa Interlude

# From Peabody, Kansas To

# Wayland, Iowa

# February, 1875

# Chapter Twenty-nine

Ben stomped his feet on the dugout doorstep then flung open the door and stepped in.

"Wait! You're covered with snow. Step outside and let me brush you off?"

Nettie laid down her mending and came to meet him. Ben stepped outside again. When he returned to the room, Andrew and Eva ran to meet him. Ben tossed Eva into the air then put his arm around Andrew.

Meanwhile, Nettie shoved a chair next to the heater for Ben. She hung Ben's coat on a peg near the door then poured him a cup of hot coffee.

Ben took a long sip, slurping noisily.

"Ah!" he sighed. "Just hits the spot. Mighty cold out there."

"What did you find out?" Nettie wanted to know.

His eyes twinkled. "Found out it's cold and it's starting to snow again."

"That's not what I mean. Did you see anyone?"

Ben nodded. "Saw Elder Jantz."

Nettie looked up impatiently.

"And what did he say?"

Ben took another sip of coffee.

"Said he thought a bad snowstorm was coming."

Anger flashed in Nettie's eyes.

"Ben, you know that's not what I mean. Do you have to be so annoying? Can't you just tell me what you heard?"

Ben's blue eyes twinkled again. "I was coming to that. You're too impatient!"

Nettie pinched her lips together. "There you go again. You'd try the patience of Job. What did you find out?"

"Some farmers from Iowa were here and asked him if there were any recent immigrants who could help them with their farmwork."

"You mean their farms are doing that well?"

"I guess so. They're our kind of people but came here several years ago and settled in Iowa. Settled near a little town called Wayland. They've done very well and now they need men for the summer, to plant crops, till the soil and help in the harvest."

"How much work is there? Is there enough for Pappa and all the others who came from Karlswalde?"

"I'm not sure they'll all want to go. A few who brought money from Russia want to buy land here in Kansas. As for those of us who don't have money, we'll need to move on. There really isn't any good land left here to claim.

"Working in Iowa would give us a chance to earn money. Maybe we can earn enough to come back here to Kansas and buy land or go on to Dakota Territory where the land is still free. They say there's a lot of good land there. It's just opened up."

Nettie's eyes opened wide. "Then there'll be Indians too!"

"They say they're driving them out. I don't know how long we'd stay in Iowa but maybe by the time we'd leave the Indians would be gone."

"When would we leave for Iowa?"

"They'd like us to be there by the first of March."

"That's less than a month away. There's no way we could do that. How far can a wagon travel in a day?"

"Fifteen to twenty miles with a good team."

"And how far is it?"

"Don't know the exact mileage but it's quite a ways. We're down here in southern Kansas and they're on the northeastern edge of Iowa."

"Then it could take a long time. Besides, where'll we get the money to buy a team and wagon?"

"We won't need to."

"What do you mean by that? We have to have some way to get there."

"We'll go by train like we did from Philadelphia."

"Where'll we get the money?"

"We have enough left."

Nettie frowned. "Ben, I'm so tired of depending on other people. I thought when we got to America, we wouldn't have to."

Ben reached over and laid his hand on Nettie's.

"Someday we won't have to. After we find our plot of land."

"I know, Ben. I shouldn't be impatient but it seems so long."

Ben's eyes brightened. "Just you wait, Nettie, some day we'll have a farm of our own. I'll build you a nice house with wood floors and glass windows. I don't blame you for being tired of this dark dugout, but if we move to Iowa, things will likely be different."

Nettie glanced at Grossmom's plate hanging on the wall. She had hung it there in January when they arrived from Russia. It was the only bright spot on the dingy wall. How long would it be until she could hang it in a proper house?

Nettie sighed a long sigh. "But it's been so long."

"Things can't get any worse. We've weathered a lot of storms."

Nettie looked down into her lap. "I know."

Nettie picked up the sock she was darning. "What about Sophia? Will she go with us? Or will she keep looking for Toby?"

"We'll have to ask her. I told Toby to meet us here but nobody knows anything about him."

"Do you think he never came here?"

Ben shrugged. "Don't know. I don't think Toby went to Iowa but he might have. Maybe Sophia would like to check that out."

"Sophia has a good job working for that family. Maybe she won't want to go."

"That's true. We'll just have to ask her. I'll walk over and talk to her after dinner."

Ben rubbed his belly. "Speaking of dinner, when are we eating?"

"We can eat as soon as I fry some potatoes. If only we had some pickles or onions to eat with them."

"Would be good but if you fry enough, we won't miss them at all. Maybe, we can move in time to plant some."

***

Ben walked into town that afternoon and when he returned, he announced that Sophia was ready to move on.

"She asked me if I thought Toby might be there."

"And what did you tell her?"

"That he might. Told her we'd just have to ask around. She says she's doing so much sewing for the family she works for, she's going to see if she can sew for people in Iowa. If they're as well off as they say, she might just make it."

Nettie's eyes brightened. "What a good idea. Sophia really does sew very well. And while she's sewing for the families, she can live with them. Elder Jantz is calling a meeting at the church and we'll discuss it there."

# Chapter Thirty

Two weeks later Nettie took Grossmom's plate off the wall and packed it in the immigrant box with their clothes and household linens. They would join the large group of Karlswalders who were going to Iowa. They would take the train.

"Remember that train-ride from Oschonin to Antwerp?" Ben asked. "We were so afraid the Russians would stop us before we could get out of the country."

"I remember all too well," Nettie said. "We were afraid they'd stop Sophia from going. My! I was frightened!"

"I was too. How different it is here in America. They say American citizens don't have to carry any kind of papers with them when they go from one state to another. Sometimes I think it can't be true that we're in America, that's it only a dream."

They boarded the train at last and arrived in Wayland. Church people met them and took them to the settlement house where they could stay until they found homes of their own. The farmers were happy to see them come and all of the men found work as farmhands.

Ben found a job working for a farmer who lived ten miles from town. They would live in the log house vacated by the owners when they moved into their new house.

Once more Nettie unpacked Grossmom's plate and hung it on the wall.

Sophia was happy to find work. When one of the women from the church learned that she was an accomplished seamstress, she arranged to have Sophia stay with them while she sewed clothes for the family. Other women soon made similar arrangements. Sophia would have all the work she wanted and

194

she would have places to stay.

In the meantime Ben made inquiries about Toby. But no one had heard from him.

Ben and Nettie had hardly settled in their new home when Uncle Tobias Unruh came to visit the Wayland church. Ben and Nettie invited him and Mamma and Pappa over for dinner. They invited Sophia too but Sophia couldn't come.

Elder Tobias Unruh, arrived in America only a couple of weeks after Ben and Nettie. But, at the invitation of the churches in the East, he remained to minister there for a few weeks.

Upon his arrival in the Midwest, Elder Unruh filed for a homestead in Dakota Territory. Now after he and his wife were settled, he came on horseback to visit his sister, and the other Karlswalders.

"Dakota is the place to go for a homestead," he told them. "There's plenty of land and it's good land. They have a bit of snow in the wintertime but now that spring is here, the settlers are in good spirits. Soon they'll be breaking up the sod and sowing their wheat."

"And is the wheat as good as the Turkey Red Wheat we planted in the Ukraine?" Ben asked.

Uncle Tobias grinned from ear to ear. "Just as good. They all brought as much as they could, which wasn't very much, and have planted it. Besides that, they've planted the local wheat."

"Will it grow well in Dakota?" Ben asked.

"Too soon to tell. Haven't been there long enough though some have been there a little longer. You remember Toby Beyer, don't you?"

"Toby Beyer?" Ben and Nettie shouted in unison.

"Is Toby in Dakota Territory?" Ben asked.

"Not only is he there but he owns a good plot of ground now that he married the Widow Tieszen."

The silence in the room was absolute. No one spoke. They were too shocked.

Nettie spoke at last.

"Did you say Toby is married?" she ventured.

"Not only married but he owns a fine tract of land with nice buildings on it. His wife's late husband, who was quite well to do, died in a farm accident. Yes, sir, Toby did himself right well."

Nettie spoke again. "But Toby was betrothed to Sophia. Don't you remember Sophia? She came with us so she could meet him and marry him here. Has he forgotten all about her?"

Uncle Tobias's chin dropped.

"That's right. She did come. Didn't she board the train at the last minute? Almost didn't make it if I remember correctly."

"And she's right here in the Wayland community. She's looking for Toby and expecting to marry him."

"Ah, then she'll have to be told."

Tears sprang to Nettie's eye. "It'll break her heart. She's been waiting for him all this time. As a matter of fact, a nice young man on the ship wanted to marry her. But she turned him down because she's waiting for Toby."

Nettie rose from her chair and walked around to Uncle Tobias's place. She put her hand on his shoulder.

"Uncle Tobias, you'll have to tell Sophia."

Uncle Tobias frowned. "Maybe *you* ought to tell her, Nettie. Women do that so much better than men."

Ben stepped in. "No, Uncle Tobias, you are an elder. Maybe it will soften the blow if you tell her. We'll arrange to have her come here and you can talk to her."

"I suppose you're right. But it won't be pleasant."

He turned to Ben and Nettie and looked at them with pleading eyes. "Will you two meet with us?"

"Of course," Ben answered. "When do you want to meet?"

"Can we do it this evening?"

"If she can get off. We'll give it a try."

And so it was settled. Ben would drive to the farm where Sophia was staying and, if he could, would bring her back for *faspa*.

* * *

Sophia was stunned when she heard the news about Toby.

"I don't believe it!" she declared. "Toby helped pay for my fare and, when my father wouldn't let me come, he said he would wait for me. I should have obeyed my father and stayed there."

"Toby apparently didn't think you were coming, Sophia." Elder Unruh said, his voice soft and gentle. "A man gets lonesome out here on the prairie alone."

"But he promised." she argued.

"You have to understand, Sophia," Elder Unruh said, "that people told him he couldn't file for a homestead unless he was married. The law actually says they had to be the head of a household or twenty-one years of age."

Elder Unruh paused a moment. "By marrying the widow, he was helping her out and he also took over a fine farm. He filed for another claim and now he owns a half section. Just think, Sophia, three hundred and twenty acres."

Sophia burst into tears.

Nettie slipped her arms around Sophia's shoulders.

"I'd like to go home," Sophia said when her tears had subsided.

Ben stood to his feet. "Of course. We can leave right away if you like."

Nettie hugged Sophia once more then saw her to the door and helped her with her coat. Ben opened the door and the two left.

Both Ben and Sophia were silent during the ride home and when they reached the house where Sophia was staying, she slipped from the wagon without thanking Ben or saying goodbye. Inside, she greeted her hostess then rushed to her room.

But as she opened the door, her eyes fell on the little angel Toby had carved for her the winter before. She had kept that little angel through all the long months of separation.

At home, she kept it by her bedside and on the long journey to America, she kept it in her pocket. In Kansas it stood on the chest by her bed.

And now, since coming to Iowa, it stood on a corner of the the immigrant box Ben had made for her. Always, it had comforted her and made her feel close to Toby.

Now it seemed to be mocking her. She snatched the little angel from its place of honor and flung it across the room.

In spite of herself, her face softened and she knelt and picked up the little angel. She held it for a moment then opened the lid of the immigrant box and shoved it to the bottom of the box.

Then she collapsed on her bed. She did not leave her bed the next morning nor the next. On the third day she tried to finish the dress she was making but she only ended up ripping out the seams. She tried the next day as well but with the same results. When Sophia did not make any progress, the farmer's wife became concerned. She hitched the horse to a buggy and called on Nettie.

Although Ben and Nettie's house was small, Nettie insisted that Sophia stay with them until the crisis was over. And so the farmer's wife brought Sophia back to stay with them. Sophia was morose and hardly spoke at all.

Weeks passed, spring arrived, trees leafed out and the grass turned green. But Sophia did not notice. The sun was shining but the light in her life had gone out and she took no interest in things around here.

By now, Nettie was pregnant again, and was fighting morning sickness. Sophia did not notice nor did she take up more responsibility. Instead, she wrapped herself in her own grief. Dark circles formed under her brown eyes and her body wasted away.

Then one afternoon a tall lanky young man on horseback rode into the yard. He dismounted and, after tying the reins to a fence post, made his way to the door of the house.

When Nettie opened the door, she could hardly believe her eyes. There standing in the doorway was Peter Jansen, the man who had fallen in love with Sophia on the ship.

Nettie flushed when Peter threw his arms around her.

"Is Sophia here?" he asked.

Nettie nodded.

"Then, please, may I come in?" He took a step forward. But Nettie blocked the doorway.

Peter's eyes darkened. "Is she married then?"

Nettie shook her head.

Peter touched Nettie's arm. "Please, I've come a long way. Went to Kansas first. Thought that's where you were going. But they said you had come here."

His grip tightened. "Please, may I see Sophia?"

"Sophia's not well," Nettie whispered.

Peter looked frightened. "What's wrong? Cholera?"

Nettie shook her head. "No, nothing like that. Her betrothed married someone else. Sophia is broken-hearted."

Peter's eyes blazed with anger. "And she waited for him!"

His eyes softened. "Please, may I see her? I think she became quite fond of me. If it hadn't been for Toby, things might have been different."

"She really doesn't care about anybody, not even little Eva. And she's always been so fond of her."

"Men like that ought to be ..." He didn't finish.

"You might as well come in and wait. She's lying on the bed."

Hearing voices, Sophia raised herself to her elbow.

Peter slipped beside her and took her in his arms. "Sophia!" he exclaimed. "I'm so glad I found you."

"Peter! Where did you come from?" Her eyes brightened for a moment then turned cloudy again.

"I've been looking for you and at last I've found you."

"But you were staying in Philadelphia," she said in a whisper.

"I couldn't live without you. Sophia, marry me."

"I ..."

"I know about Toby. But I'll help you forget. I'll make you the happiest woman in the world. Let's get married as soon as we can. I'll nurse you back to health."

"But I promised."

Peter nodded. "And so did he. And he broke his promise. This is your chance for happiness."

"I can't think. I'm too tired."

Gently, Peter lowered her shoulders to the bed and spread the quilt over her. "Rest, Dear One," he whispered then planted a kiss on her cheek.

When Sophia awoke several hours later, she looked more rested. Peter, who kept a watchful eye on her, sat down on the edge of her bed then took her hand.

"You're going to get better again. I promise. I'll find a house and we'll ask the elder at the church to marry us. I'll take care of you until you are well. Say you will, Sophia."

"How can I make such a decision? I need time."

"Take all the time you need. I'll wait as long as I have to. In the meantime, I'll find a house and when you're ready we'll get married and move in. I'll start looking for one right away."

He planted another kiss on her cheek then left.

After he left, Sophia sat up in bed then swung her legs over the side and stood to her feet.

She took a step forward but tottered precariously. She slumped back on the bed.

Nettie helped her stand then slowly, with Nettie's help, Sophia shuffled to a chair.

Sophia sniffed the air. "I smell fresh bread. Are you baking?"

"Just took it out of the oven. Want a slice?"

"Won't it make you sick? That's what they say."

"Old wives tale!" Nettie exclaimed. "I think someone made that up to keep her family from eating all her fresh bread. Do you like the heel?"

"My favorite part!"

"Mine too but I'll let you have it this time."

"Want to sit at the table?"

When Sophia nodded, she helped her to the table then cut a slice off the end of a loaf, generously buttered it then set it before her.

"Want some coffee too?"

"Haven't had coffee for a long time. Guess I'll try some."

Nettie poured her a steaming mug from the pot on the cookstove.

From that day on, Sophia began making progress.

Peter found a job and moved into a small house. He called on her each evening and urged her to set a wedding date. But Sophia was undecided. She talked to Nettie about it one day.

"Is it right, Nettie, to marry Peter when I've promised myself to Toby?"

"Toby broke the promise first. I think that frees you. Peter can give you a good life. He can make you happy again. Why don't you let him?"

"I know. Peter is a wonderful man. But I still love Toby. Will I ever learn to love Peter like I do Toby?"

"I think you will learn to love Peter. He's loving and kind. He will be good to you and you will find happiness with him."

Sophia thought about that a moment.

"I think I love Peter but in a different way."

Nettie put her arm around Sophia. "I think that's possible. And I don't think you'll be sorry."

Sophia grew stronger with each day. At last the day came when she was ready to pick up the threads of life. She moved out of Ben and Nettie's house and began sewing again.

Spring merged into summer and still Sophia could not set a date. Then one day, a few weeks before harvest, Sophia told Peter she was ready to marry him. They set the date for August twenty, just after harvest.

There was no money for a grand wedding but Sophia made herself the finest gown she could afford. It was made of finely-woven chocolate brown gaberdine with soft pleats falling from her waist. Peter presented her with the mother-of-pearl brooch he purchased for her in Philadelphia. Sophia pinned it at her throat, where it held a white crocheted collar in place.

The wedding took place in the afternoon with a full program of congregational singing, special music and poetry. Then the elder performed the ceremony and Sophia and Peter became husband and wife. After the ceremony, the church women served *zwieback*, coffee and cake.

The next day the newly-married couple made plans to celebrate again, this time at Ben and Nettie's with only Ben and Nettie's relatives present. Early that morning, Ben and Nettie butchered chickens and Mamma baked cakes. Then Nettie and Mamma fried the chickens while Nettie's sister Catherine peeled the potatoes. Mamma made the gravy and Nettie and Catherine set the table.

The guests began arriving just before noon. They ate in shifts. The children ate last. Between shifts, the women washed up the dishes so the next shift could eat.

Sophia was radiant.

"Thank you so much for a wonderful day," she told Nettie before she and Peter left.

"It was nothing," Nettie declared. "Wish we could have made it five days like a proper Hollander wedding."

"Don't need five days," Sophia countered. "Nettie, I never knew I could be so happy. I'll only be happier when we have our first child."

Nettie smiled. "And you'll make a good mother, too. I do hope the Lord gives you one soon. I'm so glad he's given us another one."

She frowned. "But sometimes I'm frightened. I'm afraid something will happen to it."

"Maybe since you haven't traveled, this one will be all right."

But that night Nettie gave birth not only to one but to two, a boy and a girl. The two little ones did not live and they buried them in the church cemetery. Nettie was devastated.

Gradually, with time and Sophia's encouragement, the gloom gave way to a measure of happiness.

Cold weather moved in and with it the snow. The ground was frozen now and the fields covered with snow. Inside it was cozy and warm. As the winter deepened, Ben spent more time at home, carving wooden figures and building furniture for their home. Sophia and Nettie spent many hours working on quilts.

Then came the news that another house was available to Ben and Nettie.

# Chapter Thirty-one

They moved the first of March. The house was built of native timber and had two bedrooms. The floors were of pine and the plastered walls were covered with white calcimine. Nettie was delighted.

The kitchen, which also served as a sitting room, was light and airy with two windows. Ben earned enough money to buy material for curtains and Sophia helped sew them. When they were finished and hanging at the windows, Nettie hung Grossmom's plate on one wall.

Ben made a rocking chair that now stood in the corner. Nettie was comfortable, indeed.

But Ben was still talking of owning land of his own.

"Remember Uncle Tobias said there was good land for the taking in Dakota. I'd like to see it. I wish we could have gone for his funeral last spring and checked it out but we were too busy with spring work."

"I know, Ben," Nettie answered, "and we couldn't afford it. Even Mamma and Pappa couldn't afford train tickets, even though he was Mamma's brother."

Ben smiled. "Maybe I could ride out on a horse. Peter might be interested too."

"And leave me and the children alone?"

Ben put his arm around Nettie. "You're right, I couldn't leave now."

"Why do you want to leave, Ben? We have a nice house, some chickens and two cows. We'll have pigs too. And I'll make a garden. We're very comfortable. I'd like to stay."

"As you wish, Nettie," Ben said, a resigned tone in his voice.

The following months were so busy that Nettie was sure Ben had forgotten about moving on. Nettie became pregnant again but thus far, Sophia had not. She talked to Nettie about it one day.

"Do you think God is punishing me?"

"Why would He punish you? You haven't done anything wrong."

"Well, I haven't done any penance for hating Toby."

"Haven't you asked God to forgive your hatred?"

Sophia nodded. "But isn't there something I can do?"

"Confess your sin, the Bible says. And if you've done that, God forgives. And you know, Sophia, God hasn't given you a baby but He has given you a very fine husband. He was good to do that. Aren't you and Peter happy?"

"Very! I couldn't have married a finer man! But I keep wondering why God doesn't give me a child."

"I think He will. Just don't give up hope."

***

Three years passed and still Sophia and Peter had not been blessed with a child.

Then, in the summer Peter became ill with a high fever and vomiting. By the third day, he was too weak to leave his bed and Sophia sent for the doctor. The doctor said it was cholera and ordered fluids.

But on the fourth day Peter went into shock. He died the next night and was buried the following day. Because it was a highly infectious disease, the funeral was a private service. Even the preaching elder could not touch the coffin.

Sophia was crushed with grief but no one could enter the house to comfort her until it had been thoroughly fumigated. Despite her grief, Sophia took care of those chores herself.

"Don't touch me, Nettie," she cautioned. "The doctor says I

could get sick too. I don't want you to get it."

She pointed to an empty chair. "Here, take this chair. I've scrubbed everything as good as I could."

"Why has God been so harsh with me?" Sophia asked when Nettie seated herself.

Nettie shrugged. "We don't know but it seems you've had more than your share."

"He didn't even give me a child to remember Peter by."

Sophia leaned forward. "Do you know what I think? I think he's punishing me."

Nettie frowned. "We've talked about this before. You had no choice. Toby had already made his decision and the wedding had already taken place. You *couldn't* marry him."

"But maybe God wanted me to be a spinster."

"If that was the case, he wouldn't have made you as pretty as you are."

"I've seen some pretty spinsters. But, if it isn't that, what is it?"

"We don't always know."

"What am I going to do now?"

"You can sew and earn your living that way."

"I don't have the heart to sew."

"Things will change. I'm sure they will. Remember when you first heard about Toby? You couldn't take up your sewing at first but eventually you did. Your work was as fine as it always had been, I might add."

Nettie smiled as she remembered what Ben had suggested a few days before.

"Sophia, I have an idea. Ben is not happy here in Iowa. He wants land of his own and the land here is all homesteaded. Besides, the prices are too high to buy. He wants to move on."

"Move on? Where would he go? I thought you liked it here and it's fine with me too."

"To Dakota. I really don't want to but for his sake, we might. A lot of the Karlswalders are talking of leaving while the ground is still frozen. Mamma and Pappa are talking of going too.

Maybe you could go with us."

"Isn't that where Toby and that woman live?"

Nettie nodded.

"I don't want to see him! I don't care if I never see him again! I hate him!"

"Sophia! You can't mean that?"

"But I do. I loved him once but my love has turned to hate."

"Jesus said hating another is the same as murder."

"Then so be it!"

"Actually you wouldn't have to have anything to do with Toby. He's married and they'll live their own lives."

"He was Ben's close friend. I'm sure we'd run into each other. Probably goes to the same church we'd go to."

Nettie rose to leave. "Well, you wouldn't have to go. You could stay here and sew. Though I would miss you."

Sophia shook her head. "No, I don't want to stay here without you. I'll think about it. Maybe I'll change my mind and go after all."

# Part Four

# The Dream Realized

# Dakota Territory

# October, 1879

# Chapter Thirty-two

The  caravan of covered wagons moved slowly through the Iowa countryside. Ben and Nettie's wagon, pulled by two sturdy horses, brought up the rear. Two crates, one carrying piglets and the other chickens, were hanging from the sides of the wagon. Milk cows and heifers tended by Andrew and other young boys on horseback trailed behind.

Ben cracked the whip. "Giddyap!" he bellowed.

The horses lurched forward jerking the wagon out of the frozen ruts. The wagon tipped precariously then righted itself again. The two crates rattled and  the piglets and chickens protested with loud squeals and cackles. Blackie, the mixed breed collie, leaped at the crates and barked.

"Well, Nettie," Ben said when the animals had quieted down, "after four years in Iowa, we're on our way again."

"That's what you've been wanting all along and now maybe you'll have it."

Ben cracked the whip. "These horses take the patience of Job. Wish we could've afforded nice horses like we had in Russia. But then we might have to trade them off for oxen. Oxen are good for breaking sod."

Ben glanced over his shoulder and smiled. "At least Andrew has a riding horse."

Nettie's eyes sparkled. "Yes, he's always wanted one. And how proud he is!"

"Good thing he was big enough. We couldn't have taken the two milk cows and the heifer if we hadn't had him to ride herd."

"Doesn't seem possible. Why, he was only seven when we left Karlswalde. He's eleven and a half now."

Ben nodded. "Yes, sir, he's nearly big enough to do a man's job. He'll be a big help on the claim."

"Will he have to go to school like he did in Iowa?" Nettie asked.

"When he's not helping on the claim. Maybe they'll wait to start school 'til the crops are in like they did in Iowa."

"And I suppose the classes will be in English too."

"Very possible."

"Then how will he ever learn proper German?"

Ben raised his hat and scratched his head. "He'll have to learn it in church. Actually, learning English isn't all bad. He'll get along better when we haul our wheat to town. It'll make it easier for me too."

He snapped his whip. "And don't forget, we're learning English from him."

"Eva's learned English from him too. Sometimes I wish we hadn't come."

"You mean that?"

Nettie looked down at her hands folded in her lap. "Sometimes. Everything's changed."

"But we still have our people, and, most important, we have our God. He hasn't changed."

"You're right, Ben. But sometimes I wish things would just remain the way they were. Do they always have to change?"

"I guess that's part of life."

"I keep thinking about the Indians."

"Are we going to see Indians? Are we Pa?" Eva chimed in. "I wanna see a papoose."

Nettie shuddered. "No, Eva, don't even think about it."

"But I'd like to see one. You said there were Indians. Why can't I see them?"

"Indians only let you see them when they want you to," Ben said.

"Are they here now, hiding?"

Nettie grabbed Ben's sleeve. "You're scaring the child! She's only six."

She turned to Eva. "Eva, go sit down."

"Do you really think it's safe?" Nettie asked when Eva had returned to her seat. "Are you sure the Indians won't attack us? You know what we heard."

"That's in Dakota Territory, in the Black Hills where nobody lives. We'll be in Eastern Dakota, a hundred miles from there. One of the generals, General Custer, has pushed the Indians, away from the settlers. First Iowa; now Dakota."

"Well what about all those rough men looking for gold. Ben, do we really want our children growing up among people like that?"

"Been thinking, maybe I ought to go looking for gold myself."     He threw Nettie a mischievous grin.

Nettie gasped. "You can't mean that!"

Ben's eyes sparkled. "You know I'm just joshing."

"It's a serious matter. Do we want our children to grow up around that kind of men? We should've stayed in Iowa with our own people."

"And work for somebody else?" Ben asked. "I'm tired of that. Working for others wasn't any better in Iowa than it was in Russia. Oh, I know I earned more money but I want to be my own boss. That's one of the reasons we came to America. Only in America can it happen. I want to make a fresh start. Whatever it takes. Someday we won't have to answer to anyone. We'll do what we want."

Nettie looked up in surprise. "I'm sorry, Ben, I didn't mean to upset you."

"Well," Ben said. He lowered his voice. "I guess I got carried away. But, as you can see, I feel very strongly about it. Nettie, this may be our last chance to own land. Our people have always kept themselves separate from the people around them and we can do it here. There are enough of us that we won't have to worry."

"I suppose you're right but I can't help worrying. The Indians might ..." She glanced behind her, then, seeing that Eva was busy playing, she finished. "They might scalp us. I'm really scared for the children. Do you really think we'll be safe? There aren't very many of us."

"We all have guns for killing game. When they see our guns, they'll think twice before attacking us. Besides, I definitely think God has led us this far and He will take care of us in the future"

Ben cast a worried look at Nettie sitting beside him on the hard wooden seat. "You all right?" he asked.

Nettie nodded. "It's kind of bumpy but I know that can't be helped."

"At least we have roads and not just trails. It's frozen so they're rough. And a good thing it is. We'd get bogged down in mud if it wasn't. That's why we're going west now."

"Andrew and Eva don't seem to mind moving. In fact, I think they're glad."

"They would! They're restless ones, they are. And, of course, Andrew enjoys riding the horse. How about Sophia?"

"Sleeping, I think. Don't know how she can sleep but her eyes are closed."

"Actually, I was thinking of you. Seems every time we move, you're expecting."

"Seems to me I'm that way all the time."

Nettie frowned. "I wouldn't mind if our babies would live."

Ben reached over and put his hand on Nettie's knee. "I know. And now we have three small graves in Iowa besides the three in Russia."

Nettie wiped a tear from her eyes. "And one at sea." She sobbed bitterly. "That was awful, that and leaving those three graves in Iowa when we were so close to where we're going."

She wiped away another tear. "Oh, Ben, who's going to take care of their graves? Who'll put flowers on them?"

Ben took Nettie's hand in his. "It's hard, isn't it? I like to think of them all together as a family in heaven with Grossmom and Jesus."

Nettie nodded. "You're right, Ben, but sometimes it's hard to believe. Other women don't seem to have trouble having babies. Some who aren't any older than I already have four or five."

"I fully believe God will give us more children. He knows we'll bring them up to love and serve Him."

Nettie sighed. "I hope you're right. I want more than two."

"He's been faithful to us, when you think about it. Giving us the chance to leave Russia, with all your family too. And then, even though it was a hard journey, we made it all right."

"Yes, and I'll never forget how good the people in Pennsylvania were. Why they were like family."

"In a way they are family. They're Hollanders just like us."

Nettie nodded again. "I never expected it to take so long to get to Kansas. Didn't know America was so big."

"Bigger than I imagined too. You know, Nettie, I really would have liked to have stayed in Kansas. Land was level and seemed to be good for farming."

"Too bad all the good land had been claimed."

"Maybe it was for the best. Some areas don't have good water. They say the railroad people dug a hole in one little *dorf*, bricked it and poured in good water. When the immigrants came through looking for land, they gave them a taste of that water."

Ben clapped his hands together to warm them. "If only we could have come when we first tried. There was land in a place called Nebraska, north of Kansas. It's good level land."

"It's my fault, Ben. I'm sorry. I didn't want to leave Mamma and Pappa. But we should have anyway."

"It's not your fault. It's Schultz and Gorbansky's fault. They're the ones who spoiled everything. If it hadn't been for them, we could be living on a claim right now. Those months would have made a big difference."

"Haven't you forgiven them? Don't start that again. What's past is past. You'll only hurt yourself by brooding over it."

"Nettie, I can't help feeling the way I do. If I ever meet them again, I'll get even."

"Ben, the Bible says to forgive our enemies."

"I know all about that, Nettie. You don't have to preach at me."

"Well, anyway, we're too late for Kansas and too late for Nebraska and too late for Iowa too. Ben, I'm so sorry. I know you've been longing to have land of your own. Maybe it'll work out in Dakota."

"Those four years in Iowa weren't all wasted. I earned enough to buy a wagon, three horses and two cows."

"Don't forget the chickens and hogs."

Ben nodded. "And now we're taking some with us. There's a little money left for machinery and a house when we get there. Then too, I learned a lot about farming here in America."

"You're right. We did quite well even though we didn't have our own land."

Ben glanced over his shoulder. "One thing does worry me," he said in a low voice. "How is Sophia going to react when she sees Toby?"

"I know. I've been thinking about that."

Before Ben could continue, Eva thrust her head between them. "Are we there yet, Pa? Are we?"

"Not yet, Eva," Ben answered. "Still have a long ways to go."

Behind them, although Sophia could not hear Ben and Nettie's conversation, she was not asleep. She was thinking. It would have been so much easier if Peter were here. What would life be like in Dakota? Would she find a place to stay? Would she find families who needed sewing? And what would she do when she saw Toby?

213

# Chapter Thirty-three

At last the first day ended and the wagon train stopped for the night. They formed a circle near a creek then unhitched the horses. Ben led the horses and livestock to drink from a nearby creek then tethered them near their wagon.

Andrew and Eva gathered dead branches then Ben built a fire. Soon flames were leaping into the air.

While Ben and Andrew went for water, Nettie cut the *vorscht* into pieces then slashed through each piece leaving the casing to serve as a hinge. She put it cut side down in the black three-legged iron spider heating over the fire.

When Ben and Andrew had finished milking and had taken care of the animals, they gathered for supper. Ben prayed and they all ate heartily.

"That was good, Nettie," Ben said as he wiped up the last bit of gravy with a piece of bread. "I was hungry as a bear."

"Are there bears here?" Eva asked.

Ben put his arm around Eva and stroked back her hair. "No bears. They don't bother land that's settled. But there might be wolves."

Eva's eyes grew wide. "Real wolves? What does a wolf look like, Pa?"

"A little like a dog."

"Like Blackie?"

"Well, maybe not as black as Blackie. More gray with some brown. And they're bigger."

"Will they hurt us, Pa?" Eva wanted to know.

"Pa wouldn't let them," Andrew said. "He's got a gun."

"Is that so, Pa?"

"That's so, Little One." He chucked Eva under the chin. "And now Little One, I think it's time for bed. Tomorrow will be another long day."

When Mamma and Sophia had finished the dishes, Sophia spread the damp dish towel on the grass to dry. The dishes done, Nettie visited with Mamma for a few minutes before retiring for the night. Ben and Andrew slept under the wagon while the other three slept in the wagon.

Some time during the night, Nettie heard footsteps on the frozen grass. Was it Ben? She waited but Ben did not appear.

Then came more footsteps. Then heavy breathing. Someone was definitely out there.

Nettie crawled to the opening at the front of the wagon and peered out into the darkness. When she couldn't see anyone, she called Ben.

"Ben," she whispered. "Ben, are you there?"

Ben did not answer.

Nettie called a little louder.

A thud came from under the wagon. Ben, rubbing his head, poked his head into the opening.

"What you want?" he growled.

"Didn't you hear?"

"Hear what?"

"Someone's outside. Probably Indians."

"Didn't hear a thing but I'll look around."

"Be careful."

Ben merely grunted.

The frozen grass crunched as Ben circled the wagon. In a few minutes his head appeared in the opening again.

"Nothing there," he reported.

"Are you sure?"

"Walked all around. You must've been dreaming."

"No, Ben, I hadn't fallen asleep yet."

"Well, there's nothing there. Now go to sleep." Ben disappeared under the wagon.

Nettie relaxed and had nearly fallen asleep when the frozen

215

grass crunched again. She sat up and listened. Someone definitely was out there.

Once again, Nettie leaned out of the wagon and called Ben. She heard another bump then Ben's head appeared in the opening.

"Go to sleep," he said impatiently. "Second time I bumped my head. Didn't hear a thing. Now go to sleep. We've got a long ways to go tomorrow."

"I know I heard footsteps. Might be Indians. Ben, what are we going to do? They'll scalp us."

"I told you they've pushed the Indians out of Iowa. And I've checked. There's no one out there. Now go to sleep and let *me* sleep."

Ben disappeared from sight.

Nettie lay very still but sleep wouldn't come. Someone had to keep watch.

Nettie had hardly fallen asleep, it seemed, when Ben awakened her. She dragged herself out of bed and fixed breakfast.

"You know those steps you heard during the night?" Ben said as they were eating. "It was the heifer. Somehow she got loose and was wandering around the camp."

They all laughed.

# Chapter Thirty-Four

Day after day and mile after mile, the wagons lumbered over the rolling plains. The adults grew weary of walking but they felt cramped in the wagon. When they were in the wagon, Sophia usually sat in the back and entertained Eva.

Only one of Ben and Nettie's cows now gave milk but it was enough for their small family. Their supply of *roesha zwieback* had given out so they ate cornbread baked in the iron spider.

Andrew still rode herd over the livestock. Without him in the wagon, Eva depended on the adults for entertainment.

"You're asking a lot of questions, Little One." Ben said one day as he ran his hand over his beard. "Tell you what, Little One, maybe Ma would like to sit with Sophia a while and you could sit up here."

Ben glanced at Nettie. "Would you mind terribly, Nettie? Will it be too crowded?"

"Oh, no. We'll push things out of the way. As a matter of fact, it would be good to have some woman-talk."

"Hope it's not too crowded. There's precious little room what with all the things we took. We really took too much."

"Only took what I had to."

"You should have let me sort your things."

Nettie's eyes twinkled. "And let me sort through yours?"

"Guess what's fair is fair."

"I thought you'd feel that way."

Nettie gathered up her knitting, climbed through the opening and sat down beside Sophia.

Eva crawled to the springboard and sat next to Ben.

"Are we still in Iowa, Pa?"

217

Ben shook his head. "This is Dakota Territory. Dakota isn't a state yet like Iowa. See how the road's changed? In Iowa we had a proper road but here it's only a trail where the wheels have worn deep ruts."

As if to emphasize what Ben had just said, the wheels veered out of a rut and the wagon tipped precariously. The piglets and chickens protested while a frightened rabbit scurried across the trail and into the tall prairie grass.

"See what I mean?" he asked.

Ben pointed to his left. "You like trees, Little One? Look over there. How about those trees?"

"Didn't you say there weren't trees in Dakota Territory?"

"The trees are mostly along the river and, as you can see, there aren't very many. Uncle Tobias said there were few trees where we're going."

"Then we're not in Dakota Territory?"

"We are but we'll go farther north."

"Why can't we stay right here?"

"Don't want trees. There's a deep swift river, too, a dangerous one. Called the Missouri. On the other side is Nebraska. Most of the land's been taken there. We're going where there's still land to be claimed."

Ben clapped his big hand over Eva's knees. "Little One, we're soon going to have land of our own. How about that?"

"But the land looks awfully level, Pa. Doesn't it ever change?"

Ben chuckled. "Don't let that tall grass fool you. It looks like it's all the same height but in places, where the land dips, it's higher than my head. You can tell how the wagon trail goes up and down."

"I miss the trees."

"Trees are nice, Little One, but they're not very nice for farming. That's why we had to raise mainly cattle and pigs in Russia. Too many trees."

"Why didn't you cut them down?"

"We did clean trees out in the yard and the field behind the

218

yard but it still wasn't good soil and it wasn't fit to raise much. Besides, it's a lot of work cutting down trees. No, sir, give me land that you don't have to clear. In Dakota we won't have to, just plow and plant."

The horses had slowed down again and Ben cracked the whip. He and Eva lapsed into silence.

"Pa," Eva said after a while, "I wish we could've stayed in Iowa."

"Now why-ever would you want to stay in Iowa?"

Eva picked at the bare threads on the edge of her sleeve. "I really do miss Greta."

"Ya, I understand. We left friends too. Not only in Iowa but in Russia."

"Then why did we leave?"

"We wanted land but most of all we wanted freedom to worship God as we please."

And in the back of the wagon, Nettie and Sophia were enjoying each other's company. "Well, Sophia, we'll soon be there," Nettie said.

"Good! I'm getting a bit weary. Tired of sitting and tired of walking."

"I agree. Sitting in this crowded wagon isn't exactly comfortable. We'll have to get out and walk again. I've had enough travel to last me a lifetime. I think once we have our homestead I'll stay there the rest of my life."

"That's what I'm thinking too."

Sophia took a deep breath. "If only Peter had lived and had come with us." She hesitated. "Or if Toby had waited."

Nettie did not immediately answer. "Yes, but that can't be changed."

Sophia wiped a tear from her eyes. "I still don't understand why he didn't wait for me. I know he loved me."

"Yes, I'm sure he did. But like Uncle Tobias said, it's lonely out on the prairie and if they told him he couldn't file for a homestead, it's not surprising he went ahead with the marriage. By then he probably had given up on your coming. Besides, most men can't look after themselves. Can't do the cooking and the cleaning and washing the clothes."

Nettie paused to take a deep breath. "And it did take us much longer to reach America than we had expected."

"Things might have been different if we could have let him know."

"They might have. Uncle Tobias said he waited until the end of winter."

Nettie put her arm around Sophia. "Sophia, you just have to trust God. We don't know why God allowed these things to happen. But God knows best."

\* \* \*

Shortly after the noon meal, they came to a frozen little stream. After the men chipped away the ice, the livestock drank their fill.

After the livestock was watered, Nettie and Sophia decided to walk for a time.

The day ended at last and they set up camp.

"Well, Nettie," Ben said as he took a bite of corn bread and fried salt pork. "Pretty soon you can bake fresh bread. Our guide said we're getting close to where our people settled."

"And a good thing it is, Ben. Our supplies are giving out. This is the last of the salt pork."

"Don't want to eat the chickens or the pigs so we'll have to shoot us some meat. I've seen birds as big as chickens, enough to make us a meal. You can fry them like you do chicken. Grouse, they call 'em. Good eating, they say."

"It will be good to eat fresh meat. I'm tired of side-pork."

"I am a little tired of it too. There are plenty of grouse and deer here in Dakota, they say."

The next day they ate grouse, browned to perfection then simmered in cream until it fell off the bones

# Chapter Thirty Five

Mid-morning, the lead wagon stopped.

"What is it?" Nettie asked. Is something wrong?"

"I don't know. I'll just walk ahead and see what's going on."

Ben fastened the reins to the wagon and jumped to the ground.

"There's a farm ahead of us," he said when he returned.

"A real farm?"

"I guess you could call it a real farm. Not as nice as some in Iowa. But there's a house and a barn and some other buildings. The house is made of wood. Pretty big for this country, I would guess. The guide says that according to the map we're getting close to the Hollander settlement. Asked if I wanted to ride along to the farm to ask directions. Told him I would."

Ben climbed into the guide's wagon. As they entered the homesteader's yard, the door opened and Toby stepped out of the house. Ben could hardly believe his eyes. Toby rushed forward and gave Ben a bear hug.

"Ben, I'd given up on you! Elder Unruh said you were in Iowa and I thought you'd stay there."

"I told you we'd come. This is our guide. Lives in Iowa and is helping us find our people."

"What took you so long?"

"Didn't Uncle Tobias tell you about all the trouble we had?"

"As a matter of fact, he did. I was sorry to hear it. Did you see my parents before you left?"

"Not long before. They're thinking of immigrating."

"I think they should."

He shuffled his feet. "I heard Sophia came with you and that she got married. How is she?"

"Then you hadn't heard that her husband died of cholera?

"No! Is she ... is she all right?"

"As a matter of fact, Sophia's with us!"

Toby's face turned ashen. "What did you say?"

"She's in our wagon."

Toby ran his hand through his hair. "But ... but ..."

He opened his mouth then closed it again.

"Won't you come in?" he asked.

The guide shook his head. "Don't have time. I figure we must be close to the Hollander settlement. Can you tell us where it is?"

"We're part of it. The immigrant house is just a few miles down the road. Immigrants can stay there 'til they file a claim. Come in and at least have a drink of cold water."

The guide reluctantly took a step forward and the two men followed Toby into the house.

A young woman, obviously pregnant, rose from a rocker to greet them.

Toby put his arm around the woman's shoulders and drew her forward.

"Ben, this is my wife, Amelia. Amelia, this is Ben."

Ben offered his hand. "Nice meeting you," he said. "We've known Toby a long time."

Amelia smiled a tired smile. "I'm so glad you came," she said. "Toby's talked about you. Won't you sit down?"

"They're in a hurry, Amelia," Toby said. "I asked them in for a drink."

"Nettie's in the family way too," Ben said as he waited for Toby to dip water into a tin cup. Toby offered the cup to the guide.

"But the baby's not due for a while yet."

Amelia smiled. "Well then, your baby and ours will likely play with each other."

Toby offered Ben the cup of water and Ben emptied the cup.

"I'm sure they will for I suspect our families will be visiting each other."

He handed the cup back to Toby and he and the guide left the house. Toby followed.

Toby laid his hand on Ben's shoulder. "You know now, don't you, Ben?"

"That you're married? At least I hope you're married."

"Yes, I'm married. But you knew that. Now you know that I'll soon be a father. Oh, Ben, I didn't mean for it to be like this. I didn't think Sophia was coming. I can't face Sophia. What am I going to do?"

"Seems to me you've already made your choice." Ben glanced up at the guide waiting for him.

"I need to explain to Sophia."

"You do owe her an explanation." Ben glanced at the guide again. "I've got to go. We'll see you again."

Toby gave Ben another soulful look then waved goodbye.

And in Ben and Nettie's wagon, Sophia had climbed onto the spring seat beside Nettie. "We're almost there. It's ..." She stopped mid-sentence and stared at the man coming out of the house. She grasped Nettie's hand.

"That's Toby," she gasped.

"Toby? How can you tell? He's a long ways off."

"I know it's him."

Sophia gathered her skirts and started to climb out of the wagon.

"Wait!" Nettie said as she grabbed Sophia's sleeve. "You can't just rush to him. Toby's a married man."

Sophia turned to face Nettie. "Thanks. I forgot for a moment."

Nettie took Sophia's hand. "This will be hard for you but his marriage doesn't come as a surprise. And you had recovered from the news."

Sophia jerked her hand out of Nettie's grasp. "But I hadn't seen him yet."

She buried her face in her hands and wept.

When she gained control again, she sat quietly beside Nettie.

"That was Toby, wasn't it?" Sophia said when Ben returned.

Ben stroked his beard. "Yes, as a matter of fact, it was."

"Then why didn't he at least come to talk to us?"

"Wasn't time. The guide wants to get to the settlement house before dark."

Ben stepped on the wagon wheel and put his hand on Sophia's shoulder. "Toby's very anxious to talk to you but he wants to see you alone."

Sophia pursed her lips. "I have nothing to say to him."

Ben's eyes softened. "You might listen to what he has to say."

"There's nothing left to say."

Sophia burst into sobs. Nettie put her arm around her. "Come let's sit in the back."

"Do that," Ben said. "Eva can sit in the front. We'll get left behind if we don't get started."

"I wish I'd never met Toby," Sophia said when they had exchanged places. "Mother was right."

Sophia covered her face with her hands.

Nettie laid her hand on Sophia's knee. "Don't be too hard on Toby. Wait until you talk to him."

"I've changed my mind. I don't want to talk to him. I don't care if I never talk to him again."

"There might be some explanation."

"What kind of an explanation could there be?"

"Yes, it seems hopeless but at least God hasn't abandoned you."

"I'm not so sure about that."

"Think how he took care of us in that storm?"

"I wish I'd drowned!"

"Sophia, you can't mean that!"

"Yes, I do."

"But you didn't drown. God preserved your life and even if things look dark now, He understands how you feel."

"What kind of a God is He to let this happen to me?"

"It doesn't mean He doesn't love you. Trust Him, Sophia."

But Sophia sat glumly, her face sullen. She refused to change her mind.

By the time they reached the immigrant buildings, the sun had nearly set. Each building was divided into three sections.

Mamma and Pappa chose the east end. Nettie's cousin and his family took the west end, leaving the center section for Ben and Nettie. Sophia would stay with Ben and Nettie.

Each section was furnished with two beds with straw ticking, a table, two benches and a small stove.

"At least you don't have to build furniture right away," Nettie said.

"And a good thing too. There's not much timber around. I'll have to look for land and that will take time."

"Well, I think time is something you won't be short of until the ground thaws."

With that Nettie began planning the sleeping arrangements.

"We'll sleep over here," she said, indicating the west side. "Sophia can sleep in the bed on the other side of the room and Andrew and Eva can sleep on the floor."

She looked up at Ben. "Now all we need is the immigrant box and the rocker."

"Your wish is my command."

He left the room.

When Ben returned with the box, Nettie took out the patchwork quilt she had pieced and tied then spread it over the straw ticking. Next she took out a checkered tablecloth and covered the table.

"I'd like to hang Grossmom's plate on the wall," she said as she sank into the rocker, "but I'll wait 'til we move into our own house."

"You rest. I'll cook supper," Sophia volunteered.

Sophia built a fire with coal from the bucket standing nearby and soon had the *vorscht* a settler had given them, frying in the spider. Ben and Andrew took the horses to the water tank. After they had enough, they took them to the communal barn, where

225

they gave them hay. When Ben had milked, they sat down to eat.

# Chapter Thirty-six

Toby watched the caravan of wagons disappear over the horizon. He stood a few minutes before reentering the house.

All those months he had waited for Sophia and now she was here. And he hadn't caught even one glimpse of her. What would life be like with Sophia? Suddenly he shook himself out of his reverie. What was he doing thinking of what might have been when he was married to Amelia? He turned to open the screen door.

Amelia, who had been watching at the window, quickly stepped across the room to the kitchen stove. She did not turn to look at Toby when the door closed behind him. Instead, she filled the tea kettle with water and set it on the stove to boil. Then she dipped more water from the bucket and poured it into a dishpan. She dropped three potatoes into the water and started peeling them.

"You starting supper?" Toby asked.

Amelia grunted.

"Sounds like the bucket is almost empty. Guess I need to get some more."

He picked up the bail and took the bucket to the door. There he took his hat from the peg and went to the well to draw water.

When Toby returned with the full bucket, he set it on the stand then dipped a long-handled dipper into the bucket and drank from it. Amelia did not acknowledge his presence nor did she speak to him.

Toby put the dipper back into the bucket and watched Amelia for a moment. What was wrong? What had he done?

"Anything I can do to help?" he asked at last.

"No," she said without looking up.

"Then I'll go do the chores."

Amelia did not acknowledge that she had heard.

An hour later Toby returned with a half bucket of foaming milk and set it on the sideboard.

"Cow's not giving much milk," he said. "Hope she lasts until the other comes fresh."

Amelia turned a slice of side-pork frying in the skillet without answering. Ben could see her profile now. Her face was sullen and her lips were pinched tightly together.

Toby tried again. "Smells good in here. What are we having? Salt pork?"

"What else? Don't have chicken this time of the year."

"I didn't think."

Toby ran his hand through his dark hair. Only tried to make conversation. What's bothering Amelia, anyway?

Toby washed his hands in the basin standing on the washstand then dried them on the roller towel.

"I see you've already set the table. Can I dish up the potatoes?"

"Yes."

Toby lifted the iron skillet from the stove and spooned the fried potatoes into a bowl then set it on the table. Meanwhile, Amelia speared the salt pork onto a plate then set the plate on the table with a thud.

When she had seated herself, Toby sat down. They bowed their heads and Toby asked the blessing on the food.

Amelia ate her meal in sullen silence. When she had cleared her plate, she broke the silence.

"Well, was she, was that woman with them?" she asked.

"What woman?"

"Sophia, your beloved. Who else?"

Toby reached out and took Amelia's hand but she jerked it away. Her eyes blazed with anger.

"Now don't sweet-talk me. You've been waiting for her, haven't you."

"No, Amelia, I haven't."

"You married me for my land, didn't you?"

"How can you say that?"

"I know all about it. My brother, Paul, told me."

"Amelia, I fell in love with you."

"Only because you thought she wasn't coming."

"Because I couldn't help myself."

"And now that she's here, are you going to leave me?"

"Of course not."

"Then are you going to make life miserable for me like Reuben did? Are you going to hit me when I do something you don't like?"

Toby looked up in surprise. "Reuben hit you?"

Amelia nodded.

"You said your marriage was a happy one."

A tear rolled down Amelia's cheek. She wiped it away with a handkerchief.

"I was afraid if I told you, you'd think it was my fault. Oh, he was nice most of the times but he had a terrible temper. I never expected it when we married. But life was hard out here on the prairie, harder than we thought it would be. I think he was so frustrated that things would set him off."

Toby shoved back his chair and went to Amelia. He put his arm around her and held her close.

"I would never hit you," he declared. "I'd never hit any woman."

Amelia looked up with tears still in her eyes. "Not even if you didn't love her?"

Toby's dark eyes looked into her gray ones. "Don't you understand? I do love you."

"Then you won't leave me for her?"

"Of course not. Remember our marriage vows? 'And forsaking all others keep thyself only to her.' Those are Elder Wiebe's exact words. I meant it when I promised to keep them."

"But will you change your mind now that she's here?"

"Amelia, I married you for life."

"And does she know you feel that way?"

229

"I don't know. I didn't see her, nor talk to her. Besides, she married someone else so she must not have cared that much about me."

"Did you see her husband?"

"No. Ben said he died."

Tears rolled down Amelia's cheeks. "Then she's free to marry again."

"But I'm not."

"Toby, I'm so afraid."

"Afraid of what?"

"That you'll leave me."

"I told you I wouldn't."

"Or that you'll want to spend a lot of time with them now that they're here. You'll want to visit with them and she'll be there," Amelia said between sobs.

"I don't think she'll live with them. She didn't in Iowa. She was a seamstress and lived with the families she sewed for."

"But she'll probably be there on Sundays."

"Amelia, you're borrowing trouble. Besides, when men and women visit, the men visit with the men and the women with the women."

"Everybody would know that she was the one you'd been waiting for."

"But you're the one I married."

Toby took Amelia by the hand. "Come, I'll help you to your rocker," he said. "You rest while I wash up the dishes."

He helped Amelia to her rocker then cleaned up the kitchen. Behind him, Amelia was sobbing intermittently. She was still crying when they retired for the night.

Just after midnight, Amelia awoke Toby.

"I think it's time, Toby," she said. "You need to get *Tanta* Ortman."

Toby threw back the quilt. "Are you sure? Will you be all right?"

"Better go," she said.

Toby dressed and went out the door.

When Toby had returned with *Tanta* Ortman, it was obvious that the baby would soon arrive. *Tanta*, murmuring reassuring sounds, gave full attention to her patient. Toby stoked the fire.

Then the baby arrived. It was a little girl. *Tanta* bathed the little baby and wrapped her in a hand-crocheted yellow blanket. She laid the little form next to her mother then turned her attention to Amelia again.

Amelia lay very still, her face pale.

"Poor child," *Tanta* said. "She's had a hard time."

At noon, Amelia had not recovered her resilience. She lay still and listless.

While *Tanta* tended to Amelia, Toby took Amelia's hand and held it. Her face was so white and she seemed so weak. Was she going to die? Her eyes were closed and her dark lashes were resting on her pale cheeks.

Then her eyes fluttered open. When she saw Toby, she strained to raise herself but her head fell back on the pillow.

"Hush," *Tanta* cooed. "You need your strength."

Despite *Tanta*'s words, Amelia tried again but without success. She looked up at Toby with pleading eyes. He bent his ear close to her lips.

"I'm sorry," she faltered. "Sorry I didn't trust you."

Toby pressed her hand. "You didn't know," he whispered. "You didn't know. I love you, Amelia."

*I do love her but it's a different kind of love,* Toby thought.

Amelia smiled then her eyes closed.

A moment later they fluttered open again. "We'll name her Anna," she said.

Her eyes fell shut then she breathed her last breath .

Toby watched helplessly. He bent down and planted a kiss on Amelia's brow then turned to the tiny infant.

"What am I going to do with a baby?" he asked *Tanta* Ortman. "How am I going to feed her? I don't know how to take care of a baby. And besides, I have work to do. I'm a farmer."

*Tanta* picked up the baby and cuddled it against her breast.

"There might be a way. One of the new immigrants lost her

baby earlier this evening. She could nurse little Anna. Maybe she'd take her."

Toby looked up in surprise. "One of the immigrants? Do you know her name?"

"Richert, I believe."

"Richert? Then it's Nettie! She's lost another baby! Come let's take the baby to her. I know Nettie. I think she'll take my baby."

"Ya. We can do that but first I must ready your wife for burial."

She rose and carried the baby to the cradle. "The baby's asleep and won't be wanting to eat. I'll lay her down and get busy with Amelia. She'll be all right for a little while."

"I'll hitch up the horses."

"Ya, you do that and while you're out there, I'll get some rags and wrap the stones heating on the stove. You can lay them in the wagon and have it nice and warm for little Anna."

Soon they were on their way. "Do you think we're doing the right thing? Will Nettie want to see another baby after losing her own?" Toby asked.

"Don't worry. Women are made to have babies. She'll welcome this little one."

They had gone merely a short distance when it began sleeting. *Tanta* tucked the quilts more tightly around them.

"Is the baby warm enough?" Toby asked.

"Ya. I've wrapped her in plenty of quilts and we'll hurry into the house."

At the settlement house, Toby fastened the reins to a hitching post then helped *Tanta* and the baby out of the wagon.

Ben, sitting at Nettie's bedside, looked up as the door opened. His eyes opened wide with astonishment. He rose to meet them. Nettie merely gazed into space.

"Toby! Where's Amelia?"

"She, she died."

"Died?" Ben put his arm around Toby's shoulder. "Oh, Toby, I'm so sorry."

232

Toby burst into sobs.

They stood embraced until Toby's tears subsided.

"And the baby lived?" Ben asked.

Toby nodded.

"A little girl. That's her in *Tanta's* arms."

"More fortunate than we. We lost another one. Makes eight. Nettie's broken hearted."

"Ben, do you think she'd take care of my little Anna?"

Ben frowned. "I don't know. We could try."

Suddenly little Anna gave a lusty cry.

Nettie heard. She raised her head and looked around the room. Toby took the baby from *Tanta* and laid her in Nettie's arms. Nettie hesitated a moment then when the baby cried again, she folded the infant to her breast.

"Will you take care of her?" Toby asked. "Amelia ..." His voice broke. "Amelia died."

Nettie looked down at the baby and nodded ever so slightly.

Toby looked down at his little one and smiled. Then, out of the corner of his eye, he saw Sophia sitting across the room. She looked up from her knitting when Toby approached her.

"Some day I'd like to explain," Toby said when he was standing beside her. "But I can't now. Have to take *Tanta* home and drive home myself."

"There's nothing to explain. It's simple. You didn't wait."

"But ..."

"No, Toby. What's past is past. I'll help take care of your little one because Nettie isn't well. Eventually you'll find another wife and she'll raise your child."

A sinking feeling gripped the pit of his stomach. With a sad heart, he walked away.

"Come," he told *Tanta* as he put on his cap, "it'll soon be dark."

"Nettie will take good care of your little one." Ben told Toby as he followed them to the door.

"I know she will. I wouldn't know how and I don't have relatives here."

"Maybe, just maybe this will be what Nettie needs." Ben said hopefully. He glanced at Nettie, who was totally absorbed with the baby. She was smiling with satisfaction.

Ben turned again to Toby. "What about the funeral?"

"I'll stop to see the elder but I'm pretty sure it will be tomorrow. I'll build a box to bury her in but I wonder if you'd come and get Amelia's body. It would help a lot. I just can't bring myself to do it."

"Be glad to."

"Thanks." Toby extended his hand. "It's so good to have you here. It's hard, Ben, it really is."

Toby took a handkerchief from his pocket and wiped the tears from his cheek. "You're like family."

Ben grasped Toby's hand in a firm grip.

"I'm glad we were here when you needed us. I'm sure we'll see you often for you'll want to see your little one."

"I'm sure I will. Thanks, Ben, thanks for being here."

Toby and *Tanta* walked out the door.

It was almost dark by the time Toby drove into his yard. He unhitched the horses and took them to the barn then returned to the empty house. Sadly he made his way to the bedroom. There, on the bed, lay Amelia's body. It was too much for him. He dropped to his knees and sobbed.

Before he went to bed, he built a box for Amelia's body.

# Chapter Thirty-seven

Early the next morning, Ben and Pappa loaded Amelia's body into Ben's wagon and made the journey to the cemetery. Toby followed in his own wagon. A small crowd had already gathered and when the elder arrived, the funeral began.

It was too cold for a long service and the elder kept it short. After reading comforting words from Scripture, he spoke some consoling words then he picked up a handful of dirt and sprinkled it on the wooden box.

"Ashes to ashes," he said, "and dust to dust." Then he prayed, committing the little family into God's care.

After the prayer, they lowered the body into the freshly-dug grave. Then two men shoveled the dirt back into the grave and the mourners drove away. There would be a fellowship dinner in the home where the church met for services.

*** 

As the weeks passed, little Anna thrived and won a special place in the Richert household. Household chores kept Sophia busy but she still found time to caress and rock the baby.

Nettie soon recovered and once more her eyes sparkled with life. Meanwhile, Toby came to dinner every Sunday after church. Sophia kept out of his way and would not speak to him nor look him in the eye.

Though the weather had turned cold and the ground was frozen, Ben went out every day except Sunday to look for a claim. Then one day in March, he returned with a gleam in his eyes.

"I've found just the place, Nettie," he announced at supper that night. "It's nice and level and it's near a lake, Silver Lake they call it. Tomorrow I'll show it to you and the children."

Nettie's eyes shone with pleasure. Then her face sobered. "But what about little Anna? It's too cold to take her out."

"I'll take care of her," Sophia quickly volunteered.

"Then it's settled," Ben said. "We'll go right after we've done the chores and eaten breakfast."

The next morning, while Ben and Nettie were away and little Anna slept, Sophia washed the dishes and swept the floor. When she had finished, she pulled the rocker next to the cradle.

Wrapped in a pink blanket edged with white embroidery, little Anna slept peacefully. Long, dark lashes rested on her plump pink cheeks and downy hair crowned her little round head.

Sophia could not resist touching the smooth, soft skin. She ran one finger over the delicate features then laid a forefinger in one tiny palm. The perfectly-formed little fingers automatically curled around the finger.

"Just like an angel," Sophia whispered.

It was then that Sophia remembered the little angel Toby had carved for her. She dropped to her knees and rummaged in the immigrant box until she found it. She held it momentarily then set it on a bedpost near Anna's cradle. Someday she would give it to Anna.

When she returned to Anna's side, she felt a rush of love for the infant. She picked the little one up and held her in her arms. When the child stirred, Sophia rocked her. Little Anna settled once more into a peaceful sleep.

So engrossed was Sophia with the little child that she did not hear the door open nor see Toby make his way to her side.

Then Toby touched Sophia's shoulder and Sophia looked up. She trembled but she did not speak.

"Beautiful baby, isn't she?" Toby said huskily, "even though

236

she is my daughter."

Sophia refused to look into his eyes.

"I know you've helped take care of her. Thank you."

Sophia did not immediately answer. "Yes," she said at last. "I couldn't love her more if she were my own daughter."

Toby took a step closer. "Then do you think you could learn to love her father again?"

Sophia did not answer, nor would she look at Toby.

Toby stood for a moment looking down on Sophia and the child she was holding. Then he saw the little angel.

He picked up the angel and held it a moment. "You've kept this all this time?"

Sophia nodded.

"Does it mean you still care for me?"

"I liked it enough to bring it with me."

"But do you care for the man who carved it?"

Sophia sighed. "That was a long time ago."

"But you've kept it all this time."

"I mean to give it to Anna some day."

Toby smiled then ran his hand over his hair.

"She'll like it especially because it comes from you."

"I hope she'll remember me."

"Why wouldn't she? You're right here."

"I'm going to Yankton."

Toby's eyes opened wide with astonishment.

"To Yankton?"

"They say they need seamstresses there."

"Can't you sew for people here?"

Sophia shook her head. "Most of the people are too poor."

"I wish you wouldn't go."

"I have to. I can't live with Ben and Nettie all my life. I have to make my own way."

Toby looked at her a moment.

"When will you go?" he asked at last.

"I'm not sure. Ben is going to ask around next time he's there."

"I wish you wouldn't go. I'll miss you, Sophia."

"There's no other way."

"I know a way."

"You do?"

"Marry me."

Sophia rose and put little Anna in the cradle.

"I'm sorry, Toby. It's been too long and too much has happened. There's been too much hurt."

Toby laid his big hand on her shoulder. "Then marry me for Anna's sake. I want her to live with me. You could be her mamma."

"I couldn't do that. I'll only marry for love."

"Well, will you think about it?"

Sophia turned her dark eyes up to meet Toby's. "Yes," she whispered.

Then her eyes closed again and her lashes rested on her rosy cheeks. A tear made it's way down her cheek.

"I pray your answer will be yes."

Toby turned and walked out the door.

When he had closed the door, Sophia burst into tears. "I do love him," she sobbed. "I've never stopped loving him."

She wiped her tears and picked up the angel Toby had made and set it back on the post.

Would the hurt ever go away? Would things ever be the same again?

Did angels really watch over God's children as Toby had said? Had an angel watched over her? One thing she was sure of. God had watched over her. He brought her to America though not without difficulty. He gave her Peter, though she loved him in a different way from the way she loved Toby.

And now she could have Toby back. Was she ready?

* * *

And out on the prairie, while Andrew and Eva romped in the

dry grass, Ben and Nettie stood arm in arm viewing the plains before them.

"This is it, Nettie," Ben said. "See how level it is? And there aren't any trees to grub out. This is our home. What do you think of it?"

"Kind of hard to make a home without a house." Her eyes twinkled mischievously.

Ben's eyes sparkled in return.

"You're right!"

"At first we'll have to live in a sod house, but as soon as I can, I'll build you a fine house, much finer than the one we had in Russia."

"I couldn't be happier."

"As soon as the office opens, I'll file a claim. We'll live there for five years and the land will be ours."

Ben reached up and snatched two hairpins from Nettie's *chignon*. The blonde tresses cascaded down her back.

"Ben! You shouldn't! You know married women don't let their hair down in public!"

Ben put his arm around her.

"Nettie, we're not in public. We're home! We've found our land!"

Ben tightened his arms around Nettie.

"You know, Nettie, it doesn't matter any more that Schultz and Gorbansky stole our first chance to leave. God has helped me to forgive them. All that matters now is that we're here and that Mamma and Pappa and their children are here too.

"We're free from the Tsar. We can worship as we please and we won't have to worry about the military lottery. Not only that but now, in eighteen-seventy-nine, four years after we arrived in America, we'll have land of our own."

# GLOSSARY

*Babushka* . . . . . . grandmother, head scarf (Russian)
*Dorf* . . . . . . . . . village
*Faspa* . . . . . . . . evening meal
*Frau* . . . . . . . . . woman, wife
*Gott ist die liebe* . God is love
*Grossmom* . . . . . Grandma
*Grossvater* . . . . . Grandfather
*Hectors* . . . . . . . About two and a half acres
*Mine kindtlein* . . My little child
*Plautdietsch* . . . Low German
*Plumemoosse* . . pudding made with prunes and raisins
*Oblast* . . . . . . . . district such as a state in USA
*Tanta* . . . . . . . . aunt
*Ukaz* . . . . . . . . . an official government decree having the force of law, a manifesto.
*Vorscht* . . . . . . . sausage
*Was ist loos?* . . . What is the matter?
*Zwieback* . . . Rich double bun, one ball of dough baked on top of another.
*Roesha zwieback* . toasted zwieback

Ruth Richert Jones and her husband, Dr. Russell G. Jones, live in Omaha, Nebraska. She is the author of *A Rose is A Rose* and *My Heart to Give*. Over one hundred of her nonfiction articles have been published.

After raising four children, three daughters and a son, she taught in the Women's Ministry Program at Grace University for nine years.

In 1995 and 1996, under Greater Europe Mission, she and her husband spent two weeks each year teaching at Zaporozhye Bible College in the Ukraine. Each two-week segment covered a semester's work.

In 1997, they returned, this time for four weeks. During this time, the author taught an exposition of the Gospel of John to a class of women. The director of ZBC stated that Jones was likely the first woman in the Ukraine to teach an exposition of a book of the Bible in a college setting.

After teaching the first year, the author and her husband visited the village of Karlswalde. The village of Gruental, from which her grandparents first emigrated, had been plowed up and planted to sugar beets.

Her great grandparents' house in Karlswalde had been replaced with a house built in the style of the original house. In 1954, the Communists destroyed the church building but nothing was ever built on that lot again. The villagers considered the land to be holy. In the nineteen-seventies, the communists plowed up the cemetery and planted the area to sugar beets.

The villagers remembered hearing about the people who came to Karlswalde in the early nineteenth century. They called them Hollanders.

According to the archivist in Rovno, Ukraine, the Hollanders who did not immigrate to America moved to the Molotschna area taking the church records with them. As far as is known, the records have been lost.

Currently the author is teaching a weekly Bible study to women in the Douglas County Correctional Center.

Besides their four children, the Joneses have nine grand-children.

# ORDER FORM

## BOOKS BY RUTH RICHERT JONES:

Land of Their Own (historical novel)  $10.95
A Rose is a Rose  (mystery)                      4.95

## PLEASE SEND THE FOLLOWING BOOKS:

| Quantity | Name of Book | Price Ea. | Total |
|----------|--------------|-----------|-------|
| _____ | **Land of Their Own** $10.95 | | _____ |
| _____ | **A Rose is a Rose** 4.95 | | |
| | **Total for books** | | _____ |
| | **Shipping** | | _____ |
| | **Total** | | _____ |

**Shipping:**
Book Rate $2.00 for the first book and 75 cents for each additional book (Surface shipping may take three to four weeks.)

**Payment:**
Please make checks payable to Ruth Richert Jones.
Canadians, please send payment in U.S. funds.

Name: _____
Address: _____
City: _____State\Prov. _____ Zip:_____

Send order to:

**THORNE TREE PUBLISHERS**
**P.O. Box 6536**
**Omaha NE 68106-0536**